MICHELLE DE BRUIN

TOMORROW SERIES ~ BOOK THREE

Dreams Come True! Michelle De Bruin

Published by Scrivenings Press LLC
15 Lucky Lane
Morrilton, Arkansas 72110
https://ScriveningsPress.com

Printed in the United States of America

Paperback ISBN 978-1-64917-082-8

eBook ISBN 978-1-64917-083-5

Library of Congress Control Number: 2020947763

Cover by Linda Fulkerson, bookmarketinggraphics.com

All characters are fictional, and any resemblance to real people, either factional or historical, is purely coincidental.

All scriptures are taken from the KING JAMES VERSION (KJV): KING JAMES VERSION, public domain.

To Tom
because we are two real hearts who share one True Love,
and because you waited a really long time.

ACKNOWLEDGMENTS

Thank you to my parents and my husband for the ways you show your unending support of me and your pride in me. I appreciate it very much.

Thank you to Christian Opportunity Center for allowing me the flexibility I needed in my schedule to get this book ready for publication. I am grateful to serve with you in doing the Lord's work.

Thank you to Shannon Taylor-Vannatter for your superb editing on this manuscript.

Thank you to Linda Nixon Fulkerson for tirelessly working to help me and the other authors at Scrivenings Press with marketing and promotion.

As an apple tree among the trees of the wood,
so is my beloved among young men.
With great delight I sat in his shadow,
And his fruit was sweet to my taste.
He brought me to the banqueting house,
And his intention toward me was love.
- Song of Solomon 2:3-4

Be Thou my vision, O Lord of my heart;
Naught be all else to me, save that Thou art,
Thou my best thought, by day or by night,
Waking or sleeping, Thy presence my light.
- Old Irish Hymn (translated)

1

Oswell City, Iowa
June 1911

"You must wear these at all times." Dr. Kaldenberg tucked the curved ends of a new pair of spectacles around Logan De Witt's ears.

The world came into sharp focus. Each vial on the shelf behind the doctor stood out in stark relief. Logan could even read the fine print on the labels.

Dr. Kaldenberg scooted away to jot a few notes in a folder. "Give these new glasses a try for a month and then come back for a follow-up appointment."

Dizziness swarmed around Logan when he stood. His new and refined depth perception would take some getting used to.

The doctor handed him a slip of paper. "Your new spectacles will help you with reading and also with seeing objects in the distance."

Both of those activities had grown more challenging since his return to Oswell City. No longer would he need to squint to make out the faces of those seated in the back pews on Sunday morning. Enjoyment should also return to his study time. He'd sure appreciate the change if it meant he no longer had to crouch over his books to make out the words.

"Thank you, Doctor." He shook hands with the doctor and headed out into the summer day.

Oswell City's main street bustled with activity as Logan followed the sidewalk to the church. He waved at Alex Zahn, who placed a supply of pastries in his bakery's display window. A whiff of sweet dough fresh from the oven carried into the street.

Walter Brinks swept the wide steps of his father's hotel. "Hey, Pastor Logan! Nice glasses," he called when Logan walked by.

"Good afternoon." Artie Goud leaned against the second story of his jewelry store from the top rungs of a ladder where he worked to fasten a red, white, and blue striped bunting to the brick wall. "Fourth of July sales begin tomorrow. Stop in if you need a special gift."

Logan smiled up at the man. He'd already spent an impressive sum of money in Mr. Goud's store last Christmas when he bought Karen's engagement ring. The businessmen downtown knew their pastor would do anything to support them, but a man also had to keep a little something in his savings. Mr. Goud would have to wait awhile before he saw Logan in his store again.

Passing the bank and the Koelman Law Firm, Logan turned the corner onto Fifth Street. The change in direction affected his balance, making one of his legs feel shorter than the other. His foot caught on the rounded curb of the asphalted street, but he grasped the trunk of a nearby tree and prevented a sprawl on the ground.

He stood still for a moment and sucked in a deep breath. Wearing these new spectacles every minute of the day would require his full attention for simple tasks he'd never given thought to in the past. Straightening his tie, Logan dared to take another step. He managed to place one foot in front of the other as he crossed the lawn and entered the church.

The door of his study hung open. He never left the door open when gone from the building. Maybe someone in need of their pastor was looking for him. He hastened down the hall.

Someone for sure had come looking for him, but she didn't appear one bit in need of a pastor. Her blue dress clung to her figure, and the neckline scooped quite low. The day was warm, but no one needed to expose that much skin to stay cool. Dark brown hair smoothed away from her fair forehead, and full red lips pouted at him. His restored vision was working far too well at the moment.

"Florence Mae Hesslinga." The sight of this young woman in his study opened the gate on a store of memories from seminary days. "What are you doing here?" He couldn't decide if he should celebrate the reunion or let his nerves take over at the way she strutted in front of him.

She trailed her fingertip across his chest. "I need your help." The invitation lingering in her words made his heart pound.

"Help ... with-with what?" His stutter had stayed behind in Silver Grove. Until now. He gritted his teeth, refusing to allow Florence any more proof of her ability to unsettle him.

"I'm staying with my aunt Clara for a few weeks."

"What about that man you married? I forget his name." Logan sought refuge in his desk chair.

"You mean Reuben? The cad. He only married me to gain a position in Father's business. Then he had an affair, and I left him. He died this spring in a drunk-driving auto accident. Aunt Clara is giving me a place to stay until I get my life in order." She claimed the corner of his desk, her clingy skirt barely covering her ankles.

Logan refused to look down. Those glasses had to go. He'd follow doctor's orders tomorrow. Blurry vision was the best thing that could happen to him right now. His ears hurt anyway. Logan slipped the spectacles from his face and laid them on his open Bible.

"Aunt Clara put me on the planning committee for the

Fourth of July festivities." Florence leaned in and murmured with her throaty voice. "It's my job to find escorts for the Miss Independence Day pageant contestants."

"Why do you ask me?" Logan leaned back, way back, in his chair.

But Florence closed the distance. "The word on the street is Pastor De Witt is the most eligible bachelor in town. You're perfect for the job."

"I see." Too bad he didn't have an engagement ring to wear like his fiancée had. Then forward young ladies like Florence could see for herself that perhaps he wasn't so eligible after all.

"I'm planning to enter as one of the contestants. Maybe you'd want to escort me." Florence leaned over far enough Logan didn't need his spectacles to catch a glimpse of what her neckline tried so hard to conceal.

He shot out of his chair. "Flora Mae." Her nickname rolled from his tongue just like memories of their failed courtship rolled through his mind. "You have to understand. I'm engaged to be married. Escorting a young woman during the pageant isn't exactly the sort of behavior I should be involved in."

"Married? You?" Florence left his desk and cornered him near his bookshelf. "You always did try to make other interests more important than me. Burying your nose in all these books of yours. Running off to lectures on topics nobody but you seminary boys cared about. Still making excuses, aren't you?"

Her accusation stole his breath. Karen was no excuse. She'd become the love of his life, at times dangerously rivaling the devotion he owed to the Lord alone. But how to make Florence understand? He hardly knew where to begin.

"Why does it matter to you so much whether I participate or not?" Logan asked.

She fingered his tie. "I'd hoped we might get back together again."

"As you can see, I'm still pursuing a career you found impossible to live with." Logan gestured at his study. The Bible was open to a passage of Scripture surrounded by pages of notes he'd taken earlier that day. Walls lined with floor-to-ceiling shelves housed his collection of priceless study materials. Chairs awaited distraught visitors.

Even the clock ticking away the seconds served as a confirmation of the careful yet fruitful choices he'd made in the time that had passed since his last interaction with this woman.

"No one is better looking than you, Logan De Witt." Her attention shifted from his tie to smoothing his shirt over his shoulders. "I was the envy of all the girls whenever I went out with you."

Her caresses moved to his hair, which needed none of her assistance to respond to the humid summer day. If he didn't get away from her, he'd soon look like the loser of a wrestling match.

"I'm sorry." He maneuvered out of her reach and stood behind his chair. Not designed for militant use, the chair possessed no ability to deter an enemy, but it was his best weapon against any more of her advances.

She sat on the corner of his desk again. "I suppose this new woman of yours tried to talk you out of the life of a pastor and into something else like I did."

Logan shook his head. "She loves me for it."

"Does she live here?" Florence slid off the desk and approached him.

He turned his chair to block her, but she kneeled on the seat and thrust her face into his.

"No. Chicago is her home."

"When's the wedding?"

"January."

"Gives a man lots of time to change his mind."

"You won't change mine." Logan gave her a solemn stare as the image of Karen's golden blonde hair and sky-blue eyes delighted his memory. Her grace and refinement formed a sharp contrast to the edges of Florence's character that had grown rough over time.

She studied him while her lips parted as if she'd go ahead and make the most of this time alone with him.

Logan took a step back and smacked up against the wall. If Florence didn't get out of his chair, he'd be trapped again. She leaned over and planted a kiss on his cheek, the layers of lipstick smearing his skin. The effect must have met her approval because she smiled at him when she pulled away.

"Happy Fourth of July. I'll see you around." Florence put all the sway any woman could muster into her hips and took her time leaving.

This unplanned encounter had wreaked as much havoc as a tornado tearing through an oat field. He settled his hands on his waist and enjoyed the feel of taking deep breaths, something he hadn't done since entering his study. Daring to believe safety belonged to him once more, he reached for his spectacles and returned them to their proper place.

A haze of dark pink smudged his white cuff. Flora Mae's lipstick! The stuff must get removed as soon as possible. He reached into his pocket for his handkerchief and dabbed at his cheek. The poor square of innocent white cloth would be a wreck by the time he finished with it. At least Florence hadn't damaged anything else. He could get over a ruined handkerchief.

SUNDAY MORNING, Logan pointed to a page in his open Bible as he preached to a full sanctuary. "If we look closely at the Apostle Paul's writings, we notice in Ephesians 5 his encouragement to be filled with the Holy Spirit."

Amazing, his stutter stayed away today. Florence's visit still rattled him. He'd awakened twice in the night from the nightmare that he stood before his congregation this morning with her lipstick smeared all over his face. And the worst part of his dream was the fact that no matter how hard he scrubbed, the smudges of color refused to come off. A shake of his head and a clearing of his throat helped him focus.

"Speak to one another with psalms, hymns, and spiritual songs. Sing and make music in your heart to the Lord; always giving thanks to God the Father for everything in the name of our Lord Jesus Christ. Let's pray."

He took a deep breath and asked the Lord to speak to the group gathered this morning. The words of the scripture he'd just read pricked him. If he took the passage seriously, he should give thanks for everything, including the discomfort Florence introduced into his life.

But he could still feel that smear of lipstick. Sometimes God really did ask the impossible from a man.

The sermon drew to a close, and he prayed once more. The congregation sang a hymn while he sat through the offering. He invited everyone to stand for the singing of the *Doxology,* and then Logan hastened to the back of the church.

Left with a few moments alone before a line of people formed to shake hands with him, he gave in to the temptation to feel his cheek. He had to know absolutely no lipstick still stained him. He studied his fingertips. Of course, he should have known they'd stay clean, but relief seeped into him anyway.

Thoughts of his fiancée helped him settle down even more. He missed Karen. Memories of the afternoons they partnered together to bring the word and worship to the congregation of Meadow Creek filled his mind. How he'd love to have her here serving with him and leading the singing. Only six more months remained, and then she'd be here with him always. He could hardly wait.

People filed out of their pews and shook hands with him.

"Good sermon today, Pastor Logan. Thank you." Clara echoed the words of many who had come through the line before her.

He smiled in response, but when Florence made eye contact with him, the smile disappeared, and his hand shot to his cheek.

He couldn't help it. Heat crept up his neck. The fear that she might try to flirt again and kiss him in spite of all these people standing around took hold of him.

But she only winked. "See ya Tuesday," she whispered in a voice belonging to a young lady who didn't know how to take *no* as his final answer. Florence moved on behind her aunt and found a cluster of women to visit with.

He sucked in a deep breath as he remembered those words he'd read from Ephesians. Thankfulness didn't describe his feelings about this encounter with Florence, even though it had gone much better than the first one.

But gratitude did come close to his relief that at least she'd made no attempt to touch him or kiss him. The Apostle Paul had issued a simpler command to follow than he'd first thought. Or maybe God was helping him steer clear of traps that could ensnare him and drag him away from the fullest blessings.

"You appear to be getting along fine with your spectacles." Dr. Kaldenberg studied Logan when the line shortened, and his turn came for conversation.

"Yes, I am. I'm very glad to have them. Didn't realize how much I needed glasses until I started wearing them." Logan reached to shake hands with the gentle and patient middle-aged doctor.

Dr. Kaldenberg smiled. "That's usually the way it goes. Soon you'll hardly notice you're wearing them at all."

When the line ended, Logan made his way to his study. He'd welcome the day when he no longer noticed his spectacles. They needed pushed up far too often, and he was always cleaning them. But they helped him read and to see into the distance.

How nice if his spectacles could also show him what lay ahead, not only as he navigated the sidewalks of town and the church building, but as he prepared for his future. The Lord had good things in store for Karen and him. Logan was convinced of it. As long as he remembered that simple truth, his vision would serve him well in the months to come.

2

July 1911
Michigan Avenue, Chicago

Morning sunlight glistened on the yards of white satin cascading over the end of the ornate drawing-room table. Rolls of lace lay nearby. Mother picked up a wide swatch in an intricate pattern and held it to Karen's neck.

"This is lovely." Mother's eyes brightened.

"Very stylish. With your daughter's blonde hair and fair skin, this lace would make a perfect complement to her wedding gown. Women with her coloring should wear white, not ivory or creamier shades." Mother's personal dress designer stepped closer and tapped her chin.

Karen preferred the white fabric to the cream one. The white was her choice for the dress she would wear to marry Logan, but mother's choice of lace, beautiful as it was, didn't fit with her desire for simplicity.

"That lace is very nice, Mother, but it's too showy. What about this one?" Karen reached for a delicate strip featuring a combination of flower buds and scrolls.

Mother's lips scrunched together. "I suppose. What do you think, Miss Rose?"

The designer wore much the same expression as Mother. She'd been Margaret Millerson's dress designer ever since the day Mother's brother Henry offered his home to his sister and her daughter. With her new life came the fashion expertise and friendship of Miss Rose.

Karen didn't even know her last name. She'd always been the woman who appeared at their home from her boutique downtown to take measurements and confer with Mother whenever holidays or a change of seasons required the newest and latest styles.

"Elegant, but not quite the right touch for the bride from a prominent family. All the society weddings this summer are going with gowns that have intricate lace on the bodice and sleeves. You'll want to do that too."

"Oh, yes. And the veil. We mustn't forget to talk about the veil." Mother hastened to the sofa where a mountain of tulle billowed. She brought it over to Karen, and, with Miss Rose's assistance, draped it down her back and across the rug.

"That should be about the right length." Miss Rose's voice carried from what sounded like the other side of the spacious room.

Karen turned, unable to restrain the twist of her brow. The ridiculously long path of tulle would reach right down the street to Uncle Henry's downtown office. If Karen were to wear a veil of these proportions in Oswell City, the silly thing would stretch all the way down the church's aisle as well as most of Main Street.

Logan's letters acquainted her with the community she'd call home once they married. It was a small town, a close-knit group of folks out on the expansive Iowa prairie who knew the value of hard work and of doing it together. According to Logan's letters, their survival depended on it, which meant Oswell City residents didn't have the time or the need for extravagance.

If the bride of their pastor were to appear in a veil five miles long and wearing a lacy dress costing more than some of their houses, she'd cost Logan a degree of respect. Not to mention set herself up as belonging to another class—something Karen refused to do. As the wife of the local preacher, she wanted to fit in and serve alongside him the best she knew how.

"No. That's too much." Karen gathered the tulle, reeling it in to form a ball. She pictured Logan working with a rope tied around the neck of a calf that had wandered too close to the creek and must return to safety.

Miss Rose wasn't exactly a Holstein calf, but she could use some convincing to return the proposed veil to a safer length.

"Right here. This is good," Karen announced when the tulle barely grazed the floor.

Now it was Mother's turn to look horrified. "But Karen, my dear, none of the brides among our friends are wearing veils that short. It won't do. It just won't do."

Karen stopped her eyes from rolling just in time. "But Mother, I'm not getting married here in Chicago in a huge stone church among guests drawn from your elite circles. I'm getting married in Oswell City. From what I read in Logan's letters, we need to keep my dress and the wedding simple. That's what he would want anyway, and well, it works for me too."

Silence drowned the room. Mother and Miss Rose looked at each other for a moment before Miss Rose gathered the tulle and returned it to the sofa.

"What about the style of your dress?" She released a deep breath. "Shall we talk about that today?"

"Let's." Mother nodded. "Settling on a dress style will help Karen make up her mind."

Karen clenched her teeth. She'd already made up her mind, but since her preferences were in the minority at this meeting, they were deemed unacceptable.

"Your mother and I talked these over last week." Miss Rose held drawings out to her.

Karen accepted the drawings and studied them. Full ruffles at the neckline and the hem. Fluffed skirts. Lace everywhere. She'd hoped for something a bit straighter and, of course, with simpler lace. But expressing her thoughts would only add to the tension between herself and the other women.

"I like the style in the neckline of this dress." She started in the least threatening place. "Maybe you could use this pattern for the dress's bodice but without that wide ruffle."

Miss Rose studied the picture Karen indicated. "I believe that will work. Shall I trim the neckline with the lace you chose?"

"Please. That would look nice. And make sure to give the dress long sleeves. Logan and I are planning on a winter wedding." Karen glanced at Mother.

She offered a smile. "Long sleeves are a good idea."

Mother's comment didn't exactly affirm Karen's suggestions, but at least she hadn't pressed for more expectations of a society wedding. Given the fact that Mother had participated in the creation of these gown ideas, Karen could understand that her changes may take some getting used to.

But really, a fancy, exclusively designed dress wasn't necessary. Karen had a white embroidered tea gown that would work just fine for what she and Logan intended to accomplish on their wedding day. Paired with a floor-length veil and a modest bouquet, Karen would make the loveliest bride her new husband could ever hope for, and that was all that really mattered.

AFTERNOON SUN SPARKLED on the lake waters. A breeze, warm with light and hope, tousled Karen's hair and rustled her skirt. She turned her face toward the current, allowing it to caress her skin, easing her nerves. The gentle wind blew over the expanse of water from peaceful shores beyond just like the wind in Silver

Grove swept across the unending fields and grasslands of Logan's native home.

The serenity of the sun sinking to the watery horizon refreshed her and restored her calm. Karen turned away from the scene with a sigh. She must arrive at home in time for dinner with her sister, her brother-in-law, and her two nephews. A late arrival would invite questions. Too many emotions swirled inside for her to offer any satisfying answers. Karen hastened across the beach as her thoughts turned to her fiancé.

Maybe Logan was also preparing at this moment for a dinner engagement. This thought perked her up a bit. Imagining Logan participating in similar activities to hers strengthened her connection to him somehow. Distance might separate them, but in the area of enjoying time spent with friends and family, they were very close.

Karen followed the streets the few blocks to the Millerson residence. As she walked, her imagination collected the facts he'd written to her about the town where he ministered, the place she intended to claim as her home. She pictured him in action among those he served.

What did he have planned for today, a Saturday afternoon in the summertime? Maybe he took a break from his preparation for Sunday morning to seek out a favorite hiding place to think of her like she did this moment, longing for him.

The street she followed intersected with the one that led to the train station. How she'd love to summon Uncle Henry's chauffeur this very minute to take her there so she might travel straight to Oswell City and marry Logan today. But she'd signed a contract to teach English at a ladies' college until the end of the year. She must see the work through to completion. Her salary would help Logan in establishing their household when they married.

Karen tore her attention away from the enticing street and kept to her route. The months marking their long-distance engagement worked in their favor. Both of them could save as they planned for the big day when their lives joined as one. If she remembered to use this time as preparation, she'd survive.

When she arrived home, Karen let herself in the side door, the one that opened into the hallway from the dining room to the kitchen. Maids scurried with cutlery and crystal in their rush to set the table.

Rita, Aunt Fran's most recent hire, surveyed Karen with wide eyes. "Miss Karen, dinner is served in ten minutes. You need to dress for guests."

"I will." Karen smiled. "It's just my sister, after all. She won't care what I have on."

Still learning the ways of the wealthy household, the young maid gave Karen a wary glance. "Don't get in trouble," she whispered.

"Not a chance." Karen laughed. The Millersons may like to hold to convention and propriety, and Karen might participate in the formality, but the atmosphere could never undermine the visit Mother and Julia had made the De Witt farm earlier that year. Bonds had formed as they sat with Karen around the table in the farmhouse dressed in the simplest of gowns while feasting on homegrown fare.

On the surface, Karen and her sister were daughters of one of the most prestigious families in Chicago, but inside, they were members of a wider community of love, as offered to them by Logan and his acquaintances. Sandy, his mother. Tillie, his sister. Pete and Anna, his friends. How she missed them all. Warmth and true fellowship flowed whenever they'd been together.

Even Mother found her place in the circle. Skeptical of Logan's character, she'd soon accepted him as deserving of her daughter's affections.

"You're doing a good job." Karen patted Rita's arm. "Don't you go and get in trouble either."

"Tryin' my best," she said as she hurried away with a stack of linen napkins.

Following the black-haired maid's suggestion was a good idea.

Slipping around the corner, Karen climbed the wooden stairs at the back of the grand house and entered her room unseen to prepare for dinner. Her gown required only a light shake to remove sand from the hem in order to look presentable enough to appear at dinner with the family.

Moments later, she entered the dining room with her windblown hair smoothed down. Mother, Aunt Fran, and Uncle Henry gathered around the table, too interested in their topic of conversation to notice Karen's sun-warmed appearance.

She gave her skirt one more shake just in case Mother glanced her way.

"You've been to the lake again." Julia clasped Karen's shoulders and smiled at her.

"How can you tell?" The lakeshore served as her own personal retreat. Too baffled by her sister's insightful discovery, Karen didn't think to conceal her afternoon wanderings.

"You look relaxed and happy. The only other time I've seen you that way since your return to the city was at our picnic luncheon with Aunt Fran on the beach in June." Julia settled three-year-old Ben into a chair and then sat next to him.

"Oh." Karen claimed the chair beside her sister. Whatever defensiveness had crept into her voice a moment ago drained away.

She leaned forward and waved at Ben. "Hello there, young man."

He returned her wave and giggled.

"Missing him, aren't you?" Julia looked at her with concern.

"Terribly." Karen lowered her voice to a whisper. "I never wanted this teaching job. I only took it because the salary will give us a good start to our marriage."

"Very noble and worthwhile in the end. You'll see." Julia patted her knee below the table.

The word *noble* fit her fiancé much better than it did any of her actions. Logan was a hero, investing all of his savings in freeing his mother from debt during his stay on the farm in

Silver Grove. He never discussed finances in his letters, but he didn't need to. Karen knew enough about the sacrifices he'd made to believe that his return to Oswell City meant starting over, building his stability a little at a time until finally positioned to support a wife.

Not only was he noble and heroic, but he was handsome too. The wind at the lake today would have tousled his blond hair into a wave that fell over his forehead, giving him a boyish, mischievous charm that matched his usual good humor and twinkling blue eyes. Those same eyes could look right into her heart with a sensitivity that convinced her beyond words of his love for her.

Karen swallowed away the thickness in her throat and bowed her head when Uncle Henry began to pray.

As soon as the meal started, Mother turned the conversation to the disagreements earlier in the day. Karen's stomach tightened. Julia might side with Mother. If that happened, everyone in her family would be against her. Karen found herself languishing more and more outside the family circle, where perspectives on upholding the expectations assumed for a wealthy family were concerned.

"Julia, my dear, what is your advice? Karen instructed Miss Rose this morning to design for her a short veil, one that barely touches the floor. The styles this summer dictate something much longer."

After a glance at Karen, Julia replied. "Mother, you forget. Karen isn't having a summer wedding. Hers is in winter. The wedding isn't in the city anyway. It will take place in a small town. You remember our visit to Logan's farm this spring, don't you?"

Mother nodded, but she appeared a bit reluctant to concede to Julia's train of thought.

"The only ones wearing expensive, style-conscious dresses were you and me. I'm sure the people in Oswell City are much the same," Julia said with a flourish of her hand in Mother's direction.

The tightness in Karen's middle seeped away during Julia's speech, but Mother still appeared reluctant, even a degree disappointed.

"I can believe things are done a little differently in Oswell City than here in Chicago." Her trademark enthusiasm colored Julia's voice. "We may have more adjustments to make. But we might like it. Maybe the folks in Oswell City will have such great ideas about how to pull off a wedding, we'll be the ones looking to them for creative inspiration." Julia laughed.

But Mother wore the same scrunched-lipped expression from their meeting with Miss Rose.

Karen laughed too. With Julia on her side in the matter, not only did she have an ally, but someone to count on to infuse fun into the wedding planning process. The relaxed, happy feeling from the lakeshore returned. She might actually enjoy herself in the months of waiting and planning that stretched all the way to Christmas.

3

Logan leaned against the trunk of an oak tree, thankful for its shade from the afternoon sun. A breeze rustled his collar. Leaves fluttered overhead. Townspeople sat in chairs and on blankets along the main street. Children clapped and pointed to the sights, adding to the cheer of the holiday. The parade inched down Main Street, featuring decorated wagons and a marching band assembled of men from town playing drums and brass instruments.

The smells of roasting meat wafted on the warm breeze as a reminder of the picnic planned for the supper hour. He'd stay downtown to enjoy the meal and socialize instead of returning to his desk. Tuesdays, he usually spent long hours studying, but he'd covered enough material that morning to allow him the rest of the day to enjoy the outdoor festivities.

The last entry in the parade, a horse-drawn cart decorated with red and blue paper and filled with elderly Civil War veterans, rolled by. Logan waved. Several of the men occupied the pews of the Oswell City Community Church sanctuary on Sunday mornings. A young girl carrying the flag followed. Soon people meandered in every direction.

"Sure was nice to see the band get back together again." A person on his right commented.

"The parade gets better every year," another replied.

"I agree. The Fourth of July parade is one of my favorite events." Logan followed them in a large crowd to the downtown square where Paul Ellenbroek, the town mayor, would give a speech.

A line formed at the stand where Alex Zahn sold cookies and doughnuts. They looked too delicious to resist. Logan took a place in line and spoke to the couple ahead of him.

"I'm looking forward to your father's speech." He smiled at Lorraine Koelman, who, along with her lawyer husband, was expecting their first baby. She was the daughter of the mayor, and a young woman he'd thought about courting. But that was before he met Karen. She was a thousand times better suited for him than Lorraine ever could have been. Logan offered the Lord a silent *thank you* for his guidance over the past year.

"He's worked hard on it. These are exciting times for Oswell City. New people arrive daily. Downtown is thriving. Father feels the need each year to welcome new residents and cheer on the businessmen." Lorraine's gaze shifted from his face to somewhere in the distance behind him.

"Pastor Logan!" The impatient voice belonged to Cornelia Goud.

He turned around.

She shook her finger at him as she approached. "You're late!"

He couldn't imagine what she meant. No one had asked him to officiate a wedding today, and no deaths had occurred requiring his services at a funeral. He stared at a total loss of how to respond.

"The Miss Independence Day pageant?" Cornelia gave him a look as if he grew dumber by the minute.

"What about it?" Dread crept into his gut.

"You're on the list as an escort." She shoved a clipboard at him revealing a list of names on the paper fastened to it and pointed to his name. We need you to come. Now."

"Oh, but I—" He shook his head.

Cornelia grasped his sleeve. "Everyone is waiting for you."

He wanted to eat a fresh doughnut and attend his friend's speech, not pair up with someone who wasn't his fiancée.

"The pageant will start as soon as the mayor finishes his speech." Cornelia's gaze traveled over him. "Why, you aren't even wearing a suit coat. Oh, dear. We need to find you one and get you ready to appear on the stage. Whatever are we going to do?" She clutched her throat.

Cornelia mentioned the third thing he didn't want to do, wear a suit coat in the heat of the day. The disadvantages fast outweighed the benefits of his original plan of staying in the park with thoughts of Karen on his mind instead of lending himself to an event where he'd end up with a young woman on his arm.

"Oh, good." Florence jogged over. "You found him." She slid her hand down the length of his arm. "You're spending the afternoon with me."

Blood boiled in his veins. Florence hadn't listened to a word he'd said, ignored every last one of his protests, and put his name on her list of escorts.

"Ladies, I'm sorry." He took a step back. "But I cannot act as an escort for the pageant."

Cornelia's eyes took on a glazed look as she glanced at Florence. "It's too late for anyone to back out. He has to do it."

"One of the other men didn't make it into town. His sister is in the pageant and said he decided to put up his hay today." Florence managed to keep her hands on him even though he now stood farther away from her.

Logan stifled a groan. Some men had all the luck. How he'd love to have a hay crop as an excuse to desert Florence right now.

"You have to come, Pastor Logan. One of our young ladies is

already without a partner. We can't afford to have that happen to any more of them." Cornelia shook her head with enough energy to make her hat bounce.

Paul Ellenbroek approached the podium and looked out over the crowd. "Good afternoon. Welcome to Oswell City's Fourth of July festival."

"Oh, dear." Cornelia's eyes widened. "The mayor is starting his speech. We don't have much time."

Florence grasped Logan's hand and tugged on him while Cornelia pressed his side. He needed to either go with these women or run the risk of creating a scene. Paul didn't deserve that sort of distraction. Neither did he want the townspeople believing their pastor an uncooperative, unsupportive influence. They would wish for him to participate in the celebration alongside them. For the sake of the town, he could tolerate Florence's company for a few hours.

He allowed the women to herd him down the street and into a tent bustling with activity. Young ladies in evening gowns scurried about, trailed by their mothers, who worked at straightening sashes and tucking last-minute hairpins into place. When the trio entered, activity halted. Mothers and daughters surrounded him while Cornelia attempted to arrange the other young men into a line.

Questions came at him from every direction, all of them demanding the same answer. Who would be the lucky woman to pair up with him? Hopeful faces gazed up at him while a couple of the young women maneuvered closer to his side.

Logan's heart pounded. Before he left town to stay on the farm with his mother and sister, he couldn't secure dinner dates or attract a woman's attention at all. But now that he'd returned, girls actually worked hard to gain his interest. His mouth dropped open. He really should explain about his engagement, but Cornelia tossed him a suit coat.

"Try this on. Hopefully, it fits well enough for you to wear during the pageant." She stood behind him and helped him ease the jacket over his shoulders.

Applause and cheers came from outside the tent.

"The mayor is finished." Cornelia stood in front of him, matching the buttons of the jacket with their buttonholes. "That's our cue." She looked over at her granddaughter. "Pearl, start the Victrola."

The grade-school girl followed her grandmother's instructions while Cornelia hustled everyone away from him and assigned them to other partners. Logan breathed in a sigh of relief. At least he was no longer the center of attention. He moved to the back of the tent to form the end of the line. The farther back he stood, the longer he could wait before fulfilling his role. Maybe Cornelia would discover she had enough partners for the women, after all.

His hopes took a nosedive the moment he dared to entertain them. Florence walked over and slipped her arm through his. She smiled up at him as if she was the one he consulted on wedding plans.

"Ready?" she asked.

No. He'd never be ready to appear with her on a stage or anywhere else. He barely had time to shake his head before she adjusted a cluster of fabric roses on her skimpy neckline. His gaze darted away. Those new spectacles really should have stayed at home today. He couldn't imagine why he thought they'd do him any good.

Cornelia motioned to him. Florence's moment in the sun had arrived. He moved forward and offered her his support, just like any true gentleman would as she ascended the stairs. Once she found her place in the line of contestants near the front of the stage, he stood in the back with the other men. He followed this pattern three more times as she got invited onto the stage to answer questions, sing a song, and model her dress.

Finally, the moment came to announce a winner. Judges narrowed the group down to three. Florence was among them.

Logan stood in the back with his ears fully tuned in to the voice of Dr. Kaldenberg, who had agreed to do the announcing. He had the attention of every last person in the crowd when he said Florence's name.

Logan's eyes widened. She'd actually won the contest. This meant he would need to join her at the front of the stage while she received her crown and then escort her down the simple runway and over to the booth where the newspaper photographer waited. Surely he wouldn't need to get his picture taken with her. Good grief. This afternoon was going from bad to worse.

The man behind the camera took pity on him and flashed half a dozen poses of Florence alone, wearing her Miss Independence Day crown and holding her bouquet of flowers. In one of the photos, she looked away from the camera. If that picture happened to find its way into the newspaper, only Logan would know the newly crowned royalty had her eyes on him.

Heat crept up his neck. Now was a good time to get rid of his borrowed jacket.

Florence finished with the photos and swept through the crowd, shaking hands and receiving hugs.

Then she came over to him and reached for his hand. "Thanks for escorting me today."

How could he respond? Never would he say it had been his pleasure. But he did have to admit that joining in the town's festivities with a companion was nice. If only that companion was his own beautiful Karen.

"Are you thirsty?" He asked in typical pastor fashion. "Would you like to get something to drink?"

"Please. Let me take these flowers to the tent so Aunt Clara can put them in water."

He followed her through the crowd and waited at the tent's entrance. In the park, he paid Alex Zahn for doughnuts and lemonade for both of them. Florence talked with a group of admirers while Logan once again sought shade beneath a tree.

A cluster of pageant contestants gathered around a nearby table, their conversation floating to his ears.

"Do you think he'd ever ask to court me?" One of them asked her friend.

"Maybe. He's been single for a long time. A man would have to start getting tired of that by now," the friend answered.

"He might decide to ask me," another woman in the group said.

"Or me," a third young lady spoke up.

"Didn't he look so handsome in that suit coat Mrs. Goud found for him? Too bad he didn't wear one of his own. But even in a borrowed jacket, Pastor Logan is one of the most handsome men in town," said the young lady who'd brought up the subject of courtship.

"And a bachelor. Don't forget that."

All the women laughed.

Logan's jaw dropped. The women at that table were discussing him! They thought him handsome, and they also believed they might have a chance to secure his attention. Something must be done. The time had come to get his engagement out in the open. He'd planned to make a formal announcement to his congregation in December, giving them enough time to get used to the idea, but not so much time for them to make elaborate plans.

A quiet, simple ceremony with only family present would suit him just fine. His wedding didn't require large amounts of pomp anyway. All he wanted were a few witnesses as he made his vows before the Lord to honor and cherish Karen until death parted them.

Florence returned. She stuck close to his side throughout the evening meal and fireworks display. Apparently, securing a guy as her escort for one event gave her special rights to his attention for the rest of the day. Logan tried not to sigh as he lounged in the park with his eyes on the sky, watching the explosions of color and sparkle above them.

DURING THE FOLLOWING DAYS, Florence stopped at the church three times. On each visit, she accomplished her mission of cornering him with no avenue of escape.

Friday afternoon, Logan took his Bible and his books to his house where he could lock the door and hide.

Pacing his parlor practicing his sermon, he noticed the same young women from the Independence Day pageant on the sidewalk in front of his house walking in pairs, meeting up with friends, or strolling alone. Either the homes farther down the street had an unusually large number of social gatherings planned for the weekend, or these girls were spying on him.

Maybe they hoped to find him in the yard or meet him on the sidewalk. Then they'd be in the right place to receive an invitation to dinner or accept his initiation of a courtship. Or at least, that line of thinking is what made sense based on the conversation he'd overheard. Even though he'd disappoint their expectations, he must break the news to them his heart was taken, and he'd already made plans to share his life with someone else.

SUNDAY MORNING, Logan instructed the congregation to sit down after the last hymn.

Instead of offering the blessing, he continued. "I have an announcement I'd like to share with all of you. This past year while I farmed in Silver Grove, I met a young woman I've asked to be my wife. She accepted, and we're engaged. Here is her picture." Logan held up the framed image of Karen he kept on his mantle. She'd had the picture taken shortly after her return to Chicago and mailed him a copy.

People leaned forward in their pews for a better look.

"We're planning to be married in January." Unsure what to

expect in response, Logan scanned the group. Many of them smiled at him. But some, mostly the young women who'd been in the pageant along with their mothers, looked disappointed. He raised his arms for the benediction before he went to the back of the sanctuary to greet people when they left.

"Congratulations, Pastor Logan! We're so happy for you."

Smiling people shook his hand. Over and over again, he heard the same enthusiastic response.

"Best wishes on your future."

The same young ladies who had talked about him in the park and spent extra time spying on his house offered these words as well, but they were said with sadness.

These women would get over him eventually. He really wasn't that great of a catch. Shy and studious, Logan was the last person to offer a woman an exciting courtship. Amazing that Karen was willing to marry him, especially considering the long-distance engagement she must endure. If these girls only knew.

Florence pouted at him with a warning in her eyes that said she may still try to change his mind. She'd get nowhere, and he'd remind her as often as necessary. He left the sanctuary and went to his study, passing the members of the Ladies Mission Society on the way.

Bits of their conversation reached him, confirming his worst fears. His wedding dominated their discussion. Oh, boy. With these ladies intently making plans, he didn't stand a chance of a quiet, simple start to his new marriage.

4

Karen faced her class of young women ready to deliver an announcement she'd received from the principal earlier that morning. "If I could have your attention, please."

The combined class of eleventh- and twelfth-grade girls focused on their teacher.

"As you know, the summer term will end in August. Emerson Ladies Academy usually tries to offer you the opportunity to participate in a performance to showcase the work you've done in English over the summer. This year, the music, theater, and English departments are teaming up to present an exhibition at the Auditorium Building with a reception following in the hotel dining hall."

A collective intake of air filled the room as the girls turned to each other with awe on their faces. One young lady in the front row squealed and clapped her hands.

Mabel, seated in the back row, shot her hand into the air.

"Yes, Mabel?" Karen called on her.

"This is the biggest event we've participated in yet. Will it really be open to the public?"

"Will the school sell tickets?" Blanche, seated in the front row, forgot to raise her hand in all the excitement.

The others in the room nodded as if they wondered and hoped for the same outcome.

Karen laughed. "Yes, the event is open to the public. A notice will go in the *Chicago Tribune* at the beginning of August. I'm not sure about tickets. The auditorium is large enough to hold everyone." She rounded the corner of her desk with a smile, "You ladies will become famous."

More squeals from the front row.

"But first, you must each take a test, which I'll administer at the end of the week. Everyone who scores high enough on the test may go on to audition for a spot in the exhibition. Only eight students across all grade levels will be selected. These students may choose a recitation of poetry or an excerpt from a book to perform at the exhibition. I'll work with you and help you prepare.

"The students who aren't selected will participate in a program on campus the last week of school. Everyone will have a reading to learn. Your performances will count as part of your grade, so do your best and take the time you need to learn your speeches and memorize them. Any questions?" Karen looked around the room. "Yes, Stella."

The young woman three rows back lowered her hand. "What is on the exam? How do we study for it?"

"Excellent questions." Karen pulled a book out from under a stack of papers on her desk. "I'll help you with that starting now, so please take out your textbook and turn to chapter three."

Karen spent the day repeating the announcement to the girls in the younger grades, answering questions, and assigning homework. She worked hard teaching her students the rest of the week, so they were prepared for testing.

Friday came. Karen followed the procedure of handing out the packets of questions to each student, maintaining quiet in the classroom, and staying late to check the answers. Her confidence rose as she turned the tests into the principal. Surely the Emerson Ladies Academy was bursting with English students ready to display their talent.

Maybe another letter would arrive from Oswell City. Reading Logan's news would help keep her mind off of the suspense. So would worship with her family at the large stone church downtown and a peaceful dinner afterward.

MONDAY CAME AND WENT. Karen heard nothing from the principal, Miss Gregory, about grades. Tuesday morning passed in much the same way. Over the lunch hour, she shared the café with other teachers.

"I was surprised by the results of the auditions in the music department," the strings instructor said before taking a bite of her sandwich.

"Did you have any students qualify for the audition?" the vocal instructor asked.

"Yes, but not the ones I expected. Two of my students will have to work very hard to get ready to perform entire pieces."

"The same happened to me," the vocal instructor said. "Most of the students I thought would qualify will be auditioning, but three students did better than I expected."

"You mean to say that the results have already been shared? When did you find out? How?" Karen looked at the other teachers in confusion.

"Miss Gregory informed us this morning." The strings instructor glanced at Karen before taking a bite of her sandwich.

Karen's stomach sank until her lunch no longer interested her. She hadn't received any information from the principal. This must mean that none of her students had scored high enough to advance. Maybe the students enrolled in the summer term weren't good enough to perform at the exhibition.

Those who stayed on campus through the summer were the

ones who needed the reinforcement of the material covered during the school year. They struggled more to retain information, even though many of them had tutors who met one-on-one to offer the highest levels of support the academy had available. Girls like Stella and Blanche in the higher grades, Gladys in the freshman class, and Jane in the sophomore class, still fell behind even with a tutor.

The English department would enjoy no representation at the highly anticipated event. She couldn't bring herself to ponder how badly this reflected on the school. She, a new teacher on staff for barely a month, had failed to produce competent English students.

Karen left the café and went down the hall to Miss Gregory's office. Prepared with an apology for her ineptitude, she knocked.

"Come in," came the response.

She opened the door and faced the principal at a loss of where to begin.

"Miss Gregory, I'm so sorry none of my students obtained high scores on the test this week."

"Whatever are you talking about? Your students did wonderfully." Miss Gregory shuffled some papers on her desk.

"Oh, but I thought, you see, I haven't received any scores." Karen sat down in one of the chairs facing the desk, weary from her disappointment.

"There must be some mistake. I saw the results. Most of your girls will be auditioning." Miss Gregory stood. "Let me check on something. I'll be right back." She left the room, her shoes clicking down the hall until fading when a door shut.

Karen's gaze wandered over the high ceiling and wide woodwork of the office. At least she and her students hadn't failed. Maybe she'd end up as a better credit to the school than she thought.

Miss Gregory returned with a sheet of paper in her hand. "Here it is, Miss Millerson. All but two of your students scored. Stella and Jane may plan to present at our campus program, but the others are eligible to audition. Auditions are July 27 in the Student Hall. Congratulations."

Karen accepted Miss Gregory's handshake, her mind spinning. The girls would be so happy. She must find a way to tell them that would make them feel special.

The bell rang. Karen thanked Miss Gregory and then returned to her class. She waited until her students arrived and took their seats.

"Ladies, I have great news," Karen said. "All of you in this freshman grammar class scored high enough on Friday's test to qualify for an audition."

Clapping and squeals followed the announcement.

"Auditions for the August exhibition are July 27, two weeks away. I want to help you prepare, so please choose an excerpt from one of these classics to memorize for the audition." Karen turned to the chalkboard and wrote a list including *Pilgrim's Progress, The Collected Poems of Emily Dickinson,* and *Confessions.* A copy of Saint Augustine's thick tome lay on her shelf at home, a duplicate copy from her fiancé's library.

The girls indicated their preferences when Karen called on them.

"Very good. I will write your names down with the title of your chosen reading." Karen made a list as she walked down the aisles.

By the end of the day, each student heard the news and made their selection. Karen stood in her empty classroom, reading the lists of names. How fun it would be to work with the students in a setting that offered more relaxation and socializing than the academy.

After she arrived home that evening, Karen sat with Aunt Fran in the drawing room. "Could you please help me with a project?"

"Why, of course, my dear. What is it?" Aunt Fran laid aside the menu she'd been creating.

"I'd like to invite some of my students over on Saturday

afternoon for rehearsal and coaching with tea and cake afterward."

"Lovely idea. I'll help you with invitations and arrange the food with our staff." Aunt Fran smiled.

Karen clasped her hands in her lap. "Thank you." No matter the outcome of test scores or selection for the exhibition, all were welcome for fun and refreshments at the teacher's house.

SATURDAY AFTERNOON, the sun shone warm. The girls clustered in the shade on the wicker furniture and on blankets spread on the lush grass. The fountain in a nearby pool spouted a crystal stream into the clear blue sky. Mid-summer flowers bloomed in the garden. Butterflies flitted around the petals and landed on skirts and hats, adding to the charm of the day. Karen poured tea into fine porcelain cups for each of the girls and served cake.

"This is the best. I haven't had this much fun since I don't know when." Mabel accepted a refill of her teacup.

"You mean you haven't had this much fun since Annie's brother shoved you off the boat into the lake." Blanche grinned at her friend.

Mabel turned red, from anger or embarrassment, Karen couldn't say. Maybe some of both.

"That wasn't any fun. Harold should know better." Mabel scowled.

The incident happened in June on an outing the ladies academy shared with a school for boys. While Annie attended the academy, her brother went to the boys' school. A serious crush had developed that day. Mabel still hadn't recovered from the attention lavished on her by the handsome and rakish Harold.

"Let's work on our samples for the audition next week." Karen steered the conversation into safer territory. "Who signed up to recite poetry?"

Five of the girls raised their hands.

Karen retrieved her Emily Dickinson book and turned to a page where her bookmark rested. "Repeat this after me. I'll help you learn it. *Our share of night to bear. Our share of morning. Our blank in bliss to fill. Our blank in scoring."*

The girls did as Karen asked, and most of them reached the end. Only two of the girls needed prompting to recall the words.

"Say it once more." Karen started them and then quit so she might listen to their progress. "Very good. We will work on this again in class next week."

She coached the others in their selections, making the same promise to help them perfect their recitations in class.

"Tell us about your engagement ring, Miss Millerson." Blanche pointed to Karen's hand.

"It's pretty. Who is the groom?" Jane asked.

The other members in the party, lagging after the efforts of memorization, snapped to full attention.

"His name is Logan, and he lives in Iowa." Karen removed the ring from her finger and passed it around the gathering. Some of the girls tried it on. Others held it in the sunlight, enjoying the sparkle.

"When is your wedding?" Gladys passed the ring to a friend.

"After Christmas, when the fall term is finished."

"You mean we'll have a different teacher for the spring semester?" Stella asked.

"I'm afraid so." Karen didn't want to quit teaching. She wanted a life with Logan and her teaching career. Many restless nights had passed in which Karen lay awake while her mind stretched the circumstance, twisting it into various scenarios.

But the outcome remained the same. Married women were not allowed to teach. She knew that when she'd accepted Logan's proposal. The time had come to make her choice.

"Where are you getting married?" Mabel asked.

"In a little town in Iowa called Oswell City. It's where Logan lives."

"Will we get to meet him?" Annie handed the ring back to Karen.

"Most likely. He plans to visit me here in the city for a week in August. In fact, I think he will be here during our exhibition." Pleasure warmed Karen's face. She could show Logan the best of her efforts in the form of talented young ladies.

Smiles broke out on the faces of many in the group. Karen never could have predicted it, but the idea of performing for her fiancé provided the girls with the extra motivation they needed to pull through the audition.

The next week, Karen worked and coached and prompted. How she'd love to see every girl rewarded for her efforts with a place in the exhibition. But only eight were allowed to participate. Two from each class. Thursday night, Karen sat in the back of the small theater in the student hall and watched the audition.

First, the vocal students performed, followed by the instrumental students, the theater students, and finally the English students. Karen rode the streetcar home that night, tired but excited. Her students had done well. Now the question remained of which girls would perform at the exhibition.

She awoke early and rushed to the school, where she stood before the trophy case in the student hall, reading the names on the list of selected students. Mabel, Blanche, Ruby, Annie, Edith, Bertha, Thelma, and Minnie. Pride swelled Karen's chest. She would announce the results today and then spend as much time helping the girls prepare as they needed to give a flawless performance.

5

Seated at the head of a long table in one of the church's classrooms, Logan read through the items in need of discussion at tonight's meeting. Topics like repair of the felt in the offering plates, scheduling the organ tuner, hiring Oswell City staff to maintain the church lawn for the remainder of the summer, and a variety of confidential issues concerning certain families in the congregation completed the list on the paper in front of him.

He raised his head, ready to call the meeting to order with a word of prayer. But prayer was the furthest thing from the minds of the people seated around the table. As soon as Logan made eye contact, questions burst forth, all of them concerning his engagement.

"Whoa, wait a minute." He held up his hand. "We have a long list of matters to discuss tonight. Let's not waste our time talking about me." Logan's gaze wandered to a separate sheet of paper detailing the situation related to the piece of property Oswell City Community Church had recently acquired. Here was the topic he wished to spend the majority of the meeting discussing.

The typed report informed him that in the month of April,

the Akerman family had given to the church ten acres of land, which included an apple orchard, a barn, and a house. Logan's brow furrowed as he read. What in the world would a church do with an apple orchard and a house? He couldn't imagine. But he wouldn't need to figure it out alone. The best leaders Oswell City had to offer surrounded him.

"But you're the talk of the town. Ever since your announcement of your upcoming wedding, downtown has been buzzing." James Koelman, senior partner in his law firm, leaned forward and pointed at Logan.

"It's been great for sales. The young men in Oswell City are taking their cues from you, Pastor De Witt. Rings are flying off the shelf." Artie Goud, proprietor of the jewelry store, clicked his tongue in delight. "If I were you, I'd expect a busy fall season filled with weddings."

Logan's face heated. The last thing he needed to keep his mind off of his own wedding and focused on church affairs was an unending stream of other people's weddings. Attending wouldn't be so bad, but he'd never get by with that. These young couples would call on him to officiate each and every ceremony.

There'd be no escape from wedding liturgy running through his mind night and day. *Do you take this woman to be your wife? Will you love her, comfort her, honor and protect her, and forsaking all others, be faithful to her as long as you both shall live?*

Logan shook his head to clear it. If he allowed his mind to stay distracted with daydreaming of his upcoming wedding like it wanted, he'd be worthless in the pulpit. Study and the delivery of meaningful messages would cease. Fragments of the wedding vows already entertained his thoughts. He resisted the temptation to clutch both sides of his head as though fighting a monstrous headache.

"Tell us the whole story," George Brinks said.

"The little bit you shared with us on Sunday morning gave us no clues." Alex Zahn rested his hands on his stomach like he was ready to settle in and listen for hours.

"How did you meet?" Doctor Matthew Kaldenberg asked.

"What made you decide to get married?" The question from his good friend Paul Ellenbroek punched Logan's middle.

"Some of the story you might already know." He relived the uncertainties and seeking after God in prayer all over again. "I took time off last year to stay on the farm with my mother. We needed extra money, so I agreed to board the school teacher. I wasn't expecting to fall in love with her or with anyone ever.

"But I did." He cleared his throat. "I believed the Lord had called me to singleness to better serve him and to serve you. When Karen came into my life, I was forced to reconsider my sense of call. She feels called to serve the Lord just like I do. We'll make a great team. She's a talented singer, loves children, and is a great teacher. I can't wait for you to meet her."

The room quieted for a moment as though his listeners soaked in the pleasant warmth of sunlight.

"What a beautiful story." Jake Harmsen, editor of the local newspaper, spoke as if in a dream. He snapped into fuller awareness. "Know what I'd like to do?"

The others at the table shook their heads.

"Let's run an article in the *Oswell Journal*. I'll include her picture and a full story. Maybe even large enough for the front page." Jake beamed.

Logan's mouth fell open, and everything that could possibly escape from it, breath, words, everything, left him. He, Pastor De Witt, orator and persuader extraordinaire, sat like a pile of rocks with absolutely nothing to say. Karen's picture in the paper? And for the one reason of eventual marriage to the local preacher? The idea never entered his head. Not even once. He really shouldn't allow such a scandal to happen.

He shook his head and croaked, "No." He cleared his throat. "No." Much stronger the second time. "Please don't."

"Not even a paragraph?" Jake pleaded.

Logan shook his head.

"Or an introduction?"

Another head shake.

"Just the picture?"

Surely enough newsworthy events took place in Oswell City to supply Jake with ample stories. He shouldn't need to fill up space in the paper with a photo of the pastor's fiancée. Logan might have succeeded as a self-proclaimed bachelor, and he might surprise more people than just himself with the sudden facts of his engagement, but he didn't need the newspaper's help in making the changes in his life more believable.

"No, Jake. I appreciate your interest. But publicity won't be necessary." Logan reached for the report on the Akerman land. "Let's turn our attention to the property the church inherited. It says here that the house is inhabited." Logan shifted his attention from the words on the page and onto the faces at the table.

They were the consistory—men who served their community as doctors, lawyers, businessmen, and farmers. Here sat men of integrity who lived their faith out in the world, honoring the Lord and testifying to his gospel message while conducting business and influencing lives. Elected by their peers, these leaders assisted Logan in shepherding and guiding the congregation. Surely he could count on them to make wise decisions in the best use of this surprise gift of land.

The group exchanged cautious glances.

Logan took the response as yes, someone most certainly lived in the house. "Who lives on the Akerman place?"

After several moments of silence, James spoke up. "Nellie. She's eighty. Lives alone. Widowed, I believe."

"Ah." Grateful for the scrap of information, Logan envisioned a shrunken elderly lady in poor health and making crucial decisions in her last days as she anticipated a new life in heaven. The image clutched his heart. "Someone should call on her."

"Not me." Three of the men said in unison.

"No way I'm goin' out there," George said.

"Me neither." Alex held both hands up as though protecting himself from danger.

"Why not?" Logan asked. An older woman, vulnerable in her loneliness and physical struggles, deserved the attention of these leaders.

"Have you ever met her?" Paul asked.

"No, I haven't." Two of the Akerman sons and their families were regular attenders on Sunday morning, but the rest of the family Logan had never seen.

"Lucky," Jake whispered under his breath.

"All right." Logan frowned. What could possibly loom so offensive about a frail widowed lady that none of these respected men would go near her? "I'll go out there and call on Mrs. Akerman." He pushed back from the table in an effort to hide his exasperation. "The church should reach out to her and determine the next step for turning this property over to our ownership. James, have you seen an abstract?"

"My office has asked for it, but it hasn't arrived yet."

"How far is the property from town?" Logan asked Paul.

"Two miles."

"Any other questions or concerns?" Logan could expect the venture to absorb half of a day out of his week. He mentally put the appointment on his calendar.

No one spoke up.

"Let's plan to meet again briefly a week from now so we can discuss how best to move forward. James, see if you can get a hold of the abstract in the meantime."

James nodded, and Logan directed the meeting to the other items on the agenda.

Monday afternoon of the following week, Logan hitched his horse to his buggy and ventured out of town on the southern road. After crossing the wooden bridge spanning the river, the road opened into rolling hills lush with the season's crops. Puffy clouds floated overhead. Birdsong drifted on the warm wind. The scent of corn pollen hung heavy in the valleys.

Paul's directions alerted Logan to a lane off to the west side of the road. He found it and turned the horse down a dirt path. Peeking out between the branches of overgrown apple trees above, a metal arch appeared with the words *Boomgaard van Liefde*.

Orchard of love. Only a friendly place would declare that sort of welcoming statement. Logan tapped the horse with the reins, eager to discover what lay beyond the sign. The lane proceeded through a thicket of apple trees until reaching a yard filled with weeds and thistles. The barn's weathered exterior displayed sparse patches of faded red paint as a testament to what it had once been.

A two-story home, complete with a porch spanning two sides and a tower at one end, looked aged, much like the barn. Logan pulled the buggy to a halt, tied the reins to a pillar, and ventured up the rickety steps and across the porch's rough boards.

He knocked on the door, but nothing happened. He knocked again. Sparrows landed on a nest near his head, chirping frantically as if to inform him loud and clear he was an impostor. He went to a window and glanced at the room beyond. Masses of black skirt on a severe black dress covered the form of an elderly woman with white hair and many fine lines on her face. She reclined on a worn loveseat. Her eyes were closed.

"Mrs. Akerman?"

Logan tapped on the window, but the lady gave no response. She had either left the earth for eternity unseen or had fallen into such a deep sleep that not even a roaring windstorm could wake her.

He looked around. If the woman no longer breathed, she needed attention, and if she slept, someone barging into her house might frighten her to death. Only one course of action made any sense to him. Carefully opening the door, he tiptoed into the parlor. He stood still and studied the woman for a moment.

"Mrs. Akerman?" he called her name loudly enough to reach her ears but quietly enough not to startle her should the sound rouse her.

Once again, he received no response.

The condition of her breathing remained hidden from his angle. She surely must have died, and he was the first person to discover the fact. He needed help, but first, he must confirm his findings. Logan sat beside her and gently lifted her wrist to feel for a pulse.

A terrific slap landed on his cheek. In alarm, he dropped her arm and rubbed the stinging area on his skin.

"What do you think you're doing?"

If looks could roast, the whole town could serve him up for Sunday dinner.

She straightened and reached for her cane. Pounding it twice on the floor, she yelled at him. "Can't an old woman get any rest around here? First, my son's hired man comes stomping through my kitchen. Then the neighbor's geese honk around in my yard. Now you."

She said "you" as if he belonged on the manure pile.

"Who are you anyway, one of them lawyers pesterin' me for information about this place?" She glared at him in much the same way the town sheriff might stare down a criminal.

Logan cleared his throat. "I'm Pastor Logan De Witt from Oswell City Community Church."

She closed her eyes. For a moment, Logan believed the announcement of his identity had stolen the life out of her. If only Dr. Kaldenberg were close by. Then Logan could turn this whole mess over to him.

A groan escaped her lips. "I knew you'd be coming. The boys told me what they've done." She leaned on her cane and stood. The shrunken lady would barely graze Logan's shoulder if he stood as well, but her presence swelled sharp and demanding, making her seem tall and strong.

She pounded her cane again. "Can you believe what my family is trying to do to me? They want to up and give my home away right out from under me, and with me still in it!" She said the last sentence like someone trapped on a boat caught in a swirling flood. Mrs. Akerman sat down in an ornate chair opposite him and looked out the window. "We were rich. Once. Rich in money. Rich in love. But that was a long time ago."

"What happened?" Logan crossed his legs and leaned back.

A cynical smile claimed her lips. "What do you care about the life story of a silly old woman?"

"I care a lot," Logan said.

"Well."

The word conceded to his interest and yet criticized him for it.

"My husband Jelmer and I married in Holland. His brothers had come to America, so he thought it would be a good idea if we did too." She gave a caustic laugh. "We made money on our orchard. Good money. But then he got the bright idea to go to war. In a new country for five years, and then he thinks he has to fight in the Civil War.

"He signed up as a volunteer with the 17th Iowa Regiment. Fought in Mississippi. Killed at Vicksburg. They shipped his body home. We laid him out right here for all the neighbors to see so they could pity me and gloat over their good fortune in this new land when my dreams had met with ruin." With a flourish, she waved her hand at the spacious, shabby parlor.

Another caustic laugh escaped her mouth. "*Boomgaard van Leifde*." The words rolled off her tongue. Distance and passing decades had not removed the natural language from her soul. "You probably saw the sign when you came."

"I did."

"It was true once, but not anymore. The sign should read *woestijn van wanhoop*." She slumped in resignation.

Desert of despair. Logan's throat ached. The physical being of this woman might sit before him living and breathing, but her heart had died long ago.

She leaned on her cane and crossed the room to a hutch where she opened a door. "Here's his sword. At least I got to keep that."

A gleaming blade reflected sunlight that broke into the house between the vines of Virginia Creeper growing over the outside wall.

"Lieutenant Jelmer Akerman." She clicked her tongue. "How proud we could have been if he'd lived. If only he'd come back to me so we could harvest our apples and continue on in love." Her gaze fixed on the window as though viewing scenes far beyond the summer day.

The world of this woman's past came alive for him. Willing to follow her husband's dreams of life in America, she'd helped him grow their farm and their family only to lose him and raise the children alone. Logan looked around the room.

Portraits of them as a family and as a couple hung on wires from the ceiling in ornate frames, the images faded and dusty. He sat quiet and unmoving as the woman wept. Today was not the time for him to ask her for cooperation in the loss of her home.

"May I pray with you?" Logan leaned forward.

"If you want to," she said with a shrug.

He petitioned the Lord for her comfort and healing. "May I call on you again?"

"I suppose, but don't come with the intent of removing me from my home. It's all I have left of him." Her voice caught.

Logan nodded and left the house. He untied his horse, thankful for the drive back to town. It offered him lots of time to figure out what on earth he might give as a report on their progress at the next consistory meeting.

6

"Mrs. Akerman won't leave her home," Logan announced to the men gathered at the church with him.

"But she has to. The church owns the property. I have the deed. Her son Fred brought it in. He also signed the papers and gave me the abstract. News of your visit to his mother today likely hastened the process along." James produced the documents he mentioned and fanned them out on the table.

The elderly woman would like him even less if his visit provided Fred Akerman with a spurt of motivation.

"She'll hate that." Logan studied James's documents attempting to make sense of the information shared in the abstract. If the Oswell City Community Church really did own an orchard, then he, as the pastor, should have a clear understanding of where the property lines lay.

"She hates most everything, including my specialty cream puffs." Alex wrinkled his nose in disgust. "Threw every one of them out the window when I last called on her. She said the puffs had too many flies landing on them. If she'd put screens on those ancient windows of hers, the flies wouldn't bother her in the first place." Alex's voice rose as if the situation happened to him all over again.

"She chased me with a broom once." Dr. Kaldenberg spoke up. "She refused to take some medication I brought for her, so she ran me out of the house."

"That must have been a few years ago. The poor lady leaned pretty heavily on a cane while I was there," Logan said.

"Only a year ago. Canes don't slow her down too much when she's upset." Dr. Kaldenberg chuckled.

"Did she show you her sword?" Paul asked.

"She did."

"Nellie didn't take it out of the cabinet and point it at you, did she?" George peered at him.

"No." Logan's eyes widened. How on earth could such a tiny shriveled woman brandish that heavy sword?

"Good. It happened to me one time when the hired man and I were talkin' on the porch. Here comes Nellie draggin' that sword along behind her. She swung it around until the point of it nicked my boot. Apparently, that day was the anniversary of her husband's death in the war. She was doin' some remembering, and I guess she wanted to make sure no one else forgot it either."

Logan drew in a deep breath. After hearing these stories, mercy had definitely been on his side. "She only slapped me."

"What did you do to deserve a slap?" Jake asked.

"I thought she'd died." He cleared his throat. "She didn't appear to be breathing, so I tried to check for her pulse, but she surprised me with a smack to my cheek."

"Slapping the preacher." Jake cackled. "It's her best trick yet. Wait 'til word gets out about that."

He laughed again, and several of the others joined him.

"Something must be done about this situation." Logan's heart ached for the lonely old woman. "Clearly, Nellie Akerman cannot continue to live on the land if the family no longer owns it."

"The place needs fixing up anyway, and she can't afford to pay for the work," James said.

"Maybe she can move in with Fred and his family. They might have room," Artie suggested.

"Good idea." Logan studied the documents on the table. "James, when will you see Fred again?"

"Tomorrow afternoon."

"Could you please visit with him about his mother moving in with him?" Logan asked.

James nodded.

"What do you think we should do with the place?" Alex's gaze traveled over the men's faces.

"Good question. We can't just let a run-down farmstead sit. The condition of the buildings will only get worse," Jake said.

"You got any ideas?" George looked at Logan.

"No, I don't. We didn't expect to inherit a piece of ground. If it came with a dairy herd, I might consider taking up milking again," Logan said as a smile tugged on one side of his mouth. "Do any of you have any ideas?"

The men looked at each other and shook their heads.

"Let's commit the question to prayer and trust the Lord to show us his plan for this property. He obviously has one, since the land fell into the hands of a local congregation. We can discuss it more in August." Logan consulted the calendar he brought with him. "That reminds me. I'm traveling to Chicago for a week in August, so we need to meet before I leave."

Knowing smiles lit the faces of the other men. Logan could guess why. Their pastor was engaged and planning to get married, deserving of time off to spend with his fiancée.

Those smiles were probably also a reflection of their happiness for him, and maybe even a clue to the conversations happening in their homes regarding the pastor's wedding. The wives of these men belonged to the Ladies Mission Society. Logan could believe the women were as happy to talk over all kinds of grandiose plans as the men were to see him get some time away.

He adjourned the meeting with prayer and went home.

On Tuesday, in the midst of a productive afternoon of study, Fred Akerman came to the church. From the distraught expression on the man's face, Logan could see he needed some attention.

"Good afternoon, Fred. Please come in." Logan gestured to one of the chairs near the bookshelves.

Fred took it.

"What can I do for you?" Logan asked.

"It's Mama." Fred hung his head. "I came from the lawyer's just now. He says Mama should move in with me, but she's determined to hang onto my father's sword. My wife won't like that. She gets nervous whenever the grandkids are around it. She won't want that thing in our house."

"Hmm." Logan had witnessed the special meaning the sword held for Mrs. Akerman. He leaned back in his chair and removed his glasses. Dr. Kaldenberg had been right—he hardly noticed them anymore. The adjustment had taken much less time than he'd expected.

"Would you come back out to the farm and talk to her? You'd have the best luck convincing her." The pleading in Fred's voice betrayed his desperation.

If he could somehow avoid swords, slaps, and brooms, he might stand a chance at a successful conversation.

"I'll come now." He stood and replaced his glasses while shutting his Bible.

"Great." The sun came out for Fred in the form of a broad smile. "We need to get Mama moved and settled before harvest. The place is too far gone for us to afford fixing it up, and Mama is growing older. The time has come to start makin' some decisions." Fred chattered on the way out the door.

At the orchard, Logan noticed a second buggy in the yard. He jumped down while Fred tied the reins and knocked on the door.

Florence answered.

What was she doing here? "Flor-Florence." Stuttering returned in full force. "Uh ... hello. I mean, good afternoon. I ... uh ... didn't expect to see you here."

She offered him a coy smile as if accustomed to producing startling effects on every man she met. "Aunt Clara and I are delivering items left over from a bake sale."

A new thought darted through his mind as his face heated. She'd better not try to flirt with him and land kisses on his cheek during this visit. He'd rather sustain a slap from the elderly lady complaining in the parlor.

Florence behaved herself, almost. That is if tucking her hand in the crook of his arm qualified as proper behavior. Left with no other choice, he escorted her to the parlor with Fred close behind. Logan shook free of Florence's grasp and claimed a straight-back chair near the blackened dusty fireplace. A seat for one offered no space for Florence's unwelcome attention.

Clara sat on the sofa, listening to Mrs. Akerman's tirade about her family's terrible betrayal in giving away her home. Patience and understanding bloomed on Clara's face.

"Pastor De Witt!" She stood and smiled when the group entered. "What a nice surprise. Nellie was just telling me of your visit yesterday."

"How are you, Mama?" Fred bent to kiss his mother's cheek. "You seem upset."

"You better know it. Of course, I'm upset. My family is doing everything they know how to oust me out of my home. Goodness. What would your father say?" She crossed her arms and glared.

"Where are you going to go?" Clara looked at Nellie and then at Fred.

"We don't know yet." He sighed. "The lawyer wants her to move in with me. We've got plenty of space."

"Don't leave your father's sword here. Who knows what would become of it. That sword must come with me." Mrs. Akerman shook her finger at her son.

"There's our problem." He sighed again. "My wife will never put up with that sword in our house."

"You need a place to live?" Clara studied Nellie.

"I suppose I do since my family won't look out for me," Mrs. Akerman said in a peevish voice.

"I have just the perfect set-up." Clara clasped her hands together. "How about you move in with Florence and me? You could have your own room right next to the sitting room with plenty of light from the windows and space to entertain guests. Why, yes. I believe it will work well. What do you say, Florence?" She turned to look at Florence, as did everyone else in the room, and found her gazing at Logan.

The interest in her eyes made him want to pull Mrs. Akerman's crocheted afghan over his head. Instead, he stood and paced to the windows.

Florence snapped her attention to her aunt. "Of course, Aunt Clara. Whatever you want."

"I've never lived in town a day in my life." Mrs. Akerman sounded terribly offended.

"But you'd be close to everything—the shops downtown, the bank, the church. Two widow ladies like us need each other's company. With a young girl like Florence around, you'll have activity and life in the house."

Mrs. Akerman rested in a solemn quiet for a few moments before the question slipped from her lips. "You'll make room for the sword?"

"Plenty of room." Clara's simple answer just might change the world.

"All right then, I'll move out of this dingy, stuffy place and go where I'm wanted." Mrs. Akerman delivered her speech with a critical eye to her son.

He merely rolled his eyes and said nothing.

Maybe the need to appease her deep loneliness prompted her sudden cooperation. The sword, a relic from her husband, had probably provided companionship in the past. Logan's curiosity grew to see if her new location in town among active, caring people might ease her severe attachments. He prayed healing happened.

LATER IN THE WEEK, after his sermon took shape, Logan took advantage of a couple of free hours on Friday afternoon and walked over to the new home of Nellie Akerman. At least Florence didn't answer the door when he knocked. But his relief dwindled as soon as Clara welcomed him into the house. Florence met him in the hall and slipped her hand around his arm once more.

"I knew you'd come to your senses and call on me someday," Florence said in her throaty voice.

Logan shook free of her grasp and glanced into the kitchen and a den as Florence led him to the parlor. Surely Mrs. Akerman hovered around somewhere. Unless, of course, she napped. He should have remembered to come in the morning instead of early afternoon as he'd done on his first visit.

"I'd hoped to check on your new house guest." Logan gave the parlor a thorough examination in hopes of detecting Mrs. Akerman's whereabouts.

"Aunt Clara settled her in for a nap and now must leave for a meeting of the garden club." Florence fingered his tie. "You have perfect timing."

"I must head back to the church." He stepped back and reeled his tie away from her.

"Stay here with me for a while." Florence's attention moved to smoothing his sleeve. "I'm sure we have lots to talk about."

"No. Really, I must go."

Logan turned around, but Florence was quick. She dogged his steps as he moved across the room. At the parlor doorway, Florence wedged herself in front of him. Cornered again. How she managed to succeed time after time baffled him.

She looped her arms around his neck. "I'm lonely too and in need of calls from my minister."

Her advances stole his speech. Never had she called him her minister before. Even when they'd courted, she hadn't used the phrase.

"I'm engaged," he whispered, looking her straight in the eye.

She pouted, but her arms remained in place around his neck.

"Good afternoon, Florence." Logan squeezed past her and untangled himself from her embrace by the time he reached the front door.

The walk back to the church was too short to calm his nerves. He stomped around in the sanctuary as he shoved furniture into new locations, thumbed through a hymnal, and rearranged the offering plates. Still, he felt rattled from Florence's attention. Would the girl never learn? Maybe he should send for Karen now so that Florence could see his engagement was for real.

If Karen didn't need to fulfill that teaching contract, he'd do it, no matter how skimpy his savings. Someday, Florence would catch on. He didn't belong to her and never would.

ON SUNDAY MORNING, he faced a full sanctuary. Off in the corner, Logan caught a glimpse of Clara and Florence in their usual pew. Seated with them was Nellie Akerman dressed in her black dress and with her white hair pulled back from her face. The skin around her mouth looked weathered and tired, but her eyes were peaceful. Maybe a little of that healing Logan prayed for had already happened.

After the service, Mrs. Akerman hobbled up to him. He shook her hand, and then she used it to slap his cheek again. Not an angry, defensive act, but one of fondness.

"I like you, Pastor De Witt. I haven't heard sermons like yours in ages. It's kinda nice to get out and go to church again. Couldn't do it without Clara, though."

I'm glad you're here. Come again."

He offered a smile that actually produced one on her face. It seemed a bit faint from lack of practice, but over time she'd remember how to use it.

Logan left for his study before Florence could corner him again. Safely inside, he removed his robe and put his sermon notes away.

The consistory may have acquired a piece of land, and Clara Hesslinga might have earned superhero status for offering Mrs. Akerman a place to live, but the question of what to do with the gift hung on his mind. His work completed at the church for the day, Logan went home.

That afternoon, he finally had the chance to take the first step toward a wise decision. He sat down at his desk in the parsonage dining room and wrote a letter to Karen, pouring out to her all his concerns and questions. He ended with these comments:

The church leaders and I wonder what we should do with an orchard. Could you please join me in praying about this matter?

I wish you were here with me. Memories of our days in Silver Grove rush in often, reminding me of how deeply I miss you and how much I need you.

Looking forward to seeing you in August.

All my love,
Logan

7

Karen lifted the teacup to her lips while her ears picked up the conversation between Mother and Aunt Fran. She had little interest in their social doings. Gatherings of Mother's elite friends usually included boasts of the week's dinner parties, the menu, and who wore what. Weddings also received a thorough talking over, in which every detail of the dress design and veil were critiqued or admired.

Mother probably embellished the facts a bit when relaying them in an effort to apply subtle pressure on Karen to change her mind. But her decisions were made. Mother would just have to suffer some humiliation when her turn came to inform her friends of her daughter's no-nonsense wedding.

Karen reached for a scone and thought through the next week's lesson plans. The girls were coming along nicely in their preparations for the exhibition. With two more weeks of practice, every young lady would be ready to perform. Talk among the students at the academy centered on the dress each one planned to wear. The dress shops were kept quite busy producing gowns and their accessories for the big event.

Ida, the housekeeper, entered the drawing room and held a tray out to Karen. "A letter came for you from Pastor De Witt."

"Thank you." Karen's heart skipped a beat. Another letter from Logan. They were the joy of her existence these days. She took the envelope and felt it. Large and puffy, it must contain several pages filled with news. Or perhaps Logan had sent her important documents requiring her signature in preparation for their new marriage. How she'd love to race out of the house right now and seek her special spot on the lakeshore to discover the contents.

Aunt Fran looked at her. "Your fiancé must have quite a bit to say. What a large envelope."

"I'm eager to read it." Karen laid her mail on the table and refilled her teacup.

"Go ahead, my dear. I don't mind." Once in a while, Aunt Fran allowed her affection to break through her proper exterior.

Swallowing one last gulp of tea, Karen gathered up her mail and left the room. The brief walk to the lake took much longer than she wanted. Finally, she reached the sandy hill at the water's edge and slit the envelope.

Dearest Karen, the letter began. She could almost hear Logan's warm voice in the greeting. He went on to write of an orchard his church had acquired, using several pages to acquaint her with a lady named Nellie and to share his thoughts about the gift.

Could you please join me in praying about this matter? The sentence pierced Karen's heart. So many times, Logan had requested her prayers for one concern or another. If they were in Silver Grove right now, Logan would call her to the farmhouse parlor, ask her to share the sofa with him, and then he'd share his heart with her, ending the discussion with a quiet yet fervent request for her prayers.

Tears welled in her eyes. Separation was insufferable. They belonged together. Logan affirmed this truth in the last sentence of his letter, where he'd written how much he needed her. She needed him too. Their lives were already so closely intertwined. Her time in the city had better not weaken the bond. Praying with him and for him would help.

Her heart took in his last words. *All my love*. Then he signed his name.

The tears came. She worked hard in her teaching position at the academy, instructing her students and guiding them. But her hardest work lay in seeking contentment. She might succeed in finding enjoyment and satisfaction in her work if reminders of her approaching wedding didn't arrive almost daily. There were decisions to make, flowers to choose, and questions to answer about her dress.

Julia, in her well-meaning enthusiasm, brought little items she'd purchased for Karen's new home, unaware how much the thoughtful gesture tortured her sister. And just when Karen got her heart settled and decently satisfied with her life in the city, a letter from Logan arrived, calling her into a new life with an invitation to share in his work and daring her to dream of a secure future filled with love.

She allowed the tears to fall for only a short while before settling her heart once more, this time with a walk down the shore. The shallow waves lapped at her feet, splashing her shoes and skirt. After covering a good distance, Karen pulled Logan's letter out again. She reread the section about the gift of land.

The information contained a hole. He wrote all about acquiring the land, but he didn't say why the family wanted to give it away. Surely no one was trying to deceive Logan and his church. Uncle Henry might have some ideas.

Upon her return to the house, Karen went to his library. Uncle Henry sat at his ornately carved desk with an account book open before him.

"Uncle Henry?" Karen called from the doorway.

He glanced up. "Come in."

"I'm sorry to bother you. I just want to ask you a question. In the letter I received from Logan today, he mentions land given away to the church. Why would anyone do that? Wouldn't they sell it instead and keep the money?"

At the sound of Logan's name, Uncle Henry tensed. He and

Aunt Fran were the only ones in the family who hadn't yet met her fiancé. Surely memories of her father's mistakes didn't cloud her uncle's acceptance of the man she planned to marry. Uncle Henry still latched onto his low opinion of preachers, but Mother had completely changed her mind. And it happened after only knowing Logan for one day.

If Mother could change, so could Uncle Henry. Logan's visit to the city might be exactly what Uncle Henry needed. Then he could see for himself Logan's good character and understand why Karen wished to marry him.

"People gift land for various reasons." He tented his fingers. "Since they are giving it to a church, maybe it is an offering of sorts."

Karen took the information with her to her room. Logan must know she most certainly would pray for him, and a good place to start was in helping him find some answers. She sat at her writing desk and pulled out her monogrammed stationery to begin a letter at that very moment.

THE VIEW from the windows of the pastor's study gave Logan a full panorama of Main Street. He watched now, recalling a valuable bit of information he'd overheard on Sunday morning. Florence and her friends had scheduled a time to meet for coffee downtown. Ten-thirty Thursday morning. Logan glanced at his clock. Right on time. His attention returned to the window just as Florence and three other women entered the café.

Now was his chance. He sprinted around his desk, gathered up his Bible, and took off for Clara's house.

She answered when he knocked on the door. "Good morning. May I see Mrs. Akerman please?"

Clara smiled her greeting and admitted him into the house. A deep breath filled his lungs as he followed her down the hall. How nice to do his calling on these ladies Florence-free.

"Pastor De Witt is here to see you." Clara moved the curtain aside, allowing sunlight to stream into the room.

Mrs. Akerman had made herself at home. The same portraits from the parlor in her old house adorned the walls. Her love seat rested against one wall. The hutch occupied space nearby. Logan couldn't help himself. He eased a door open. Sure enough, the long, shiny sword hung within.

He turned his attention to the woman in the rocking chair. "How are you, Mrs. Akerman?"

"All this light is giving me a headache." Her hand rested on her forehead. "My house in the country is shaded. Too much sun in town."

Logan eased into the other chair in the room. Since Mrs. Akerman was in complaining mode, he should settle in for a long stay.

"Didn't realize town was so stuffy. This house can get so hot. But do my children care? No. Fred's only been to see me once. I'm still waiting on the others. But now that their mother is living in town, they probably think I don't need anything and will forget all about me." She waved her handkerchief in the air as though dismissing her clan as careless.

"Do you really think that's true?" Logan asked. "Living in town is a chance to make new friends. Your family won't forget about you just because you live in a different place."

Mrs. Akerman stared at her lap and gave no response.

Maybe talking about the sword would cheer her up. "I see you brought your husband's sword."

"Oh, the time Fred and the boys had moving that heavy thing in here." She pointed at the hutch. "Chipped the paint. See?" She pulled back the curtain to reveal nicks in the wall.

Bringing up the sword didn't work. "I was glad to see you in church on Sunday. Will you try and come again?"

"If Clara makes me, I suppose I'll have to. I'd forgotten how hard church pews are. Not sure my back can take it."

Clearly, Mrs. Akerman's mood didn't allow for any cheer

today. He needed to get back to the church anyway and make his escape before Florence came home.

"May I pray for you?"

"If you want to," she said with the same shrug she'd used the last time he'd asked.

He bowed his head and petitioned the Lord for his blessings in her life today. Logan couldn't cheer her up, but chances were good that God could.

Clara met him in the hall and showed him to the door. At the precise moment he turned the knob, the door swung open with no effort from him. Logan stumbled out of the house. When he regained his footing, he stood face to face with Florence. A smile quickly replaced her startled expression.

"Logan!" She rested a hand on his shirt front. "Looking for me?"

"I ... uh. I was just leaving. Have a good day." He sprinted into the street, not looking back during his entire walk to the church.

Seated in his chair behind his desk, Logan worked to catch his breath. That was close, but it was the best he could do. The only chance he had at an obstacle-free visit with Mrs. Akerman was to call in Florence's absence.

When the noon hour arrived, Logan went home to eat his lunch. Noticing the new supply of mail, he took it to the table and leafed through it as he ate. A letter from Karen caught his attention. He ripped the envelope and unfolded the stationery with an elegantly scripted -*KM*- in the corner.

She shared news of her students and details on wedding preparations before writing her response to the news Logan shared in his last letter. *Why does the family wish to give away their land instead of selling it?* He straightened away from the page for a moment. This is a question he should have thought to ask. Karen was a wonder. She completed him, and in doing so, helped him see with sharper vision.

Thank goodness he'd been smart enough to tell her about the

situation related to the property. His thoughts had been too preoccupied with Mrs. Akerman and convincing her to move out of her home to wonder for himself why the Akermans didn't sell the land. Now that she was settled in town, Logan and the other leaders had time to ponder this question and decide how to move forward.

He finished reading, while in the back of his mind, he ticked off the days until his visit to Chicago when he would see Karen again.

After lunch, he walked to the mayor's office in the city hall. As he entered, Paul looked up from his desk and greeted him.

"Did anyone mention a reason why the Akermans are giving their land away instead of selling?"

Paul thought for a moment. "No. I don't believe I ever heard one. We were waiting for you to return, so didn't ask many questions."

"Hmm." The desire to know claimed a strong grip on Logan's heart. "Thanks. I'll see if James knows anything."

With a nod to his friend, Logan strolled down Main Street to the Koelman Law Firm. Brandt led Logan to his father's office. They held a conversation similar to the one he'd had with Paul. It was also just as brief. Like the others, James hadn't stopped to wonder why the land was gifted to the church instead of sold for profit.

Only one other person could help him, and that was Fred himself.

LOGAN SOUGHT Fred out after church Sunday morning and invited him to his study.

"What can I help you with?" Fred asked.

"I should have thought to ask you much sooner. We've been caught off guard by your generous gift of land and so concerned about your mother that no one thought to ask why you want to give your land away. I'm not sure we should take it. Can you afford the donation? Wouldn't you rather sell it and have the money?" Logan folded his hands on his desk, eager to hear Fred's answer.

"You see, Pastor, it's like this. The land my father settled is rough. It's too rough to farm. There's cliffs along the back of it from a creek that runs through it. If we sold it, the land might bring a little money. Someone might be willing to try and make a living from it. But the truth is, my brothers and sisters and I talked this over, and we want the church to have it, and we want it given in memory of our father.

"He was a devout man, more religious than any of us. And he had big dreams of what he hoped to do for the Lord. But he died before getting started on those plans. So, take the land and do with it what you feel is best. Use it for the Lord's work as my father hoped to do someday. If you do, it will help us all remember him. Even Mama will find comfort in watching the changes. She doesn't act like it now, but it will mean the world to her, just like it will to the rest of us."

The long speech from the usually reserved man deserved a standing ovation or a column on the front page of the newspaper. Faith and vision shone in Fred's words. The quiet and unassuming farmer possessed more of both of those qualities than Logan did on some days. The gravity of the moment crowned the meeting with solemnity and honor.

"Thank you, Fred, to you and your family for your generous gift." In the absence of the brass section of Oswell City's marching band, Logan rounded the corner of his desk and held out his hand for a ceremonious handshake. "I'm honored, and I assure you the consistory and I will take very seriously the decisions we make to put your land to the best use possible for the kingdom."

"Something I've always wanted." Fred shook Logan's hand and mumbled as one lone bead of moisture formed in the corner of his eye.

8

Logan hastened home after the morning service to pack before catching the four o'clock train to Chicago. He rushed through his simple lunch. Too many Sundays he spent eating bacon, potatoes fried in the same pan, and slices of his own homemade bread. Never would he want anyone to find out he knew how to make bread. Mama had shown him how during a quick trip to the farm for Christmas, his first year as Oswell City's pastor.

'Anyone living alone should know the basics of how to make their own food,' she'd said during the lesson. 'You'll likely get married soon anyway. Then you'll have a wife to cook for you.'

Every Monday morning before tackling his laundry, Logan plunged his hands into sticky dough and kneaded it as he rehearsed the truth his heart knew so well. He must serve as a single man, unattached to anyone except the Lord and his calling on Logan's life. Without a wife or family, he made himself even more available to the Lord and his work.

Or, so he'd thought.

Karen had come into his life and demolished that bulwark of conviction. And here he sat eating his own bread with four years of practice to his credit while his mind journeyed ahead of him to the fiancée who awaited his arrival tonight. Mama's words would come true. Eventually. After a delay that took much longer than she'd wanted.

Logan smiled after gulping down half a glass of water. Five more months and Mama would have the daughter-in-law she'd always dreamed of. He cleared the table, washed the pan and the dishes, and rushed to the spare room in search of his suitcase. With it open on the bed, stacks of socks and trousers went in first. Then two ties. Next, his best dress shirts.

A knock came on the door.

Logan opened it to find Walter Brinks, son of the family who operated the hotel. The boy stood on the front step with a wild look in his eyes.

Memories of the last time Walter sought him on a Sunday flooded his mind. On that day last summer, Walter had delivered the worst news Logan had ever received. Only Mama, Tillie, and her husband remained as reasons for Walter to deliver more bad news from Silver Grove.

Or maybe the news came from Chicago. What if something had happened to Karen?

He licked his lips. He could take whatever Walter had to say. "What is it?"

"The hotel. You gotta come quick. Dad sent me." Walter tugged on Logan's arm.

"What happened?" Thank goodness the news involved no one in Logan's family or in Karen's. But a crisis downtown demanded his attention.

"A fire in the kitchen. Someone's been burned. Come on!" Walter led the way.

Smoke billowed from a window on the main floor. Dr. Kaldenberg examined the arm of a young woman seated on a bench. The fire department's engine arrived, its bell clanging and the siren blaring. The group of firemen jumped off as soon as the engine came to a stop and hooked a hose to a nearby hydrant. Alex and Paul came running, along with a crowd of neighbors.

George stumbled out with his nose and mouth buried in his sleeve. Walter ran to him. Logan followed along behind, trying to decide where he could be of the most help.

"So glad you came." George thumped his back.

"What can I do?"

"Help the doctor. More people have burns." George pointed to a cluster of people exiting the hotel and gathering in the yard to wait for the doctor's attention.

Logan nodded and went to the doctor, who by now had bandaged the woman's arm.

"Ah, Pastor Logan. Good to see you." Dr. Kaldenberg leaned in and spoke in a low voice. "Grease caught fire in the kitchen while the staff cooked the noon meal. Several of them worked to put the fire out, but the curtains caught fire, and soon the flames spread through the entire kitchen and into the dining room."

"I suspect all these people have injuries." He pointed at the cluster nearby. "Could you please talk with them and help them settle down as they wait for treatment?"

"Of course."

Logan spent the afternoon listening to the story of how the kitchen caught fire, worries over the damage done to the hotel, and concerns for their jobs. He prayed with each one. The last person joined the doctor on the bench when George came over.

"I think we've got it under control now."

"Good."

George watched the firemen reel up their hoses and jump back on the fire engine. Blackened squares on the ground floor marked the window openings to the kitchen, dining room, and lobby. Tendrils of smoke wisped to the sky. He stood still, his gaze distant and empty.

"Would you like to pray?" Logan rested a hand on George's stooped shoulder.

With tired movements, George turned. "Yeah. I'd like that."

Right there in the heart of town with a hot wind blowing the scent of charred wood across the trampled lawn, Logan asked the Lord to provide comfort for the Brinks family today and resources to rebuild in the days to come.

"Stop by the church next week if you need to talk. I'll be gone for a few days this week, but will have time when I return." Logan would be gone for a few days if he hadn't already missed the train. He hadn't heard a whistle from the direction of the depot in the chaos of George's tragedy. But his departure time surely drew near.

In an attempt to stay calm on the outside, Logan shook hands with George, but on the inside, everything quivered. He had to catch the four o'clock train.

George moved off down the street, and Logan jolted into action. He sprinted home and glanced at the clock. Three forty. Twenty minutes until departure. He could do this. He raced to his room and changed out of his smoky clothes. A quick combing of his hair and a toss of last-minute items into the suitcase, and he was ready to go.

A train whistle cut through the air. Logan slammed his suitcase shut, sprinted from his room, and locked the door of his house. Four blocks stretched between his home and the train station. He took off on a run waving to townsfolk who still milled around after the hotel fire and tried his best to avoid a collision with anyone in his path.

Panting, he entered the station, presented his ticket, and found a seat on the coach as the train began to chug in a slow pull away from the platform. When the train increased in speed, Logan leaned his head against the seat, allowing his mind to settle and his breathing to return to normal.

Karen anticipated his arrival on the other end of this journey. A whole week stretched before him in which he had no other cares except to enjoy her company. He could hardly wait.

THE LAMP GLOWED on the street outside the drawing room window. Mother thrust a needle and thread through the cross-stitch sampler in her hands. Uncle Henry read the newspaper. Aunt Fran held a book. Karen had tried to read, too, but her mind stayed distracted with thoughts of Logan. The train ride from Iowa required six hours.

As each hour of the afternoon passed, Karen remembered her own travels and envisioned when he crossed the Mississippi River, reached the outskirts of the city, and arrived at the station. His train was scheduled to arrive at ten o'clock. She checked the time. Nine fifteen. His train couldn't be late. She'd die if Logan didn't appear on time.

Maybe he'd arrive early. If he did, someone should be at the station waiting for him. How awful if he came to a strange place at night and no one met him.

Karen straightened. "We should go."

"Go where?" Uncle Henry peered around his paper.

"To the station. Logan could arrive any minute."

"Hank is planning to leave in fifteen minutes. Plenty of time." Uncle Henry disappeared behind the paper.

Karen stood. "But what if the train is early?"

"The Chicago and North Western is rarely on time. Why, just last week, Bertha Reynolds told me of a cousin coming to the city for a visit. They stood around for two hours waiting on his train." Aunt Fran held up two fingers to emphasize her point.

"But, someone should go with the chauffeur to meet Logan." Karen's chest tightened. The railroad didn't dare to keep her waiting until the wee hours of the next day for her fiancé to arrive in town. The delay would kill her. "Aren't you going, Mother?"

"No, my dear. By the time Hank gets him loaded up and takes the time to drive here, eleven o'clock will have come and gone. I'm going to bed soon. I plan to meet Logan at breakfast in the morning."

"Aunt Fran?" Karen attempted to keep the desperation from her voice.

Fran rose from the sofa. "Your uncle Henry and I are going to bed now."

"Like your mother, we'll meet Pastor De Witt in the morning." Uncle Henry folded up his paper.

"Then, I'll go." Karen clenched her fist and refrained from stomping her foot.

Uncle Henry's brows rose. "No, Karen. That's not a good idea. It isn't safe for a young woman of means to be out after dark."

"We don't want you venturing out alone." Mother's eyes held worry.

"Oh, no. Certainly not." Aunt Fran's voice held alarm.

"But I wouldn't be alone. I'd be with Hank. And on the return trip, Logan will be there too." Why did her upperclass family make her feel like a grade-schooler?

"Stay home." Uncle Henry lifted her chin with his index finger and looked into her eyes. "Wait for Hank to bring Pastor De Witt to you."

He should quit referring to Logan in such a way. Use of his formal name made Logan sound cold and strange, pushing him away to a manageable distance. Maybe that was what Uncle Henry wanted. Then he wouldn't have to make the effort to know Logan for who he really was. If Uncle Henry truly felt that way, he'd miss out on a relationship with the warmest, most kind-hearted man who'd ever lived.

Mother folded up her sampler. Sympathy replaced the worry in her eyes. Mother liked Logan and accepted him, but she lacked the influence with Uncle Henry to help him do the same. Mother valued many good things, but if they differed from Uncle Henry's priorities, she dared not cross him by speaking up or acting out.

Uncle Henry's opinions and preferences received the last word in the Millerson home. If Uncle Henry's opinions of Logan differed from Mother's, conflict and unrest would take up residence in their otherwise harmonious household. Mother may give in and let Uncle Henry's ideas rule, but Karen could not. She loved Logan, and she loved her family, but her heart told her who held her allegiances. This time they did not belong to Uncle Henry.

"Have a good night, my dear." Mother kissed her cheek. "Listen to your uncle," she whispered before taking the stairs, leaving Karen alone in the lamp-lit drawing room.

She held her breath. The moment of reckoning had come. Ever since the day of her father's death, Karen had done her best to listen to Uncle Henry, to respect him, and to follow his advice. He was a good man, a generous man, deserving of this response from his niece.

But another man had completely claimed her heart. In a few months, she would say the vows that committed her to respecting him and listening to him. Whatever consequences resulted from Karen's devotion, she'd accept it. Slipping into her shawl and pinning her hat in place, Karen eased out the kitchen door and headed to the garage.

Hank arrived at the Chicago and North Western terminal at nine forty-five and waited with her in the spacious lobby. People milled about, checking schedules, buying tickets, and dealing with the same impatience Karen felt. The clock suspended from the wall ticked away the minutes.

"The ten o'clock train from Omaha has pulled into the station. Passengers will arrive shortly." Finally, an announcement boomed through the air.

How lovely if she could burst into gleeful jumping this very moment. Logan had arrived. She'd see him any minute. A stream of people carrying satchels and other luggage entered the waiting area. Karen spotted Logan before he saw her.

His blond hair lay perfectly combed, even at this late hour. The black suit coat hung at crisp angles on his broad shoulders. He wore the spectacles he'd written of in an earlier letter. They made him look distinguished and more manly if that were even possible. He turned as if searching for her. A smile lit his face when their eyes met. He waved.

Karen could hold back no longer. Her legs propelled her across the waiting room. Tears streamed from her eyes, and laughter burst from her mouth as he caught her in a tight embrace. Kisses landed on her lips, her nose, her forehead, and back on her lips again.

"Oh, I've missed you!" Logan crushed her to his chest.

The same fervor swelled in Karen's heart. She struggled with finding the best way to tell him, but words failed. She curled her arms around his neck, bringing his head down to her height. The love her heart held for him filled the kiss she placed on his mouth.

Logan returned it.

"Come on," she whispered in the loudest voice she could muster. Her insides were jelly, and so were her legs. If Logan hadn't kept his arm around her as they walked, she surely would have fallen.

"Let me take your bag." Hank reached for Logan's satchel. After locating Logan's suitcase, the three of them went to the car Hank had parked on a side street.

Logan assisted her into the back seat. Then he went around to the other side and climbed in next to her. "You'll never believe what happened this afternoon. I nearly missed my train."

"What?" Karen couldn't decide if she should laugh or cry. Logan missing the train? Unthinkable.

"The clock said three-forty when I returned home. I had exactly twenty minutes to finish packing and get to the train station." He delved into an action-packed story of a fire at the Oswell City hotel and his assistance to the doctor for the better part of the afternoon. "But I did it because here I am." He held his arms out as if starring in a show.

Karen reached for one of his hands and rested her head on his shoulder while Hank chauffeured them through the dark streets. The touring car's motor purred as they navigated through the tall buildings of downtown Chicago on a summer night. No streetcars ran. Shop windows were dark. A breeze blew in from the lake, rustling the trees in Karen's neighborhood.

Logan was here. She'd cherish each day he spent with her. Contentment found her at last.

9

Karen hastened down the hall and knocked on the door to the room designated for Logan's use. He opened the door and stood before her wearing slacks, a white shirt, and a tie. His spectacles were in place, and his hair was combed. He looked ready for a day of church business.

The professional appearance might work in his favor toward a good impression on Uncle Henry. But then again, it might work against him. Logan looked every inch the pastor, all the way down to the studious spectacles perched on his nose. Uncle Henry may very well choose to throw her fiancé out after the first glance.

"Good morning, sweetheart." He bent to kiss her cheek.

Flutters claimed her stomach. Logan shouldn't be so calm and self-assured until he secured Uncle Henry's good opinion. The group joining them downstairs required more than a winsome smile to welcome him fully.

"Ready for breakfast?"

"Lead the way." Logan placed the prayer book he'd been holding on the dresser.

Karen took him to the landing, down the staircase, through another hallway, and into the dining room.

"We waited for you." Mother patted the empty chair next to her.

Karen winced. Arriving late to breakfast was not a good way to start.

"Good morning, Pastor. I mean, Logan." Mother smiled at him.

"Good morning, Mother." Logan took the chair at Mother's side as he greeted her according to the arrangement they'd worked out during her visit to his farm.

"Uncle Henry. Aunt Fran." Karen cleared her throat. "Please meet my fiancé, Logan De Witt."

Uncle Henry nodded. "Welcome to Chicago."

"We're happy to have you." Aunt Fran gave him a smile.

So far, so good. Logan already received a bit of warmth from Aunt Fran. Karen claimed the chair at the end of the table and bowed her head while Uncle Henry prayed. A maid brought a platter from the kitchen covered with a silver dome. She set it on the table and lifted the dome to reveal ham slices and pancakes. Mother offered the platter to Logan, who helped himself and passed the food to Uncle Henry.

"Tell us about your trip." Aunt Fran put food on her plate.

"The trip went well. I arrived on time, but the biggest adventure happened before I even boarded the train." Logan recounted the story he'd told Karen last night. Small-town characters and big-hearted acts of heroism filled his account.

"The mayor came to help put out the fire?" Uncle Henry asked.

"He sure did. George is a good friend of his. Plus, the Oswell City Hotel is the only one in town. We can't afford to lose it."

"How charming." Aunt Fran's glance at Logan held a hint of condescension.

Karen paused in eating as her nerves struck again. Logan just gave away the fact that his experience with city life was limited, perhaps even non-existent. Silence settled in for a long while.

When Aunt Fran's plate was empty, she asked for more coffee. Rita brought a silver carafe out immediately.

"I could use some too. Thanks for bringing that out for us." Logan flashed his trademark smile at the maid.

Poor Rita, still trying to learn her job and her place in the household, blushed a bright pink. The blush was followed by a bewildered expression since she wasn't used to receiving a response for serving the table. Especially from such a handsome guest of the Millersons who'd paid even the slightest attention to her.

Logan glanced at Rita as she left the room, but she turned away, too flustered to respond. Uncle Henry stared while Aunt Fran poured coffee into her cup and introduced a topic of conversation.

"Karen, you do remember the engagement party planned for this evening, don't you?"

"I do. I have my dress already chosen."

"A good number of our friends are coming. We'll serve the meal at seven with cake to follow. I'd like to have you and your fiancé stand with me in the foyer to receive our guests. That way, you can introduce him, and he can meet every one of our acquaintances here in the city. A string ensemble is coming at eight to provide music for the dance. Logan, you'll want to make sure and wear your tuxedo."

Logan set his coffee cup down. "I uh ... I'm afraid I don't own a tuxedo."

"Oh." The word popped out of Aunt Fran's mouth as though the world stopped spinning. "But I've designed this engagement party as a formal event. All the men will wear tuxedos."

"What about Arthur? Logan is close to his size. Maybe he can borrow a tux from Arthur," Karen suggested.

"But he and Julia are invited to the party. What will Arthur wear if he gives his tux to Logan?" Mother sounded worried.

"Doesn't Arthur have two tuxes? I thought I remembered hearing Julia mention it," Karen said.

"Maybe you and Logan can drive to Julia's after breakfast to check. If he is unable to borrow from Arthur, call on Miss Rose at her dress shop downtown. She may know where one can be found." Aunt Fran sipped her coffee as she continued to scrutinize Logan. "I don't suppose you dance either."

Logan shook his head. "Not a day in my life."

"Logan doesn't have to dance tonight if he doesn't want to." Karen sent a concerned glance his way and clenched a fist in the hand resting on her lap. Her family should quit imposing on him. They should let go of their expectations for him to squeeze into roles he was never meant to fill.

"But he is attending with you. Your engagement is the reason we are hosting this party. Both of you are guests of honor. It will never do if your fiancé doesn't dance. That means you will have to dance with someone else. Oh, dear." Aunt Fran patted her cheek in distress.

"Then I won't dance either. If Logan doesn't dance tonight, neither do I." Karen sat a little straighter in her chair.

"Or she can dance with me." Uncle Henry gave Logan a solemn gaze as if Logan had somehow slighted him in his lack of dancing skills.

"Why don't you go over to Julia's? See what you find there. We can worry about the dance portion of the party later." Eager to keep the peace for her brother, Mother urged Karen ahead with morning plans.

An hour later, Karen traveled with Logan in the car once again. This time Hank chauffeured them down streets that took them north to Julia's large, comfortable home in another area of the city.

A member of the Bauman household staff admitted Karen and Logan into the house. Julia greeted them with enthusiastic hugs that couldn't be outdone by her just as excited children.

"Unca Wogan!" Ben yelled as he careened down the hall and wrapped his arms around Logan's knees.

Everyone laughed as Logan reached for the little boy and tossed him in the air. Ben responded with a squeal and a tight hug of Logan's neck.

Ten-month-old Sam left his place on the rug and crawled over to Karen. She reached for him and settled him on her hip.

"Come in, come in!" Julia led them to a beautiful parlor. Sheers hung at the large windows. Ferns thrived in the light streaming into the room. Furniture upholstered in a rich berry color bordered a rug of complementary hues.

Karen sat on the sofa and looked around. If the Oswell City parsonage required any redecorating, Karen would adopt her sister's style.

"How was your trip? What time did you arrive?" Julie fired off her questions for Logan as she settled into a straight back chair.

Logan joined Karen on the sofa. "The trip went well, and I got into Chicago last night at ten o'clock."

"Glad that went smoothly. Aunt Fran shared with us her friend's horror story of waiting two hours for a cousin to arrive. Thank goodness that wasn't you."

"I wouldn't have survived a two-hour delay." Logan shook his head.

Karen heard in his voice the same misery she feared at the possibility of a late arrival.

"Aunt Fran probably also told you about the engagement party planned for tonight."

"She did, which is why we're here," Karen said. "Could Logan borrow a tux from Arthur?"

Julia bit her lip. "I'm afraid Arthur will need to wear his, but his father has one. Let me send a message to his parents. I'll be right back."

Julia disappeared down a hallway leaving Karen and Logan alone.

"What is the parlor like in your house?"

Logan looked around. "Much smaller than this one but just as nice, I suppose."

"What color is it?"

"Navy blue."

"That sounds nice."

"Did you want to change it?" He grinned at her.

"Only if it needed it, but I like blue."

"Then you will like the dining room too, because the rug and chair cushions coordinate with the parlor décor."

"I can't wait to see it."

Logan smiled and leaned in to whisper. "And I am more than ready to show it to you."

"A neighbor boy is on his way." Julia returned. "Let's have tea while we wait for him." Julia invited them to stay before giving instructions to the kitchen staff for tea.

They passed the morning sharing stories about Julia's children, Karen's students, and Logan's life in Oswell City.

The doorbell rang, and Julia rushed to answer it.

"Here you are, Mrs. Bauman." A boy in his teens handed a suit on a hanger to Julia as well as a note.

She read it out loud. *You're welcome to borrow this tuxedo from Arthur's father. We will need it Saturday night, so please return it soon.* Julia handed the suit over to Logan, and he tried it on to discover a near-perfect fit.

"Thank you, Julia. We appreciate it." Logan waved to her on the way out the door.

Hank delivered Karen and Logan home in plenty of time to join the family for the noon meal.

"Hey, Karen." After the meal had been eaten, Logan beckoned her out of her chair in the drawing room to the background noise of clinking dishes as two maids cleared the table.

Uncle Henry had returned to his downtown office. Mother and Aunt Fran went shopping for a few more items for the evening's party. Kitchen staff bustled between the dining room, kitchen, and parlor in preparation for the evening's festivities. She and Logan were left with quiet afternoon hours to enjoy.

"I've been thinking about the dancing situation." Logan scratched his head.

Karen held her hand up. "If you don't want to dance, I completely understand."

"But it is important to your mother and your aunt, isn't it?"

Karen couldn't deny the truth. At other engagement parties she'd attended, the honored couple opened the evening with the first dance. She nodded.

"I have an idea." He led her into the dining room and stopped in the corner before the Victrola. "I'll bet you know how to dance."

"I love to dance."

"Then teach me."

"What?"

"We've got a few hours. Show me how it's done."

"Um ..." Long ago, she'd dreamed of floating along in the sight of a house full of guests in the arms of the man she hoped to marry. Her skirt twirled around her ankles. The man wore black and stood tall and strong. Like Logan. She stepped back. "All you need to remember is the box step. It goes like this." In slow motion, Karen moved her feet in the pattern. "You try."

Three attempts later, Logan's movements grew smoother.

"Good. Then you turn and do it again."

Logan mirrored her movements as she outlined the steps.

"At this point, you as the man can stand still and give me a twirl. Like this." Karen took one of Logan's hands, raised his arm, and spun in a circle. "Then turn once more and make the same pattern over and over again."

They moved through a series of steps together with Logan mirroring her actions.

"Got it?" She glanced up at him.

"I think so."

"I'll start the music." Karen started the Victrola. The melody of a waltz filled the room.

She faced Logan. "Put one hand here." She guided his hand into her palm. "And put the other one here." With her help, his hand rested on her back above her waist. "Ready?"

He nodded.

"1-2-3. 1-2-3. Go." Karen counted in rhythm to the music coming from the Victrola and then followed Logan's steps as he moved with the music.

They did well until he brought her back into his embrace after the twirl. Logan began on the wrong foot and nearly knocked Karen over.

"Sorry." He caught her in an instant before she hit the floor.

"I'm all right. Try it again."

Logan gave her another twirl, and this time when he fell into rhythm with her, he used the correct foot. "I think I'm getting the hang of this."

"You're doing a wonderful job. A fast learner." Karen kept pace with him as he followed the music.

When the waltz ended, he paused and offered a grand bow.

Applause broke out. Karen turned to find the entire household staff crowding the room with their eyes on the dancers.

"Well done, Miss Karen." Ida gave her a smile.

Karen took a deep breath and smiled back. If their informal training session had impressed so many, surely their efforts tonight at the party and dressed in their finest would gain Logan a degree of influence with her aunt and uncle.

10

Karen stood with Aunt Fran beneath the chandelier in the foyer of the Millerson home. Her dress of blue brocade satin swished around her feet with every movement she made. She loved this dress with its square neck and tiers of fabric gathered at her waist by a rosette. Aunt Fran's maid had helped her with her hair by sweeping it up into an elegant puff of curls. Karen felt like a queen in her gorgeous dress and hairstyle. All she needed was a crown to complete her royal look.

People streamed into the house, shaking her hand and offering congratulations.

"This is Pastor Logan De Witt from Iowa," she introduced him over and over again, as the guests shook Logan's hand and received his sunlit smile.

Whenever a gap occurred in the line, Karen took a step back. She really didn't need to move out of her place in the receiving line at all, but it gave her a better view of Logan. The borrowed tuxedo made him look positively dapper. The long tails and crisp cut of the jacket accentuated his height. The white shirt beneath and the white bow tie gave him distinction and also spoke of his natural appreciation of the finer things.

"That tux looks nice on you. No one would ever know it belongs to Arthur's father." Julia gave his shoulder a playful punch when she arrived.

"It's the most formal suit I've ever worn. I hope I don't spill something on it." Logan brushed at the jacket while his brow furrowed.

"A damaged suit wouldn't affect your looks any. You're too handsome for that." Julia offered him a smile and followed Arthur down the hall.

The frown stayed in place as if Julia's compliments confused him.

But Karen knew the truth. A farm boy he might be, but the Logan she had grown to love read classics and history. He spoke with charm and intelligence. Wisdom abided in his soul, and depth of character expanded beyond his six-foot frame. The tux outfitted him in just the right way to bring to the surface what might otherwise remain unseen.

At the call to dinner, Logan offered her his arm and escorted her into the dining room as if he were a king. Floating along on the arm of such a gentleman, Karen might as well be royalty. No one else loved her as gently or honored her so nobly. He pulled a chair out for her at the long table and then settled in next to her. Arthur and Julia sat across the table.

"This is all so exciting!" The pride in Julia's smile seemed to release its own energy. The flames on the candles in the centerpiece between them flickered.

If the disturbance came from Julia's airy radiance, Karen wouldn't be a bit surprised. Mother sat near Uncle Henry at the head of the table. Aunt Fran occupied the chair across from her. Friends from their church, their neighborhood, and a few of Uncle Henry's business associates filled the other seats.

Uncle Henry prayed to begin the meal. Household staff brought multiple silver platters to the dining room and stood alert for the slightest need of replenished drinks and any other service the guests required. The meal passed with pleasant conversation shared over delicious food.

When the time came to serve the cake, Uncle Henry and Aunt Fran led the gathering to the parlor where a layered cake sat on a stand near the window. A waiter circulated with a pitcher of punch and a tray of glasses.

After everyone had been served, Uncle Henry cleared his throat. "At this point in the evening, I should offer a toast to my niece and her fiancé, but the truth is I don't know what to say. Toasts are for the purpose of sharing happiness with the guests of honor. I want to do that, but I cannot. I'm more concerned for you, Karen, than I am happy for you." He cast a solemn glance at Logan. "The best I can do is to say that I hope you aren't making a mistake."

A span of silence followed Uncle Henry's words. Guests looked at each other, uncertainty on their faces and in their voices as low murmurs spread throughout the room.

Mother stepped forward. "What Henry means is that he wants only the very best for my daughter and for Logan. Isn't that right?" She glanced at her brother, but he didn't answer her question. Mother's voice shook as she raised her glass in the air. "A toast to Karen and to her fiancé. May misfortune never find you, and blessing and joy always follow you." Mother's choice of words spoke as loudly of her past as the lift of her glass did of her hopes for Karen's future.

The others in the room raised their glasses as well and then followed Mother's lead in enjoying the first sips of the rosy-hued punch.

Mother blinked moisture from her eyes. Once again, she had saved the day for her brother with grace and tact. Karen swallowed her drink as a wave of affection for her mother rolled over her. Mother had lived through some difficult times of struggle and humiliation. But those dark days had only served to make Mother strong and beautiful.

In that moment, Karen made a silent but determined choice.

Whatever sufferings she and Logan might encounter in their years together, strength and beauty would become the mark of her character too.

Cheer returned to the gathering while maids busied themselves cutting the cake. Aunt Fran gave plates of cake to her guests as everyone stood around to eat it. Soon the strains of classical music floated in from the dining room.

"Time for dancing," Uncle Henry announced. "Karen and Pastor De Witt, the first dance belongs to you."

Karen's stomach fluttered. She loved waltzing, but Logan might have forgotten everything she taught him earlier in the afternoon. He didn't dare stumble in front of Uncle Henry and everyone else and make a fool of himself.

Logan escorted her to the dining room, where the furniture had been moved to transform the space into a ballroom. He settled his hand on her back and held her hand in his other one. A flicker of nerves crossed his blue eyes.

"Logan, really. We don't have to do this if you don't want to."

"Shh." He smiled at her. "I've got the steps down."

"Are you sure?" she whispered.

"Perfectly." He winked at her just like he did in the old days when she'd boarded with his family on their farm. "1-2-3. 1-2-3. Here we go." He swept her into a confident dance around the room. Even the twirl he accomplished with grace.

"You're doing well. I think you missed your rightful destiny, Logan De Witt," she teased. "Dressed in a tuxedo, dancing a waltz at an upperclass party—you were born for city life."

"Only because I've had a good teacher." He gazed deeply into her eyes.

The music ended. Couples joined them on the dance floor. Logan guided her through two more songs. Ready for glasses of punch, they moved to the side of the room and drank from cut glass cups as they watched the other dancers.

A cluster of household staff stood nearby watchful for the tending of guests' needs.

"This is a nice party." Logan turned to them. "Thank you for serving us at dinner."

The group stared at him. Karen could believe none of them knew what to do with a guest of honor who not only paid attention to them but thanked them for doing their job.

A grin claimed his mouth. "Have any of you ever ridden a train before?"

One of the men nodded. "Once."

"Let me tell you about yesterday afternoon. Can you believe I nearly missed my train?"

One young woman shook her head. Interest glowed in the eyes of each person.

Logan launched into an entertaining retelling of the fire in the small town where he lived.

Just then, another staff ushered a group of young ladies into the dining room.

"Miss Millerson!" Blanche waved from the middle of the group from the academy.

Karen rushed over. "I'm so glad you came."

"Where is he?" Annie scanned the party guests.

"Over there." Karen pointed at Logan. The girls had kept up a constant string of questions about Logan ever since their last visit to Karen's home. She didn't need to ask who they wanted to see. Their anticipation answered the question for her.

"Whoa," Mabel said under her breath. She blushed dark red.

"He could star in movies." Minnie's voice expressed dramatic admiration.

"That he could." Karen inhaled a satisfied breath.

"Come this way, girls, and help yourselves to some punch." Ida gestured to the punch bowl as she welcomed the students.

Karen followed along behind. Except for the night of Logan's marriage proposal, she'd never been happier. She slowed to a stop and watched the party going on around her. The girls from the academy sipped punch and chattered with each other. Mother conversed with elegantly dressed friends. A pleased expression shone on her face. Aunt Fran danced with Arthur. Julia visited in the corner with some women from church. Logan told his story to the staff.

At that moment, they all burst out laughing.

"I never thought I'd see the day when you welcomed another preacher into your family."

Out of the corner of her eye, Karen noticed Archibald Reynolds, husband of Aunt Fran's friend Bertha, and business colleague to Uncle Henry.

"No welcoming." Uncle Henry harrumphed. "Only observing. Karen can do better. The day will come when the boy messes up. It's just a matter of time. That's how it is with most who call themselves men of the cloth."

"Well, well." Mr. Reynolds thumped Uncle Henry's back as he chuckled. "It does my heart good to see you keeping up the old pep, Henry. For a moment, I thought you'd gone soft."

"Not me, my friend. Not me." Uncle Henry peered at Logan and the group of staff over the top of his second glass of punch. "See him over there, rousing up my staff? They shouldn't carry on so. I must find Fran and tell her to put a stop to it."

"Come now, Henry. Let him have his fun. He's probably got more in common with them than he would with us anyway." Mr. Reynolds fell into silence as he too sipped on his glass of punch.

The nerve! Uncle Henry and his arrogant friend had no right to look down on her fiancé. Logan was the finest man who ever lived. He left his group of attentive listeners and came to find her. Karen held her breath as if keeping her air inside could also contain her irritation.

"I have some people I'd like you to meet." She took Logan's hand and led him to her students.

As the girls noticed Logan and her approach, bright pink stained their cheeks.

"Ladies, please meet my fiancé." Karen gestured to Logan before she pointed to each girl and said her name.

"Do you enjoy your English classes?" Logan asked the group.

"Oh, yes. Miss Millerson is our best teacher at the academy," Blanche spoke up.

"Are you coming to the Exhibition?" Annie asked.

"Miss Millerson said you'd be in town during our performance," Mabel said.

"I'd love to come to your Exhibition. Miss Millerson wrote and told me all about it."

The song from the string ensemble ended, and a new one began. "Do any of you ladies enjoy dancing?"

"I might if I knew how," Ruby answered. The others nodded in agreement.

Logan glanced at Karen. Surely he didn't expect her to teach them right now with her family and their friends watching.

He looked back at the girls and held his hand out. "I'd be honored to help you learn."

Ruby cast a shy glance at Karen as if seeking her approval.

"It's fine. Go on." Karen watched Ruby place her hand in Logan's and step with him onto the dance floor. She inhaled more satisfied breaths as she enjoyed the scene of Logan, the rookie dancer, tutor Ruby in a similar fashion to how she taught him earlier in the day. Ruby caught on quickly. Her eyes grew round, and the blush persisted on her cheeks as she glided around the room with Logan.

He took turns with each girl teaching them new steps or helping them refine their skill according to each one's abilities.

"Only a matter of time until he slips up. You just watch." Uncle Henry's voice carried to Karen's ears. She turned to find him and Mr. Reynolds at the refreshment table. Uncle Henry glared at Logan as he spoke. "And when he does, Karen will believe me when I say marriage to a preacher is a mistake."

His words brought on a case of light-headedness. She and Logan together would prove him wrong. But Logan should not have to tolerate that sort of pressure during his stay. She watched him now as he twirled Minnie around the dance floor. Nothing should diminish the joy they found in the time this week allowed them to spend together.

When the song ended, Logan returned with Minnie to the group and bowed to them. "Thank you for the honor of dancing with me, but now your teacher should have a turn." He held his hand out to Karen.

She accepted his invitation. He held her in his arms and led her through the steps he'd mastered.

"Having fun?" he asked.

"I am. This engagement party will always be a wonderful memory." She'd choose to store away the beautiful parts of the evening and work to forget the unsettling ones. Her fingers went cold, and her legs wanted to tremble.

She leaned her forehead on Logan's shoulder. "I just wish my family could understand why I love you so much."

His hand left her back and patted her shoulder. Though he said nothing, the simple consolation assured her at least one person in the room understood.

11

Karen descended the stairs, humming a strain from a Strauss waltz, the same one she and Logan had danced to the evening before. He'd remembered every step she'd taught him. They had glided around the room beautifully as if they'd danced together for years.

What a shame Logan's occupation in Oswell City didn't provide him with opportunities to use his new skill. He danced so well, but he might forget how after he returned home. Even if he did, Karen would never forget the evening she spent waltzing in his arms. The moment belonged to them alone.

"Good morning, my dear," Aunt Fran greeted her when she entered the dining room for breakfast.

Furniture was restored to its usual places. Glass dishes and punch bowls were put away. No traces remained of the vibrant party the evening before.

Logan stood and pulled a chair out for her.

Karen smiled at him. Ever since his arrival, their hours had been filled with preparation for the engagement party and with family. Enjoyable as Karen found these pleasures, she wanted nothing more than getting Logan all to herself. A nice leisurely day of strolling in the gardens and exploring downtown shops suited her plans very well.

"The anniversary of your father's death was last week." Mother's words shot a spear through Karen. Why did Mother have to go and bring that up? She completely ruined Karen's lovely memories of the previous evening.

"You know I always visit his grave on that day."

Yes, Karen knew. Mother continued to honor a husband who had failed to honor her.

"I didn't go to the cemetery last week but waited for Logan to arrive. I'd like to ask both of you to join me on my visit today."

Activity at the table halted. Everyone stared at Mother.

"No." Karen gave her head a determined shake. "I've never gone with you in the past, and I won't go now." The whole miserable story of her father's crimes was behind them, where Karen would make sure it stayed.

"Really, Margaret. Is that necessary?" Uncle Henry's voice held impatience.

"Yes, I believe it is." Mother's gaze passed from Karen to Logan. "I trust you learned of my husband's misdeeds at some point while you shared your home with my daughter."

Logan gave her a solemn nod. That Christmas supper, when Karen had exposed her father for who he really was, probably sat heavily on Logan's mind at this moment as it did for her.

"You know how hard we worked to erase any memory of your husband from this family," Uncle Henry muttered with gritted teeth. "If you want to pay him tribute, go ahead. But I see no reason to drag Karen back into the mess." He shook his head and returned to eating his scrambled eggs.

Father's memory still caused pain for Uncle Henry too. He'd bailed the man out of jail and given him a job, but the efforts hadn't been enough to eradicate scandal. Not until his brother-in-law died did the suspicions of mishandled finances quit following him.

Offering his home and his name to his sister eased the doubts of most of his business associates, but the passing of time operated as his best ally. People had finally forgotten, or at least no longer held Uncle Henry guilty by association. He wasn't any more willing to stir up the past than Karen.

"Logan, will you join me?" Mother once again heeded Uncle Henry's wishes and directed her question at Logan instead of her daughter.

"I'd be honored." He glanced at Uncle Henry. "With all respect, sir, I think it would be a good idea for Karen to come along."

If Logan had slapped her, she couldn't have been more offended. She sent him a look that let him know.

Unwavering sincerity glowed in his eyes. Her gaze flew from him to Uncle Henry. He scowled. Logan's request had not been interpreted as respectful.

To defy Logan meant taking sides with Uncle Henry. That would only strengthen his unaccepting position against her fiancé. But to go along with Logan's suggestion guaranteed a morning of misery. How nice if she could release the groan building in her throat, run out of the room, and throw herself on her bed.

"I'll be there," Logan whispered as he reached for her hand and held it.

If only his presence could erase the past. But the memories still haunted her, and the pain found plenty of chances to prick her heart. Karen's mind shifted back to the Christmas supper around the dining room table in the De Witt farmhouse. Her story hadn't frightened Logan away then. Surely he would prove his words true and stay with her through not only this dreaded visit to the cemetery but through a life with a wife whose father had been a well-known criminal.

Karen closed her eyes and took a deep breath even as her stomach sank. She'd chosen to spend the rest of her life with Logan. He hadn't forsaken her yet. Whatever shadow she might cast over his spotless reputation, they'd work out together. For better or for worse began now.

Karen sucked in a breath. "I'll come, Mother."

Mother smiled, but Uncle Henry reached for his copy of the *Chicago Tribune*. He made much noise in rustling it open and spent the remainder of the meal behind it.

An hour later, Hank drove the three of them south to the cemetery, passing through the neighborhood where Karen lived as a child. Brick storefronts lined one side of the street. People milled about on the sidewalk doing their morning shopping and looking in store windows.

Carts hitched to horses were parked along the street. The names painted on the sides advertised a variety of goods available for delivery, such as items from a bakery, dairy products, horseshoes, and furniture. Farther down the street, a stalwart brick church building towered to the sky. Next door stood a white clapboard house.

"That is where we were living the night Father got arrested." Painful memories rushed in as she pointed to the house. Logan's knowledge of the scandal gave her the courage to show the house to him.

Logan glanced at the house and then looked at her with an expression that said he felt her sorrow.

Karen slumped into the seat. Surely no one would recognize her. Father's siblings and their families still lived in the area. The only reason they might have to acknowledge her as a relative would be to admit the shame Karen and her mother still brought upon them. Separation was best. Yet another reason why an Oswell City wedding appealed to her. A different set of wedding guests gave her a fresh start to a new life in a small town she'd claim as her true home.

At the entrance to the cemetery, Hank turned right and followed a path through the rows of stones. The path sloped to a small valley in a copse of evergreen trees. Hank parked the car, and Logan helped Karen to the ground. Mother led the way down a row of stones and stopped before one of them. She reached into the basket on her arm and gathered up a bunch of flowers from Aunt Fran's garden. She knelt and placed the flowers at the base of the stone.

Logan kept his hold on Karen's hand and led her to stand nearby. Resistance stiffened her movements as she forced herself to walk at Logan's side.

Her gaze passed over the familiar information revealed on Father's stone. "Do you remember what I shared Christmas night with you and your family?" Karen glanced up at Logan through her tears as the horrors replayed in her mind.

"I do." Logan's voice carried quiet and soothing to her ears.

"Father got arrested for embezzlement. The offering had to wait until Mondays to be deposited, and the leader of a local gang attempted to rob the church, but Father caught him in time to prevent it.

"The police came, but the gang leader got away. After this, the gang grew more dangerous in their attempts to get the church's money." She was rambling, and her words were ones Logan had heard before. Words that she didn't want him to have to hear again, but somehow talking helped ease the grief she still carried. His patient presence at her side gave her the strength to keep facing the pain.

"Father didn't want to put his wife and two small daughters in danger, so he never brought the money home with him. He gave in when threats were made on his life and offered to give the gang a certain percentage each week if they would leave him and the church building alone.

"But he started gambling. He gambled to make up the difference, I guess, and he finally got caught when someone he owed visited our house. Father couldn't pay, so the man had him investigated." Karen wiped her eyes as she relived the memories. The policemen at the door. The handcuffs. Father leaving the house. Their names in the paper. A move to a smaller house. Father's sickness. Father's funeral.

"Then, we moved into Uncle Henry's mansion." Memories of her trip to Iowa and meeting Logan assailed her.

She looked up at Logan. "Everything about you represented scandal to me. I'd fought so hard against the feelings of love for you that flooded my heart. Not until I surrendered my life to the Lord did I welcome a future with a preacher."

Karen reached into her pocket for her handkerchief and wiped her nose. "I'm sorry, Logan, that I took so long to let myself love you."

He gathered her in his arms and rested his chin on her head. The simple display of compassion melted her, and she wept against him.

CLOUDS GATHERED and shielded the sun removing the shadows from the letters and numbers etched in the stone Logan read.

Simon Van Deursen
1860-1903
Aged 43 years
Departed to glory

Many little truths bubbled with insight of Karen and her family. Her father's stone lay next to two other stones of people with the same surname. Those other two people surely were his parents. The dates of birth and death placed them in a generation older than Simon. They likely immigrated to America at some point during their lives, like Logan's father did. But instead of settling farm ground out on the prairie, they chose the city. Simon married a woman in America, and his daughters were born here.

Then he fell into trouble, which probably contributed in some way to the deterioration of his health. This man might be gone, but his deeds still lived on in the hearts of his wife and her family. Margaret, her daughters, and her supportive brother were still being shaped by the poor decisions and early death of one man. It saddened them, and it hindered them.

Karen's need for security made complete sense to him. Marriage would provide this for her. She deserved a man in her life that was stable and would never surprise her with irresponsibility. Logan prayed at that moment he could be that man, a husband she could count on to care for her and not fail her.

"I'm so sorry you had to see this gravestone with my father's name on it." Karen's quiet voice held tears. "If learning about my heritage causes you pain, I can understand."

"Why would it cause me pain?" Logan kept her wrapped in his embrace in an effort to demonstrate that he endeavored to be the stable man in her life.

She looked up at him through eyes glassy with tears. "When my family looks at you, they still see him. I don't know how you will ever break through that perception and prove you're different."

Logan looked down at her. "If you remember, I asked your mother for her blessing, not your uncle. She has granted it along with her acceptance of me. Julia has too. I can't prove my character or anything else to your aunt and uncle. They will need to decide for themselves that I'm worthy of you."

"So far, they have not. Oh, Logan. Why can't they approve of you? Uncle Henry is the only true father I've ever known. He has to like you and give us his blessing. He just has to." She clung to him as she spoke through fresh tears.

Logan held her for a long time. He wanted the approval of each member of Karen's family too, but he could do nothing on his own to make it happen.

Henry Millerson must be a deeply devout man for the failures of his pastor brother-in-law to hurt him so much all these years later. Logan had witnessed Henry's generosity in sharing his home with Karen and her mother, his prayers before meals, and his good judgment in choosing friends. His approval would mean much and was well worth earning.

In a gradual calming, Karen's tears ceased. She rested quietly in his arms. Her stillness alerted him to the fact that she may feel ready to leave for home. The visit to the grave had been healing for her, even if it had been difficult to accomplish.

He looked down at her. "Are you ready to go?"

"I think so." Karen nodded her head against the front of his suit coat.

"Your mother is waiting in the car." He offered Karen his handkerchief since hers was soaked, took her hand, and led her away.

12

"Come with me to the plant this afternoon." Henry extended his invitation to Logan over the noon meal. "I need to attend a meeting there, and I can easily take the time to give you a tour."

"I'd enjoy that. Thanks."

"Perhaps stepping into my world for an afternoon will give you a proper appreciation for the life Karen enjoys as a part of our family." Henry's brow lifted as if the invitation carried a degree of challenge.

Logan hardly knew how to respond. He didn't need a tour of Henry Millerson's business to catch on to the standard of living he showered on his niece. The size of the house alone nearly made Logan's knees buckle when he caught sight of it in the daylight. Oswell City's City Hall, the church, and most of the homes in between could fit within its walls.

The Ellenbroek residence was considered the finest home in Oswell City, but it ranked as little more than a child's playhouse compared to Henry Millerson's mansion. The food, the luxury touring car, even the borrowed tux reminded Logan he'd only ever been a farm boy making his living in a small town where his salary depended on the giving of others. God provided for Logan regularly, and he provided well, but even the best of years would not supply the money for Karen to have her own household servants.

All the tasks of cooking and looking after a family would fall on her. Sharing his life asked much from her. The fact that she'd even accepted his proposal humbled him and had driven him to his knees more than once since his arrival in Chicago. If she still wanted him, along with the simplicity and the hardships his lifestyle offered her, then the Lord alone deserved all of the credit.

After the meal, he walked with Karen to the corner to catch the streetcar.

"With the Exhibition only two days away, I want to help the girls rehearse at the academy this afternoon. Are you sure you'll be all right spending the afternoon with Uncle Henry?" Karen glanced up at him with a wrinkle in her brow.

"I'm not sure how the tour of the plant will go, but I'll do my best to act respectfully." He kissed her forehead.

"I wish he could say the same. I have a feeling he's only inviting you to come along so that he can show off to you. What if he says something to make you look bad in front of his colleagues?" Karen adjusted her hat against the breeze that worked it loose from her hair.

Logan smiled. "That might happen. But don't worry, sweetheart. Just remember, I have your mother's approval."

Karen nodded, but she looked doubtful of a positive outcome.

A clanging bell announced the streetcar's swift approach.

"You have to go." Logan pressed her shoulder as though the reminder of her appointment with her students would ease her concern.

"See you later." She offered a quick wave and stepped onto the streetcar.

Logan made the short walk back to the house and arrived in time to accompany Henry downtown. Hank deposited them on the street in front of a massive stone building that seemed to reach above the clouds floating in the blue summer sky.

The elevator carried them up many floors before the doors opened into a hallway. Desks and cabinets lined one wall. Large windows admitted entrance to afternoon sunshine on the other side.

"Good afternoon, Mr. Millerson." The greeting echoed from the people seated at the desks. One young man brought him a stack of envelopes.

Henry breezed down the hall until reaching a door with a sign on it that said *Henry Millerson, President, Millerson and Company Steel Works.* He unlocked the door, and Logan followed him into the office.

A polished desk filled the center of the room. Cabinets occupied the space near the windows. A grouping of chairs and a small table sat in one corner.

"Welcome to the administrative operations of the steel works." Henry dropped the case he carried onto the surface of the desk. "I need to collect some papers, and then we'll get on our way to the plant." He bent to open a desk drawer and shuffled through files until a knock sounded on the door. "Come in."

Two men in three-piece-suits entered.

"We realize you have to get to a meeting, but we'd like for you to take a look at this report." One of the men thrust a sheet of paper at Henry.

The other man spoke in a low voice. "It's about the Stuart account. They still haven't paid."

"Excuse me." Henry glanced at Logan a moment before he focused on the report. "I need to deal with this."

Logan nodded as Henry left with the other men. Shoving his hands in his pockets, Logan sauntered over to the window. The distance to the street below made his head spin. This office certainly stretched higher than the haymow of the dairy barn on the farm in Silver Grove. He blinked and wandered around.

Too bad he didn't have anything along to read. He settled into a chair and reached for Henry's copy of the *Wall Street Journal*. By the time Henry returned, he'd completed the paper and started on the *Chicago Tribune*.

"There you are, sir. I was about ready to come looking for you." Logan stood and dropped the newspaper on the table.

"Yes, well. I got detained. We must get going." Henry stuffed papers and files in his case and left the room.

Logan followed through the hall, down the elevator, and into a lobby where Hank paced.

"Sorry to keep you waiting. But everything is taken care of. Let's go. I'm already late." Henry rushed ahead of Hank to the door.

"Yes, sir." Hank hastened onto the street, opened the car door for Henry and Logan, then claimed the front seat.

He navigated busy Michigan Avenue while Henry pointed out buildings and told Logan their names. Hank drove south through residential areas and industrial sections of the city.

"There it is." Henry pointed to a sprawling building surrounded by railroad tracks. Smokestacks spewed steam and black smoke into the air. A river ran nearby. One bank appeared mountainous with dark hills of coal and ore.

Hank drove into a lot at the front of the building and parked.

"Come back for us in two hours," Henry instructed as he left the vehicle.

Logan followed him into the building and discovered a cluster of men standing near the door.

"We've been waiting for you," one of them said.

"I know. I'm sorry. I got held up at the office downtown." Henry turned to Logan. "This is Pastor De Witt. He's my niece's fiancé and is in the city visiting for a week. Junior, could you give him a tour? I'd hoped to do it, but now this meeting will run late," Henry said to the young man at the desk.

"Sure." He stuck his pencil behind his ear and joined the group.

When the other men left for the meeting room, Junior handed Logan a hard hat. "Here. You'll want to put this on to go out to the foundry."

Logan took it and settled the heavy gear on his head.

"You're a preacher," Junior said while they walked down a long corridor.

"I am."

"It's a known fact Mr. Millerson doesn't like preachers. I'm surprised he likes you."

"I don't know that he likes me." Logan laughed. "It's more accurate to say he's putting up with me."

Junior peered at Logan much like a student would study a textbook in preparation for an exam. Logan's neck heated, and he fidgeted under his suit coat. Maybe his inexperience with city life was starting to show, giving him away as a country bumpkin who didn't know the difference between refined living and backwoods survival.

Or maybe it was the glasses. He'd debated about leaving them at home since he wouldn't need to study this week. Those spectacles probably made him look like a bore. They screamed at everyone he met about his enjoyment of study and long hours reading. He should have left them at home. His adjustment to city life and making friends there needed no extra challenge.

Junior brought him to a room with windows on the side facing a huge cauldron. Sparks and flame shot out of it as it swayed from side to side. He'd read about volcanoes erupting in other parts of the world. The scene before him must surely resemble the phenomenon.

While Logan watched, Junior explained the process of making steel. They moved on to other parts of the plant while Junior continued his explanations and pointed out items of significance.

"I need to ask you something," he said in a quiet voice while he walked with Logan through a spacious room resembling a warehouse.

Steel beams lay stacked on shelves almost to the ceiling. Horses pulled wagons through the space, and men yelled to one another as they loaded the wagons.

"What's on your mind?" Logan asked.

"I'm happy with my job here. Truly I am. But I ..." Junior's voice trailed off as he studied the rafters. "One of those men who met Mr. Millerson when you arrived is my father. He is part of the *and company* portion of Millerson Steel Works. He and two other men partner with Mr. Millerson. They have contacts with the railroad and construction companies. Father wants me to fill his role someday and take over his portion of the ownership, but I'm not so sure."

"What would you like to do?"

"My mother taught me how to cook. I like it. That's what I really want to do—cook."

A grin stretched across Logan's mouth. He'd just discovered another member of the secret society of bread bakers. At least this young man admitted to enjoying it. That was more than Logan could say for himself.

"Then do it." Logan smiled at the younger man.

"I don't know. I'd have to take culinary classes. Get a job at a hotel or a restaurant." Junior slumped.

"It might not be as difficult as you think."

"Maybe you're right." A smile eased the tension from Junior's face. On the route to the front of the building, Junior took Logan around the warehouse and across a set of railroad tracks. As they entered the empty lobby, a smile still remained on Junior's face. "I'm going to tell my father. Today. Thanks, Pastor De Witt."

Logan shook his hand.

THAT EVENING, Logan stood in the foyer of the Millerson home dressed in his suit this time, not the tux. Tickets to the Chicago

Symphony Orchestra were tucked securely in his pocket. Karen descended the stairs wearing yet another new gown. The fabric was plum colored. It stretched gracefully off her shoulders, revealing even more of her flawless fair skin. Sparkly jewelry hung at her neck.

In that moment, he forgot how to breathe. The fact that she chose to give her heart to him when she could secure the attention of any man in the world sobered him.

She reached for a shawl and smiled at him as he offered his arm.

"Have a nice time," Margaret called from another room.

"Thanks, Mother. Don't wait up for us," Karen called back on their way out the door.

Hank drove them to Orchestra Hall and assisted Karen's exit from the back seat of the car. Logan led her into the building and helped her find the seats indicated on his tickets.

"Are the girls ready for their performance?" he asked when they were settled.

"I believe so. I was most concerned about Blanche. She has trouble with memorization, but I expect her to do well. The practice today helped."

"Pastor De Witt!" A man raced down the row in front of them, stopped before Logan, and reached to shake his hand.

Yes." The reply carried a wary tone. He'd seen this man before, but where?

"I'm Theodore Croft. My wife and I were at your engagement party."

"Oh, yes. I remember now."

"I wanted to tell you not to let Henry get you down." He shifted his attention to Karen. "You won't be making a mistake if you marry this man. Let me assure you." He put his attention back on Logan. "My sister lives in Oswell City. She's heard you preach and knows who you are. We receive regular letters from her. Keep up the good work, and congratulations. I'll put a good word in with Henry for you whenever I can." He gave a hearty laugh and disappeared.

The exchange left Logan a bit dizzy. Karen stared at him in wonder. Theodore had caught the attention of the people seated around him because they stared at him too. Not with wonder, but with amusement and maybe even with a little admiration mixed in.

"I'm almost afraid to ask, but I have to know. How did your day go with Uncle Henry?" Karen held his hand.

"Better than you expected." He grinned at her.

"He didn't brag or insult you in front of anyone?"

"Not that I noticed." Logan pushed his spectacles up on his nose. Here he was, looking like a complete bore again. Even at an event with as much class as a symphony concert, he still had to wear the silly things. But they did refine his vision. Better to use them in the enjoyment of the evening ahead of him instead of in looking back at problems he couldn't fix.

Karen gave him a playful nudge with her elbow. "You can tolerate a lot, Logan. Why do I get the feeling that Uncle Henry was as belligerent as ever?"

He shrugged.

"You're just choosing to overlook some things, aren't you?" Karen studied him.

"Henry has a right to his own opinions. He doesn't have to like me. But his disfavor won't stand in the way of me marrying you." Logan gave her hand a squeeze as confirmation that nothing and no one would come between them.

THE NEXT MORNING, Logan sat on the veranda where he read from a systematic theology book he'd brought along. The sermons he planned to preach that fall required a fresh angle on old truths. He might as well make use of a quiet morning while Karen taught at the academy.

Karen's mother claimed the chair across from him. She

brought along a tray with two cups of coffee and a small platter of biscuits.

"Please have some. I remember how Sandy brewed your coffee dark on the farm, so I asked Evelyn, our cook, to make it for you in the same way." Margaret set a cup in front of him.

"Thank you." He closed his book and laid it in his lap.

"What are you reading?" She tilted her head to catch a glimpse.

"Just some stuffy scholar only a preacher would find interesting." He sipped coffee. It tasted perfect. Better than Mama's if that were possible.

"I want to apologize to you on behalf of my brother. I honestly don't know what has happened to him. I thought his happiness for Karen getting married would help him welcome you into the family, but he's grown more callused. I'm sorry."

Struggling to find words to offer as a reply, Logan remembered the previous day's interactions with Henry. Formality served him well, but underneath the introductions and conversations, there existed no warmth, no affection, and no acknowledgment of Logan's new and permanent place in the family.

"He must still be hurting. Very much." Logan set his cup down and looked at Margaret.

Margaret settled back in her chair and peered at him in much the same way Junior had done the day before. "See." She shook her finger at him. "There's something about you. Henry knows it. He just doesn't know what to do with it."

Logan blinked. Margaret's words made little sense, but they settled in deep, raising questions Logan hadn't known needed answers.

Before speaking again, Margaret sipped her coffee. "You know our family's story."

Logan nodded.

"Two men. Same occupation. Similar backgrounds. Two very different personalities." Margaret spoke softly as though thinking out loud. Her gaze remained on him. "Henry is still trying to make you fit the mold. I trust the day will come when he gets the chance to see you for who you really are. Like I did."

While Logan ate a biscuit, they sat in silence. His heart was still absorbing the truths he'd learned about his fiancée. She had the same cultural background as him. Karen and Oswell City would understand one another very well. They would hit it off. He anticipated a good relationship right from the start.

Last summer, when he made the last-minute decision to offer the schoolteacher a home, he couldn't have known it would lead to him sitting here at this moment, prepared to marry a woman so well suited for him. Karen had come into his life when he wasn't looking, and now, she made the most ideal and perfect partner for him.

"Don't fit his mold, Logan. He needs you to be different. We all need you to be different." Margaret took her time eating a biscuit and drinking her coffee. After a while, she returned inside, leaving him alone once more.

Questions swirled. The mold she talked about probably referred to his inexperience with the city. Henry was sophisticated and cosmopolitan. Logan was not. Henry had perfect eyesight. Logan did not. His interest in boring subjects like systematic theology, and his country simplicities must be what Margaret noticed.

He waited for Karen to come home and then rode the streetcar with her to explore a few downtown shops. When evening arrived, Logan and Karen went with the rest of the family to the home of Archibald and Bertha Reynolds.

According to Fran, the Reynolds had sent the invitations months ago for their annual late-summer party. Too many plans had been made to cancel, so even though the Millersons also hosted a party the same week, Bertha stuck with her original plan.

Logan had been in attendance for only a few minutes when he discovered the guest list enjoyed quite a large overlap with the engagement party. He'd barely filled his glass with punch before a group surrounded him. Among the men in the cluster were Theodore Croft, Arthur Bauman, and Junior's father.

He held his breath. These men were all friends with Henry Millerson. What could they possibly want with him?

"Junior is attending cooking school in the fall. We worked it out last night." Junior's father thumped Logan's back. "We have you to thank for it." The man beamed.

"You're thanking me?" Logan guessed the man would get upset for counseling his son to go against his wishes.

"We are. My wife and I knew something bothered him. The best part is, he's going to work at the plant and go to school at the same time. We'll adjust his hours so he can accomplish both." He turned to the others in the group and announced the plan with great enthusiasm.

Logan smiled, happy to hear the family had worked out an arrangement that benefited everyone.

Theodore and Arthur shook the man's hand and heaped exaggerated compliments on Logan. His face heated. He'd not done all that much. Not really.

Conversation turned to another topic Logan knew nothing of, so he quietly drank his punch. His gaze landed on Henry across the room, who scowled at him. Logan's heart thumped. He couldn't imagine what he'd done to provoke such a look of displeasure. Excusing himself from the group, he went in search of Karen. She sat at the piano in the Reynolds' drawing room.

A maid arranged chairs in rows while Bertha called for the attention of her guests. "Come in, everyone. Karen has agreed to entertain us with some piano music."

Guests flowed into the room and sat. Logan slipped into the corner that offered him the best view of his talented fiancée and leaned against the wall.

The room quieted as Karen played. The Chopin nocturne washed over him. Its mesmerizing and lyrical melody spoke a message to his heart. It told him Karen was gracious and lovely beyond words. She wore her blue dress, the same one she'd worn for his sister's wedding in May.

The sight of her had stolen his breath that day, just like it did now. His heart seemed to quit beating, and his lungs stilled as he hung on every note. He listened with the longing to seize this moment and remember it forever.

The music eventually faded away. Everyone applauded. Karen started another nocturne, just as soothing and every bit as romantic. He must find a way to put a piano in the parsonage. Karen should have the opportunity to play this music in their home. He couldn't imagine how she learned to play like that or where she got her talent from. He'd do everything he possibly could to help her nurture it.

Later that night, after they arrived home and the other members of the family went to bed, Logan sat in the parlor with Karen enjoying the crackle of the fire he'd lit. "You were sensational tonight."

She smiled, a bit self-consciously. "Thanks, Logan."

"I want you to be able to play as much as you like after we are married."

"I'd love that. Your house on the farm didn't have a piano. I missed it."

"I'll see what I can do about finding one for us to keep in the parlor when I return to Oswell City." He'd need to move some furniture around to make room for a piano, and the end result might feel a little crowded, but the reason was well worthwhile.

She reached up and stroked his cheek. Appreciation shone in her eyes.

"Karen, may I ask you something?" The question had grown stronger as the day progressed. Perhaps the time had come for a lesson in self-awareness.

"Sure."

"Be honest with me, all right?" His voice took on a hint of pleading.

A tiny frown wrinkled her brow.

"I don't know how ... I mean ... I feel silly asking, but I'd like for you to help me." He stopped and rubbed his forehead. "Your mother talked with me this morning. She told me I don't fit your uncle's mold, and it sounds like she doesn't want me to.

"Tonight, his friends sought me out. You saw Mr. Croft at the symphony and heard what he said. Earlier in the week, your mother wanted me to know about your father and invited me to the cemetery. It's a big puzzle, and I can't figure it out. I don't know what any of this means."

Karen gazed at him for a span of time that seemed to drag on for half an hour. "You have a look about you."

Logan frowned. "You mean it's obvious I know my way around a dairy farm better than I do Michigan Avenue."

"No. I don't mean that at all. You have a way about you that exudes compassion and makes people feel valued. You somehow know how to get people to trust you without even saying a word." Her words soaked in satisfying his questions like raindrops nourished tender roots.

"So, it isn't the glasses either. I wondered if maybe they made me look like the boring preacher I really am."

"No." Karen laughed softly. "You look studious, distinguished, and even more handsome than you did before."

"You actually think that?" His gaze flew to her face.

Karen nodded. "You're also winning over Uncle Henry's circle of friends. My guess is it doesn't feel so good to him."

"Your mother said something similar this morning when we had coffee together." The conversation came rushing back to him.

"I'd also guess you are quite popular in Oswell City. Everyone loves you here in Chicago, and that has happened after only a few days. Think how much people must adore you after spending those three years with them until you took that break to stay on the farm."

Logan's mouth dropped open as he stared at her. "You mean ... you think ..." He stood, wandered to the fireplace, and leaned on the mantle. His heart wrestled with the information stretching it this way and that to see if it really was true. Apparently, truth resided somewhere in what Karen told him because a large colorful picture was getting painted in his mind this very minute. He must try to put it into words.

"People in Oswell City follow me because there's no one else to follow. They don't have a choice. I mean, they have to tolerate my preaching and put up with my counsel. I'm all they've got."

"Maybe not." Karen came to him and wrapped her arms around his neck. "I have a feeling you are more popular and respected than you think you are."

He frowned and looked past her as various scenarios played through his memory. The town he served just might choose him even if they were given more options. He counted many of them as his friends. They might see him that way too.

The popularity and respect Karen mentioned may lie at the source of that conversation he overheard in the park between the Miss Independence Day contestants. Karen's observations pressed him to view his role in Oswell City in a different light. But even if the townspeople loved him as much as Karen claimed, the Lord was the only one who could see all of Logan's deeds.

He shrugged. "I'm not sure why it even matters. I shouldn't get too concerned about my levels of popularity."

"Then think of it as influence. People listen to you, and they trust you. That's what matters. It's also what Mother means about not fitting Uncle Henry's mold. Father lost his ability to win people over and influence them for good. Uncle Henry is watching you, Logan. He's expecting you to end up the same way. Don't ever change. Please. Keep being you, the man I trust, and the man who makes me feel special."

He wanted to do all of those things for her, but he never imagined she felt he already succeeded at them. "I try my best."

Wedding liturgy filled his mind again. Karen deserved his faithfulness, his protection, and his love. In offering those to her, he might avoid the failures that destroyed her father. Fidelity at home might translate into fidelity in every other area of his life.

"I may not have an accurate gauge on my popularity, but I do know one thing." He settled his arms around Karen's waist. "When you arrive in Oswell City, you will be the popular one in the family. Everyone will love you and think you're beautiful. I've already had the newspaper editor begging to put your picture on the front page."

"Really?" Karen's eyes grew round, and she gave a laugh.

"It's the truth." Logan allowed a tiny bit of swagger to taint his voice. "With you at my side, anyone who doesn't already love me will melt at my feet out of their deep devotion to you."

She rolled her eyes. "Now, you tease."

"Maybe I do about the melting at my feet part, but I don't about the devotion part." He grinned.

Karen's solemn gaze met his. Logan's grin faded, and his heart pounded as he looked into her eyes. He tightened his embrace in the hopes of coaxing a kiss from her.

It worked. The moment his lips met hers, his heart pounded in his chest, and the warmth from the fireplace penetrated to his insides. If anyone was going to do any melting around here, it would be him. Karen's kisses had that effect on him.

But he didn't care tonight. The romantic music, the stunning blue dress, and the encouragement told him what a lovely young woman he was about to marry. He put every effort into this moment so that Karen knew without a doubt how special she really was.

13

"Help me with this section. I keep forgetting the words." Annie held a paper containing a portion of a Dickens story out to Karen.

"My sash keeps coming loose." Minnie reached for the ribbon at her waist to retie it, but the effort failed. She turned to her teacher. "You try."

Karen worked to tie Minnie's sash as she prompted Annie on her script.

Edith joined the cluster backstage. "Is he here?"

"Yes." Any time one of her students asked about a *he* or a *him* with a slight flush to their cheeks, Karen knew exactly who they meant. "Logan is seated with my mother, aunt, and uncle in the fourth row. He's looking forward to hearing your selections."

Like the other girls gathered around, Edith tried to hide her smile, but the satisfaction they felt about the news of their teacher's fiancé in the audience could not be concealed.

"Hurry and find your names on the schedule. The Exhibition is almost ready to start." Karen pointed to the paper taped to the wall as she caught a glimpse of Miss Gregory slipping through the curtain onto the stage.

"Good afternoon, ladies and gentlemen." Her voice carried to the group left behind. "Welcome to the Exhibition of the Emerson Ladies Academy. We are pleased you have joined us for a program filled with the most-talented students enrolled in our summer term. First, you will hear recitations of poetry and excerpts of classical works from our English students. These ladies will be followed by our vocal students.

"Last, a variety of ensembles showcasing our instrumental students will perform. I hope you'll enjoy the Exhibition. To get started, we will hear from Miss Mabel Norton, a junior at Emerson. She will recite a portion of George Washington's farewell address. Please help me welcome her."

Applause followed.

Mabel's eyes grew wide.

"It's your turn. Go on," Karen whispered.

Mabel reached for the curtain, pushed it aside, and ventured out into the sight of all.

"She has it mastered. She'll do just fine," Blanche whispered as she crowded in close to listen.

"Of all the dispositions and habits which lead to political prosperity, religion and morality are indispensable supports." Mabel's voice held clear and steady.

If the girl felt nervous, a listener would never know. Karen took a deep breath and listened to every word. Mabel had worked hard. She deserved to enjoy the success of a well-delivered presentation.

"The experiment, at least, is recommended by every sentiment which ennobles human nature." Mabel finished, and applause rang through the auditorium. She appeared from around the curtain with a large smile on her face.

"You were wonderful." Karen squeezed her in a quick hug. "Well done."

"Thanks, Miss Millerson." Mabel joined her friends, who also offered her hugs.

"Blanche, you're next," Karen prompted.

She took the stage and gave her recitation of a collection of poems from Emily Dickinson. Applause rang for her as it had for Mabel. Watching the performances of these older girls helped the younger ones with their anxieties. Each one performed to the best of their ability, making their teacher quite proud.

After the students from the freshman class finished, the girls went with Karen to find their families in the audience and sat with them through the musical performances.

When the Exhibition was over, Karen's students sought her out during the reception in the hotel dining hall. She showered praise on them, but they beamed under her fiancé's generous compliments.

Once again, Karen took a step back to observe Logan. Had he really not known how charming he was until she pointed it out to him the evening before? How a man could remain so blind to his own abilities amazed her. She could see quite plainly the effects his sincerity and kindness had on others, even if he could not.

From the way her students gazed at him in full adoration, his charm worked wonders yet again. He mustn't change. Not ever. Logan De Witt must go on displaying to the world what true compassion really looked like. He must go on in genuine sincerity, sharing that gentle and loving heart of his with the world, changing it by remaining the same, just exactly who he is, unwavering from who she knew him to be.

"I'm so proud of all of you. Very nicely done, ladies." Karen wiped a tear from her eye and rejoined the happy circle talking and laughing with Logan and her students.

LATER IN THE DAY, Karen sat at the dining room table with Mother and Logan as Uncle Henry and Aunt Fran made preparations to attend a performance of the Chicago Symphony Orchestra. Aunt Fran returned downstairs after she'd finished dressing. She wore a stunning chocolate-colored gown with a fur stole wrapped around her shoulders. Karen caught a glimpse of her as she stood at the end of the table, chatting with Mother.

"Have you seen our tickets?" Uncle Henry leaned his head into the room and looked at his wife.

"No. Are they in your library?"

Frowning, Uncle Henry left. After a few moments, he came back. "Didn't see them."

"Maybe they're in the bedroom."

He thought for a moment. "I don't think so, but I'll look."

A few minutes later, he returned to the dining room, checking his pockets. "I can't find those tickets anywhere. I distinctly remember purchasing them and then taking them to my office downtown. I'm sure I kept them in the desk drawer, but when I checked today, they were gone."

With wide eyes, Aunt Fran stared at Uncle Henry. "You don't suppose one of your employees took them."

Uncle Henry shook his head. "No one else has a key to my office, and it is never open when I'm not there. I can't think of anyone who would've been in it without me."

Looking at Logan, his speech slowed. "Wait a minute. You were in my office on Tuesday. The next evening you took Karen to the symphony. Maybe you're the one who took my tickets."

Karen's eyes grew round, and her pulse throbbed. Her uncle had just accused Logan of stealing!

"Uh ... no, sir. Honest. I didn't even know you kept tickets in your office, nor did I go exploring. The entire time I waited for you, I read the newspaper. The tickets I used to take Karen to the symphony were ones I ordered and had sent to me ahead of time."

Karen released the breath she'd held through Logan's speech. Thank goodness his stutter had cleared up quickly. If he'd stumbled his way through an explanation, Uncle Henry would suspect him of deception. He'd grown shrewd in that way from the years of working with people who lost all propriety when dealing with the subject of money.

"They were good seats. I paid a high penny for them." He stared Logan down as if the pressure of his gaze had the power to squeeze out a confession.

But Logan continued to eat his meal with complacency. The only indicator Karen received of any discomfort he might experience showed in the red tint of his neck above his collar.

How dare Uncle Henry put Logan on the spot and blame him for theft! This was Logan he spoke to, the same young man who'd slept in a barn through the early months of their engagement. This was the same young man who drained his own savings in order to free his mother from financial stress. Uncle Henry had no right to treat Logan in such a way. Karen struggled against the temptation to stand up and tell him so.

"You have to believe him." Aunt Fran tugged on her husband's arm. "We can go to the symphony another time." Her gaze met Karen's. Warmth and approval shone in her eyes.

At some point during the past couple of days, Logan had won her over too. Perhaps, like Karen, Aunt Fran had stepped back and paid attention to Logan at one of the week's social events. Or maybe she just knew how to recognize good character after spending enough time around it.

Karen offered her a tiny smile, and Aunt Fran responded with one of her own.

"But I'm out those tickets." Uncle Henry turned gruff.

"I'm sure they'll turn up. Let's still dine out at least. We're all dressed up and have missed dinner." Aunt Fran led him from the room.

FRIDAY AFTERNOON, Karen sat next to Logan on a stool at a counter in the kitchen of the Millerson home.

"The leftovers from the evening meal will make chicken salad sandwiches for your outing to the beach tomorrow." Evelyn, the cook, stood nearby, scooping little balls out of a watermelon.

Rita did the same with a cantaloupe. Ida, the housekeeper, polished silverware. Other staff bustled in the background laundering table linens and keeping watch over the delicious-smelling chicken in the oven.

"Thank you, Evelyn. Your chicken sandwiches are the best." By observing Logan over the past few days, this new habit of saying *thank you* came more naturally to Karen.

Evelyn smiled at her. The practice no longer embarrassed the staff. Instead, a cozy camaraderie had grown between Karen, Logan, and the household staff, and led to the friendly gathering around the counter.

Tomorrow was Saturday, Logan's last day in the city. Karen could no longer deny the end to his visit would come. Of course, he couldn't stay here forever, but the thought of facing the next week, the next month, the entire fall season without him made her light-headed and sent a sharp pang through her mid-section.

Karen inhaled and pushed those gloomy thoughts away. As long as Logan remained here with her, she'd relish the time they had and store away special memories. The days and weeks to come would provide her with ample time for loneliness.

She shifted her focus onto him in time to watch him toss a melon ball in the air. He maneuvered to the anticipated landing destination and caught it in his mouth. A grin spread across his face while Ida and Evelyn shared a laugh. Rita smiled a quiet smile as if still unsure how to respond to the Millerson's handsome and entertaining guest.

"Well done," Ida cheered.

Logan claimed his stool, picked up another melon ball, and studied it. "Alex Zahn back in Oswell City makes items in his bakery about this size. They're like doughnut holes and have raisins in them. We call them *vet bollen*. Whenever I'm in need of a study break, I buy a dozen and work on perfecting my accuracy. No one in town has caught on yet to my talent, so don't give away my secret." He winked at Rita.

Her face might as well have caught fire for as red as it turned.

"Here, you try." He handed her a melon ball from the very pile she'd created.

"I don't think so." She lowered her eyes and kept working.

Logan took the ball, tossed it in the air, and caught it in his mouth with precision. "There you go." A teasing smile broke out on his face. "See? Now I'm ready to spend hours and hours creating profound theological concepts. That's all it takes."

Ida produced a grin of her own as she turned to Karen. "Looks to me like you will have your hands quite full when you marry this character."

"Speaking of Oswell City, the church there recently inherited an orchard complete with a house and barns." Logan settled on his stool once more. "What should we do with it? Any ideas?"

"Make apple cider," Evelyn offered.

"Host a fair and give demonstrations," Ida said.

"How about you? Have you thought about it at all?" Logan asked Karen.

"I have. Oswell City Community Church should start an outreach of some sort. Make a place for people who don't have a home."

"There, you see." Logan gazed into her eyes for a moment as a grin soon took over his face, and he pointed at her. "That's why I want to marry her. Creative. Thoughtful. Keeps me focused. I need that."

"She's good for you, I'll agree." Evelyn smiled at them.

"You were made for each other," Rita said while she worked.

Voices echoed in the hall, and footsteps clipped the wooden floors. Mother and Aunt Fran had arrived home from the ceremony they'd attended that afternoon. Uncle Henry had given money to the art center. The construction project for which the funds were designated was finished and ready for service to the city.

Karen had not wished to attend, and Mother didn't mind. The event didn't affect her anyway, so Karen took advantage of a

Friday afternoon with no classes scheduled and spent her time quietly at home with Logan.

Mother and Aunt Fran paused in the doorway as they took in the scene.

"What is Logan doing in here?" Mother asked.

"As our guest, he shouldn't be in the kitchen." A frown wrinkled Aunt Fran's brow.

Logan stood, and Rita slid melon rinds out of sight as if a cleaner countertop could somehow rectify the situation.

"Logan is one of us. Do we really need to concern ourselves with formalities?" Karen couldn't keep the pleading from her voice. Surely Mother could remember back to her visit to Logan's farm. Everyone sat around in the kitchen, talking and sharing in the work.

"I suppose not. I'm just unaccustomed to finding a minister in the kitchen with our staff." Aunt Fran ventured into the room.

"Forget he's a minister. He's my fiancé, and someday soon, he'll be my husband." Karen clutched Logan's hand.

"Of course, you're right, my dear. I'm still trying to get used to all of this. Henry and I will be sad to lose you."

Karen nodded as tears welled in her eyes for Aunt Fran. Unable to have children of her own, she had truly adopted Karen and Julia as if they were her own daughters.

"Oh, Aunt Fran. I'm going to be sorry to leave you too." She shared a hug with her aunt as her heart stretched with every emotion that twisted it. Joy and gaiety from a moment ago. Love for Logan. Love for her family. Sorrow over leaving them. Sadness over Logan's Saturday night departure. Her head ached. Lying down for a bit before dinner sounded like a good idea. She excused herself and went to her room.

THE NEXT DAY, the family gathered together with Julia, Arthur, and their children at the lakeshore. The sun shone, and wind blew off of the water, splashing little waves in the sand. Karen wore her white tea gown and carried her parasol as she and Logan explored the low dunes near the water's edge.

For their luncheon, Aunt Fran and Julia spread a quilt in the shade near the base of a cluster of trees. They snacked on chicken salad sandwiches, melon balls, cheese, tarts, and iced tea as warm breezes blew overhead. Gulls called to one another as they soared in the sky. Sailboats rocked among the waves on the horizon. A lighthouse anchored a pier far into the distance.

Logan left the quilt when the group finished eating and stood at the water's edge. The breeze tousled his hair, giving it permission to frizz into waves that abandoned the controlled style he usually convinced it to comply with. His top buttons were undone. The shirt sleeves were rolled up. Wind billowed in the white fabric at his back. His gaze remained fixed on the sky, far out to the horizon, beyond the frolicking sailboats.

This trip to the lakeshore must be a reprieve to him with the similarity to the open spaces where he thrived on the Iowa prairie. The city, with its tall buildings and crowded streets, surely posed a challenge for a man as unfettered as Logan in both his physical location and disposition of spirit. Confinement lost any power to limit him or stifle him. The city must surely represent that to him, and Karen couldn't blame him if he felt eager to leave it.

"What are you thinking about?" She came to rest at his side.

"I remember my last visit to Lake Michigan. Pete and I would go in the afternoons when we were in seminary. I loved the blue waters and lapping of the waves. They make me think of Dad and how he loved the water. The lake looked the same during those visits as it does today. I needed to come back, so I'm glad your family decided to plan a visit while I was here."

"I'm sorry we won't be able to have that great lakes honeymoon we talked of." A winter wedding limited their options for outdoor honeymoon locations.

"We could have been married by now if our original plans had worked out," Logan murmured as he continued to watch the waves on the horizon.

"Maybe we can come back for a visit next summer." Karen's heart constricted. "Make it our yearly tradition." They'd planned for a July wedding, but Logan's financial struggles during his stay on the farm prolonged his responsibilities there. Karen accepted her teaching job to help him build their savings, further canceling any possibilities of a summer wedding.

"I like the sound of that." He shifted his attention to her and walked with her down the length of the beach as they leisurely passed the afternoon.

Around four o'clock, Uncle Henry called for everyone to gather and prepare to return home. Hank came to pick up the group headed for the Millerson house. Julia and Arthur loaded their family into their car and came as well so that they might stay for dinner and spend the evening with the family on Logan's last day in the city.

When they arrived home, everyone scattered to their rooms to wash the sand from their feet and change their clothes. Karen stayed in her dress and went instead to help Julia bathe two little boys and prepare them to appear at the table.

"You're getting your auntie Karen all wet." Karen made her best attempt to rub a towel over the head and shoulders of Ben, who'd managed to keep one hand in the water and splash it out of the tub.

He giggled.

Karen moved him away from the tub so that he'd help the process instead of hinder it. The sooner she got this little boy dressed, the sooner they could go to dinner.

"GOOD EVENING." Karen addressed the group gathered at the table when she entered the dining room.

Logan came to dinner wearing his suit and tie, his hair

smoothed of any frizz, and his spectacles perfectly in place. He looked prim enough to attend a meeting of Uncle Henry's executive friends. No evidence of wind or waves hung about him.

Karen was a bit windblown and sun-warmed in comparison, but tonight promised a simple, intimate gathering of family. No need for her to dress up or act formally. Way too soon, the train would carry Logan away.

"This is a delicious dinner, Mother," Julia said between bites.

"Thank you. Evelyn outdid herself with the lovely food for our luncheon as well as this succulent roast and the cheesecake she made for our evening meal." Mother touched her cloth napkin to the corner of her mouth.

When the dinner was finished, the party moved to the parlor, where everyone visited until Julia announced their children must go to bed. Even Uncle Henry joined in the conversation. He'd done well the entire day, considering the fact he was still convinced Logan had stolen his symphony tickets.

Karen's heart cried over the reality that Logan would leave the city before resolution had been reached. The relationship between the two men had grown more strained and hadn't improved.

Julia hugged Logan. Ben took his turn next, and Arthur shook his hand. The family left.

Mother turned from waving to them at the door to glancing up at Logan. "I guess this is when I must say goodbye."

"Goodbye, Mother." Logan nodded and welcomed her into an embrace. "Thank you for hosting me this week."

She stepped away from him and smiled in spite of the tears sliding down her cheeks.

"We've enjoyed having you." Aunt Fran also offered him a hug.

When Uncle Henry's turn came to say goodbye, he gave Logan a formal handshake, the same kind he used for business associates he hadn't yet learned to trust.

Logan produced a stiff smile. "Thank you for hosting me, sir. I've appreciated your generosity and your hospitality."

Uncle Henry nodded but said nothing. He went with Mother and Aunt Fran upstairs, leaving Karen and Logan alone. She ventured a glance at his face. Maybe he would kiss her again like he'd done when he arrived and on Thursday night.

"How would you like to say goodbye?" He asked in a quiet voice.

Karen considered the question. "Take a walk with me." There was still one place she wanted to visit with him. A peaceful evening and a spacious garden awaited them.

She led him to the door she used when she slipped out to read his letters. A brick path curved around the house to the garden's gate. Karen opened it and strolled at Logan's side through hedges of hydrangea, groupings of lilies, butterfly bushes, and a wide variety of late summer flowers. They reached the scrolled iron table and chairs on the far side of the fountain.

"I could marry you tonight." Logan draped his suit coat over the back of one of the chairs and took her in his arms. "You know that, don't you?"

"Of course I do."

"Then we wouldn't have to part. I could take you with me to Oswell City and begin our life together right now."

"I'd quit my teaching job and go with you."

A grin spread across his face in the darkness. "We have a preacher. You're wearing white. We could make a bouquet from your aunt's flowers and have a little ceremony right here."

"Who would be our witnesses?" Karen's brow wrinkled.

Logan's gaze moved to the stars overhead. "The moon ... and the Lord." His eyes traveled the darkened sky before returning to her face, and the grin appeared once more.

"Good enough for me, but Julia would never forgive us."

"Neither would the Ladies Mission Society." Logan chuckled. "They're all making big plans for you and me."

"It sounds like we'd better hold off before you have the entire town in an uproar." Karen raised a brow to match his teasing mood.

He laughed again, a happy, unfettered sound consistent with his nature and relaxed outlook. "You know I love you." His tone grew serious.

"I know." Karen closed her eyes before the tears came.

That kiss she dared to hope for came forth in complete reinforcement of the words he'd just spoken. It ended too soon. A breeze picked up scattering petals from a nearby bush across the moonlit lawn. Logan reached for his jacket and accompanied her inside the house with just enough time left for him to gather his luggage, kiss her once more, and go with Hank to catch the ten o'clock train to Iowa.

14

Logan rubbed his eyes for the fiftieth time. The words Apostle Paul wrote to the Corinthians refused to lodge in his brain. Fatigue lingered through Sunday and Monday and into this afternoon. He'd tried his best to catch a nap on the train as he traveled home Saturday night, but the Scriptures and texts for his sermon kept his mind too active for him to rest.

At five in the morning, he'd arrived in Oswell City. Then, he'd gone home for a cup of coffee. He spent the early morning hours at church in prayer prior to delivering the gospel message. Later in the day, he'd taken a nap and had slept well that night, but Monday had been filled with pastoral care demanding much of his energy.

Poor Nellie Akerman had tripped and hit her head. A colorful bruise bloomed over one side of her face. Mrs. Ellenbroek had fallen ill during Logan's absence. She'd done so well ever since her recuperation from pneumonia a year ago, but the symptoms had returned. Dr. Kaldenberg was keeping a close eye on her.

Logan offered another prayer for each woman. Closing his

eyes for the brief intercession felt nice. He attempted to focus once again on Paul's faithful words, but bleariness persisted. Spectacles offered no help. The time had come for a snack from the bakery. A walk downtown might wake him up a little. Logan left his desk, eager to discover what delicious items Alex had on display.

Alex stood on the sidewalk in front of his bakery, deep in conversation with the mayor, Jake Harmsen, and George Brinks. A younger man Logan didn't recognize completed the group.

Jake waved as soon as he saw Logan. "I'm glad to cross paths with you because I wanted to ask if I could run a story on your trip to Chicago in next week's paper."

Sneaky Jake. Even with a foggy brain, Logan caught on. Jake still tried any possible tactic to get Karen's picture in the paper.

"No." Oswell City had more interesting topics to choose from than what the preacher did on vacation.

"But I'm sure you took in some evening entertainment. Saw the downtown. Maybe even visited the lake. People around here would find a story like that really fascinating."

If Jake's opinion were true, then he should go to Chicago and gather material for his own story.

"I did all of those things, but I don't want them in the paper."

"No pictures to share?"

Logan shook his head.

"No tidbits of information about your fiancée?"

Again, Logan shook his head. A trend had emerged in his relationship with the town's newspaper editor. Jake asked too many questions, and Logan gave the same old answer in the form of a repetitious shake of his head.

"There must be something from your time in Chicago we could put in the paper." Jake crossed his arms and peered at him.

Memories of Karen flowed. He could supply Jake with a whole month's worth of information. Like how Karen looked in her evening gowns, or how well she played Chopin, or how much he wanted to kiss her again. Not just once, but every day for the rest of his life.

"Just say I'm back in town and looking forward to the arrival of my bride. She'll be here in January."

"Everyone already knows that." Jake's mouth scrunched to the side of his face. "What I need is a story."

"No story here." Logan held his hands up.

Jake grumbled and assaulted the notepad in his hand with the pencil he always carried in his pocket.

"I'd like for you to meet Mick Farnsworth." George clasped Logan's shoulder. "He's here from Des Moines to inspect the hotel and create an estimate of how much I'll need to spend in the renovation. A few of us talked it over while you were gone and thought it might be a good idea to have him take a look at the buildings on the Akerman farm. That way, we know how much money we'd need to spend to fix the place up."

"Fine idea." Logan smiled as he reached to shake Mick's hand. "Take a look around and stop in when you have a chance to let me know what you find out."

Two days later, Logan sat at his desk once again, attempting to concentrate on Corinthians. Mick appeared in the doorway of the pastor's study.

"Come in." Logan invited the sandy-haired young man with alert brown eyes into his study. "What do you have to share?" Logan studied him in a search for papers with numbers and dollar figures written on them.

Mick dropped into one of the chairs and grasped the sides of his head as a groan accompanied his words. "I've got it so bad."

Logan frowned. Either this man complained of the general condition of his life or he was terribly sick. From the way Mick held his head, Logan believed the theory about sickness. Maybe he should send for Dr. Kaldenberg and have him examine the suffering young man.

Mick shot to his feet and paced, talking out loud all the while. "I came to town to do this job. I was only going to stay for a few days, complete the paperwork, talk with George, and go home."

Whether the words were meant for Logan's ears or Mick just needed to ramble, Logan couldn't say. He sat quietly in his chair and allowed the man to roam.

"But I saw *her*. Out on the street one day. Walking past my table at the café the next. She's the most amazing creature I've ever laid eyes on. Oh." Mick groaned again before he flung himself into the chair and sprawled his arms over the desk. Pure, untainted desperation hung on his features.

"You're engaged to be married. How did you do it? I mean, how did you get a woman to pay attention to you long enough to court her?" Mick stood and thrust his fist into the air. "That's what I want to do! Starting today, I am courting Florence Hesslinga." Mick flopped into the chair again and stared at Logan as if every last bit of sage wisdom on the subject resided right here in the study of Oswell City Community Church with its shy and studious pastor.

If the Fourth of July could happen twice in one year, then the second set of fireworks was going off on Logan's insides. Mick Farnsworth wanted to court Florence! This meant she'd stop chasing him and set her sights on someone else. Oh boy. If he had any cash with him, he'd hand it over to Mick and personally fund their first evening of courtship. Flowers, candy, a meal at the café. Logan didn't care. Anything to divert Florence's flirtations.

Logan had all he could manage in restraining himself from leaping over his desk, shaking Mick's hand, and launching him from the church in an unashamed pursuit of Florence.

"You gotta help me." Mick folded his hands as if saying a prayer or two could further secure Florence's attentions.

His year on the farm claimed Logan's memory. If he told the raw truth to Mick, he'd have to admit he'd never courted Karen. He hadn't been looking for a wife. All he'd done was find ways to generate income so that Mama would have her debts paid.

One of the ways he'd done that was by offering the teacher room and board for the school year. Karen had lived with him for nine months. That's how he got to know her and decided to marry her. Logan's face heated. His experiences included the worst advice a preacher could possibly give to an eager and restless young man. He cleared his throat and leaned back.

"Give it time." He nearly choked on the words slipping from his mouth.

No way did he want a delay in Florence's chances at a new opportunity. He wanted her settled with Mick or anyone but himself this minute. But Mick needed to slow down. For his sake, Logan would venture some counsel.

"If you handle it right, Florence will look at none but you."

A smile bloomed on Mick's face, making him look young and quite naïve. Florence could very well be his first attempt at a serious courtship.

"Let her know how special she is. Buy her gifts." This time Logan did allow experience to inform his counsel. Florence loved presents. Expensive ones. Another reason why the serious seminary student hadn't kept her attention. Any money he had was already spoken for in buying books and paying tuition.

"I can do that. Yeah." Mick said, straightening in his chair.

"Take her dinner." This would provide Mick with a nice, slow event to help him set a sustainable pace in this new courtship.

"Visit the jewelry store." Mick's eyes brightened, and a smile broke out.

"Not yet." Logan shook his head. The idea of going slow obviously had not yet caught on with Mick.

"Call on her at home. Afternoons are good." More experience Logan hadn't asked for concerning Florence, but it was turning out to be useful to her benefit.

"Wow. Thanks, Pastor De Witt. I wouldn't have known the first thing about where to start without talking to you." Mick shook his hand and raced from the study.

Logan couldn't resist. He swiveled in his chair to watch Mick out the window. The young man turned onto the lawn of Clara Hesslinga's home. Florence answered the door. After a few moments, Mick followed her inside. Humming one of the hymns from Sunday's service, Logan turned back to his notes on Corinthians. Maybe he did know a little something about courtship after all.

SEATED at the head of the table, Logan addressed the group of men gathered for another meeting. "Mick Farnsworth has compiled some costs for us. I'll invite him to share those with us so we can make a decision tonight of what should be done with the house on the Akerman farm."

Mick cleared his throat and stood. "The house has a leak in the roof. It needs a new coat of paint, new windows, and boards replaced on the floor of the porch. I estimate the total cost of renovation at five hundred dollars."

"We don't have enough funds in the church's budget to cover those costs," James said.

"Do we need that old house anyway? We might as well tear it down and start over with a new building to fit our purposes," Artie said.

"That's part of our problem. We don't know what to use the property for." Logan's conversation with Karen replayed in his mind. "I've heard the suggestion we should start an outreach of some sort."

"But to whom, and way out in the country? That doesn't make sense." Artie crossed his arms.

"Artie's right. Any location for an outreach should be downtown on Main Street so people can find it easier," Jake said.

If only there was a way for Karen to see the property. She'd know what to do and give him good suggestions.

"Could you take a picture of the house, Jake? I want to send it to Karen and her family. They might have some ideas on how to use the property." Logan glanced over at the newspaper editor.

Jake shrugged. "I guess. I'll go out there tomorrow."

"I have an idea," Paul Ellenbroek spoke up for the first time. Everyone shifted their attention to him. "Last week while Pastor Logan was gone, the Van Drunens and the Haverkamps both had relatives arrive from Holland. These folks need a place to stay until they can secure permanent housing, and neither family has room for them.

"With the hotel shut down for renovation, Oswell City could really use a place for people to find accommodations. What would you think of using the Akerman house as our temporary hotel?"

"A regular bed and breakfast," Alex said. "I'd be happy to supply bread for meals."

"The arrangement would put my housekeeping and kitchen staff back to work," George said. "But what about the place being so far out of town?"

"We could arrange for someone to drive people back and forth," Paul suggested.

"What about the leak in the roof?" James asked.

"We might be able to come up with some city money to fix the worst places," Paul offered.

"It would still require a lot of cleaning to make it comfortable for guests. Those upstairs rooms haven't been used in a long time," Dr. Kaldenberg said.

"Our wives can help out," George replied. "I'm sure folks

new to Oswell City will prefer their own rooms in an old house to cramming in with their relatives."

Others at the table nodded.

Logan followed the train of thought and approved. "The resourceful and generous citizens of Oswell City will have their guests comfortable and feeling at home in no time."

15

The Ladies Mission Society descended upon the old Akerman home with brooms, mops, and feather dusters. They spiffed the place up so well, Logan believed Mick could knock a couple hundred off his estimated costs of repairs. A little paint and patching of a few cracks in the walls, and the house would look as nice on the inside as any other home in Oswell City.

The outside was another matter. Much work still waited in order to restore the place to its original glory, but for a town in need of some form of hotel, the Akerman house was plenty adequate. Once the cleaning had been completed, the consistory gave Logan approval to call on the Haverkamps and the Van Drunens, welcome them to town, and invite them to take advantage of the new accommodations.

He went to the Haverkamps first. The small home on the north edge of town appeared cramped with adults and children. Two families of relatives had immigrated to Iowa over the course of the summer.

"Oh, thank you. Such a thoughtful offer!"

The adults in the family expressed their gratitude with English spoken in a heavy brogue. They loaded up the wagons at once and made the trek to the orchard where George's hotel staff was ready to serve them and look after their needs.

"Watch for us at church on Sunday. We'll be there." The couples waved to Logan.

"Happy to help out." He waved back and drove to the Van Drunen home.

A young man opened the door to Logan's knock.

"Good afternoon. I'm Pastor Logan De Witt from Oswell City Community Church," Logan announced.

The man smiled at him but gave no other response.

He should have stopped to consider that not everyone who immigrated to Oswell City would understand English within the first week.

Logan recalled the few words his father had taught him and tried again. "*Goode middag.*"

The man's face lit up. He reached to shake Logan's hand and repeated the greeting.

"I'm the *dominee van het kerk* in Oswell City." Logan winced. That was terrible Dutch, but it was the best he could come up with at this moment of improvisation.

The man nodded and pointed to Logan. "*Dominee?*"

"That's right." The man wouldn't understand that reply. What was the word for *yes*? He hesitated for a moment as his mind spun through his limited vocabulary. A simple syllable lodged in his mind. Now he remembered. "*Ja.*"

The man laughed and called over his shoulder. "Angelien! *Ik ben met het dominee. Comen!*"

A slim blonde woman appeared at the door. She smiled. "You're the minister?" A heavy brogue slurred her words, but at least she spoke them in English.

"Pastor Logan De Witt." He reached to shake her hand.

"I'm Angelien, and this is my *echtgenoo*t, I mean my husband, Conrad." She pointed at herself and then at the man who had answered the door.

"Welcome to Oswell City." Logan offered them his warmest

smile. "I've come by to tell you that the church owns a large house out in the country. You are welcome to stay there if you like. We serve meals and provide housekeeping. Stay as long as you want."

Conrad and Angelien exchanged glances and held a subdued conversation using words Logan no longer remembered.

"We accept," Angelien announced.

"Great. The house is clean and spacious, but I'll warn you that the roof leaks and some boards on the porch need to be replaced. We hope to fix it up soon."

"He is carpenter." Angelien pointed to her husband. "Maybe he help with repairs." She turned to Conrad and repeated to him everything Logan had said.

Conrad pointed to himself as a broad smile crossed his face. "*De timmerman*."

Logan nodded. This newcomer to town would sure come in handy as the church restored the Akerman house. He should let the other men know as soon as possible.

Two children trotted up to Angelien. She picked up the smallest one. "Pastor De Witt, please meet our daughter, Betje, and our son, Markus."

Logan smiled at both children and offered to help the Van Drunens with their move.

IN THE WEEKS THAT FOLLOWED, Conrad proved to be of much assistance in the roof repairs and other odd jobs around the property. From time to time, George brought hotel guests for overnight stays. The system the consistory had devised worked well and satisfied a large need.

Jake developed the picture of the house and gave it to Logan. He wrote a letter to Karen describing the house's current function and asked her to continue joining him in prayer about the property's long-term purpose. She wrote back, encouraging him to still consider the possibility of some form of outreach. He appreciated Karen's reply and kept the matter in prayer. The Lord would reveal to them at the proper time what he intended for the house and barn.

As the autumn season progressed, Artie's prediction about weddings came true. Logan was called on to perform at least one every week. The liturgy didn't have a chance to fade from his memory. Constantly, he stood with a couple at the front of the church, asking them if they promised to love one another, cherish one another, and care for each other in sickness and in health, until death parted them. His heart answered every time with its own resounding *yes*.

In only three more months, he'd finally say his own vows to commit himself to Karen as her husband. Each wedding he officiated served as a confirmation of the happiness awaiting him.

He kept watch on Mick and Florence. Perhaps they might be one of the couples following his example in matrimony. Mick must have figured out how to slow down because he hadn't yet made an appointment with Logan to plan a wedding service. Florence had better still welcome Mick's attention. Logan didn't want to think of what might happen if she refused his offer of courtship.

She hadn't cornered him lately or thrown her arms around his neck, so Logan accepted that as a good sign Florence had decided to give her attention to another. Mick had returned home to Des Moines in recent weeks. The distance separating him from Florence may lead her to decide Logan right here in town was much more convenient than the extra effort required to keep in touch with a man living farther away.

As the holiday season grew closer, one large project dominated his list of tasks to complete in his preparations for getting married.

"Do you know of anyone with a piano for sale?" Logan asked Paul Ellenbroek one Sunday morning when they shook hands after the service. "The parsonage needs one. I checked at the Akerman house, but it doesn't have one. If I'd found one there, I'd devise a way to move it into my parlor. My fiancée is quite an accomplished pianist, so I would like to have a piano for her to play when we're married."

"Hmm. A piano. Let me think about that. Lillian knew of a woman east of town who moved away. She had a piano, but I believe all of her furniture is sold by now. I'll start spreading the word and see what turns up." Paul went to help his wife into her coat.

Now that the matter was put to rest, Logan could channel his energy into the Advent season. He'd have to work extra hard helping his congregation prepare for Christmas because the excitement growing on his insides did nothing to help him preach. It actually worked against his attempts to study and deliver a message.

The slightest thought of Karen threw him into distraction. Stutters crept back into his sermons until Logan could hardly pull himself together enough to function as the devout and sensible minister.

He wanted to run up to everyone he met and shout the news, 'I'm getting married. Get excited. Did you hear? I'm getting married!'

Running around and yelling was hardly necessary. The entire town was already terribly excited.

"Mildred and I will bake the cake for your wedding reception." Alex Zahn smiled at him and shook his hand after Paul left.

"Oh, yes. We'd love to do it." Mildred, standing in line behind her husband, gave an enthusiastic nod.

Talk of the wedding introduced sudden disorder to the line of complacent people filing out of the sanctuary. People flocked around him with offers to help.

"You are planning on the Ladies Mission Society providing

the meal for the rehearsal dinner, aren't you?" Grace Koelman asked.

"The repair work is done on the hotel, which means I'm ready to rent out rooms again and open up the dining room." George Brinks inched past the others until he stood at Logan's side in his best effort to be heard. "Let me provide accommodations for your family from Silver Grove, and your bride's family from Chicago."

"Please let me give necklaces to your bride and her attendants." Artie Goud pressed in next to George.

"I'll help with transportation," Paul called out as he and Lillian passed by on their way to the door.

"I'll bring a bowtie from my own collection over to the parsonage for you sometime this week." Dr. Kaldenberg joined the group and gave Logan a handshake. "You might like one to wear with your suit for the wedding service."

Dizziness made Logan's head swim. He was still getting used to the idea of more people than just family in attendance at the wedding service, but the rest of the town saw this important event quite differently. Anticipation mingled with the festive feel of the season put everyone in a mood for celebration.

Even Mrs. Akerman had an encouraging word to say. Her bruises had cleared up, returning her skin to its normal color. Clara helped her maneuver through the crowd so she could reach Logan.

She landed a playful slap on his cheek as had become her usual greeting for him, and looked him in the eye. "Enjoy every minute you have with your new wife, Pastor De Witt. We never know how long the Lord will allow us to hold on to our good gifts before he takes them away from us."

He gave a sober nod. The elderly lady spoke from painful experience. Her words stayed with him long into the afternoon. He most certainly would enjoy every day he had with Karen. Next to God and his word, she was his greatest treasure. He couldn't wait to have her and to hold her for as long as the Lord allowed.

FRIDAY NIGHT, Logan worked by lamplight at his dining room table, putting the finishing touches on his Christmas Eve sermon. Snow fell outside his window, covering Oswell City in a pure and sparkly layer of white. The fire crackled in his fireplace, making the parsonage a cozy haven on this winter evening.

A knock came on the door. Logan rushed to answer it. Someone might want him for an emergency or a death.

A man and a woman bundled in coats and scarves stood on his front step.

The woman pushed her scarf away from her mouth. "Is this the preacher's house?"

"It is."

"We got a delivery for ya. Conrad Van Drunen bought the house next door to us. It had a piano, but his wife don't play it none, so they wanted to get rid of it. The word around town is the preacher is lookin' for a piano. Ya still interested?" The woman studied him as snowflakes collected on her scarf.

"Uh ... why ... yes. Yes, of course. I'm still hoping to find a piano." Logan craned his neck to catch a glimpse of the street. A wagon box on a sled was parked behind a team of horses. Blankets bound with twine covered an object in the wagon box.

"Mind if we back it up to your door?" the man asked.

"No, not at all. Let me get my coat, and I will help you unload." He hastened into his wool coat and went to enlist the help of his neighbors.

After much pushing, shoving, and furniture rearranging, the piano rested along the dining room wall near the hutch. His desk and a couple of chairs were pushed out of the way to make space for the new instrument, but the dining room didn't look as crowded as he'd expected.

"Thank you for delivering the piano." Logan shook hands with the couple while he made a mental note to stop in at Conrad's new place and offer him a payment.

The man waved on his way out the door as if to say he'd enjoyed the exertion.

Logan shut the door and returned to the dining room. Except for admiring his fiancée's talents, he knew nothing about music. But he sat at the piano anyway. Plunking a few of the keys told him the instrument was in pretty good shape with its keyboard in tune. He stared at the keys envisioning his wife seated here and playing a lovely melody. His heart swelled.

Christmas Day, with its flurry of gift-giving, was only a few days away. But for Logan, the season of receiving gifts had just begun.

16

"I am going to miss you so much." Mabel threw her arms around Karen's neck.

"You're the best English teacher we've ever had." Blanche dabbed the corners of her eyes with a handkerchief.

"Are you sure you can't stay and teach longer?" Ruby clasped her hands and pleaded.

These girls knew how to rip a heart out.

Karen swallowed back her own tears before she spoke. "I'd love to. Really I would. Teaching each of you at Emerson Ladies Academy has been the most rewarding experience I've had during my teaching career. Watching it come to an end is hard."

"I guess if I was marrying a man like your fiancé, I'd want to quit teaching too." Annie shrugged and looked at her.

A small hope flickered in her prayers these days that just maybe an opportunity to continue teaching lurked somewhere in the life she and Logan hoped to build together. Her future husband championed her teaching talents, as well as her desire to use them. She could trust him to help her find a way to satisfy her sense of call to teach.

Miss Gregory joined the group. "Miss Millerson, please come

with me to the refreshment table. The faculty and I would like to present you with a gift."

Karen and her students followed the principal across the room. Miss Gregory lifted a wrapped box from the table and handed it to Karen. She unwrapped it while her colleagues watched. Opening the box, Karen discovered a shiny brass surface. She pulled the object from the box. The brass surface formed the top of a clock. It would look perfect on the mantel of the fireplace Logan had told her about.

"Thank you." Karen glanced around at the kind people who had welcomed her earlier that year onto their staff. "This will look very nice in my new home."

Miss Gregory expressed her appreciation for Karen and invited everyone to enjoy the food laid out for the reception.

Karen ate, but her chest ached. Today was the last day of the semester, the last day at the ladies' college, and the last day of her career. She didn't dare think about the facts here, surrounded by her students and other teachers. Tonight, alone in her room, she'd allow the tears to fall and draw on her courage to face her loss. Right now, she must put all of her energy into this gathering.

"Congratulations on your upcoming marriage." The vocal instructor gave Karen a hug.

"Thank you."

"We're so happy for you." Miss Gregory gave her a hug too. "Who is the groom?"

"Logan De Witt. We will live in Iowa after we are married."

"All the best, Karen. We've enjoyed having you on staff here at the academy with us this semester." The strings instructor shook her hand.

"I've enjoyed it too. I wish I didn't have to leave."

The others smiled at her.

"We wish you didn't have to either, but we understand. Getting married is a good reason to quit your job," Miss Gregory said with a light chuckle.

Final encouragements given and one more round of hugs exchanged, Karen left the campus and rode the streetcar for the last time.

Along the route home, shoppers bustled in and out of downtown stores looking for Christmas gifts. Bells jingled. Horns honked. A light snow fell. Karen's heart carried too much weight to enjoy the festive aura of the city on this Friday afternoon three days before the holiday. The arrival of the new year would bring change. As much as she wanted to marry Logan, the somber endings marriage required reminded her that even good changes came at a price.

She stepped off the streetcar at the corner nearest Uncle Henry's mansion. Cold accompanied her walk when a wind blew in and swirled snow around Karen's face. She pulled her scarf snug to her ears and hastened down the street.

"Miss Karen, they're waiting for you." Ida stood on the top step with the door wide open.

"Who is waiting for me?" Karen asked as she climbed the steps.

"Your mother and Miss Rose. Julia is in there too. So is your Aunt Fran." Ida followed her into the foyer.

At the top of the stairs, Julia bounced on her toes. A squeal escaped when she called down to Karen. "Oh, it is just beautiful! Come and see."

Karen frowned as she removed her coat and scarf. Julia's actions reminded her of Aunt Fran the day Ben was born. No one in the house that Karen could recall was expecting a baby. She couldn't imagine why everyone was so excited. She ventured up the stairs. Julia caught her by the hand and took her to Mother's room.

On a dress form, the most celestial creation of shimmering white Karen had ever seen flowed to the floor. Her breath caught as she crossed the room and dared to touch a lacy sleeve. Her wedding gown, perfect with just the right amount of lace and tucks, cast its own glow over the room.

"Didn't she do a nice job?" Mother stood nearby with an intent gaze focused on Karen as if she'd been assessing her daughter's response.

"It's lovely." She could hardly believe she'd really wear such a masterpiece.

"Try it on." Miss Rose sounded as giddy as Julia.

Karen blinked. Yes, of course. She should put this dress on and try to convince herself this day of endings and new beginnings was truly happening.

Before Karen could respond, Mother and Miss Rose worked to loosen her skirt. She slipped out of it while someone unbuttoned the row of buttons on the back of her blouse.

With great care, Miss Rose removed the gown from the dress form and slid it over Karen's head. While Karen slipped her arms into the sleeves, Miss Rose moved to fasten the buttons on the back.

"Oh, Karen." Julia's breathless words escaped from behind the fingers she held to her lips.

Karen turned to look in Mother's full-length mirror on its decorative wooden frame. The image reflected back at her swept all gloominess away. She couldn't help but welcome the changes rushing into her life with this scene before her.

A scooped neckline, low but not too low, dipped between her shoulders bordered by the lace Karen had chosen during Miss Rose's initial consultation. The skirt gathered at her waist and fell to the floor in elegant waves. Tiny white rosettes secured the gathers.

If only Logan could see her. She couldn't imagine what he'd say or do. Life as she had known it for the last six months, might have come to an end this afternoon, but this dress held promises of the new life about to begin. In shining silence, it asked her to release her hold on the past and allow the Lord to introduce into her life relationships and adventures that were larger, and perhaps even better.

"Make sure and try this on." Miss Rose roused from admiring

the reflection in the mirror and retrieved a mound of tulle. She placed one end of it in a twist of Karen's hair.

The tulle cascaded to the floor and stopped at the hemline. "A shortened veil."

Mother smiled. "Yes, my dear. The length of the veil doesn't matter. I want you to be happy on your special day."

"Oh, Mother." Karen hugged her. Already her relationships were expanding in readiness for what was yet to come.

When the smell of good food wafted into the room, Miss Rose helped Karen change into her other clothes so the family could go to the dining room and eat the evening meal.

Over the course of the next few days, the Christmas season swept in with parties and social gatherings. Karen enjoyed them all. She went with her family to church for the Christmas morning service. The rest of the day was spent in the decorated parlor with Julia's family eating candy and exchanging gifts.

Karen received many nice items for her new home. She added them to the collection she'd received from a shower Mother and her friends had hosted in November. As soon as the new year arrived, these gifts would travel with her to Oswell City.

After Christmas, Karen spent the day packing a trunk of her household items. If she completed the task early, she'd have one less responsibility when the time came to pack her clothing and other possessions. She finished the job and retired to the drawing room with a book later in the evening. The fire crackled toasty warm as Mother worked needlepoint, and Uncle Henry and Aunt Fran played a game.

The doorbell rang.

Uncle Henry startled and looked around. "Who could possibly be out calling at this hour?"

"And the day after Christmas." Aunt Fran looked at Mother.

"Did you invite any guests?"

"No, I did not." Mother shook her head.

Ida came into the room. "There's a caller for Miss Karen."

A frown claimed Karen's forehead as she rose from her chair. Mischief twinkled in Ida's eyes when she passed by, adding to her confusion. She ventured into the darkened foyer, caught her breath, and pulled the door open. After one glimpse of the man outside, she shut the door and leaned against the wall, her chest heaving.

It couldn't be him.

Pounding came on the door. "Hey, Karen?"

It was him. Logan's voice carried to her ears and made her heart thump. She collected her wits and opened the door once more.

In one motion, Logan stepped into the house, gathered her into his arms, and landed a kiss on her mouth. His winter-chilled lips soon warmed from the contact. When he finally released her, Karen's mind swirled with one hundred questions, but all she could do was stare.

"I had to see you." Logan's low voice carried urgency and intensity. "I've been to Silver Grove to spend Christmas with Mama and Tillie, but before I returned to Oswell City, I needed to spend some time with you."

Karen backed out of his embrace while Logan fished in his coat pocket. He produced a small wrapped box which he handed to her.

"It isn't quite as expensive as last year's gift, but I hope you like it anyway. My larger gift for you rests against the wall of my dining room. I'm happy to tell you the parsonage has a piano."

Karen's eyes widened while more questions joined the ones swirling in her head. "You bought me a piano?"

"Not bought exactly. Conrad wouldn't let me pay him for it. And since a piano wouldn't travel too well on a train, I brought you that instead." He pointed to the little wrapped box in her hand.

Her limbs went numb. Logan had spent time deciding on a gift, shopping for it, and wrapping it, but she had none to give to him. "I don't know if I can take this. You've even spent money on train tickets to get here, but I didn't think of buying you a gift. With our wedding next week, I wasn't expecting to see you for Christmas. I'm so sorry."

"Oh, Karen, it's all right. You didn't have to do anything. I just ... well, we became engaged on Christmas last year, so I wanted to come celebrate with you." A tiny smile tugged at one corner of his mouth.

Not only was her fiancé compassionate and charming, but he was filled with grace as well. She could think of no response to give except to abandon all reserve and throw herself into his arms.

"Karen, my dear, who is at the door? Who is your caller?" Mother spoke as she entered. "Oh." She stopped short, and her hand fluttered to her chest.

Uncle Henry and Aunt Fran followed close behind and almost ran into her.

"I'm going to bed." Uncle Henry headed up the stairs.

"I think I will too. Come on, Margaret." Aunt Fran tugged on Mother's arm.

"What a pleasant surprise to see you, Logan. How long can you stay?" Mother asked as she followed Aunt Fran up the stairs.

"Until tomorrow afternoon."

"Such a short trip."

"I'm afraid so. I need to get back to Oswell City to prepare my sermon and preach on Sunday."

"You are welcome to the same room you used on your last visit." Mother called out as she reached the top stair.

Logan nodded his thanks and then turned his attention on Karen.

"How did you get here?" Karen studied his dark coat and red scarf while her brain worked to absorb the fact that Logan stood here with her in Chicago.

"A streetcar still operated, so I hopped on and rode until it stopped at your street. My previous visit to the city helped me know my way around." Logan shifted his arm from her waist to her shoulders and walked at her side as she led him to the drawing room.

The fire still burned in the fireplace. Mother's needlepoint lay where it fell when she went to inquire about Karen's guest. Karen folded up the piece of fabric and put it in a drawer to free up space on the loveseat. She tucked in next to Logan when he sat down.

"I come from Silver Grove with good news."

"Oh, really? What is it?"

"Tillie announced at our family gathering yesterday that she and Andrew are expecting a baby. It's due next summer."

"That's wonderful." Karen shifted to look at him. "I'm so happy for her."

Logan chuckled. "Mama's pretty happy too. She made sure I got the message that the job of supplying her with grandchildren didn't belong only to Tillie."

"Good thing you're getting married then." Karen punched his arm.

Instead of responding with some form of orneriness as Karen expected him to do, Logan gazed at her while a solemn expression overtook the grin on his face.

In a quiet voice, he said, "Yeah, it's a good thing."

Karen's breathing grew labored as Tillie's news sank in. She and Logan could be the ones making the same sort of announcement next Christmas, or even sooner. The look on Logan's face told her he guessed her thoughts and shared them.

She looked away. More changes. More new beginnings. The realm of joy opened up too quickly for Karen to keep pace. She must think about more immediate concerns before happiness overwhelmed her.

"I think I'll take a look at this now." Karen held up her gift.

Logan smiled, so she unwrapped the box. No writing on the

outside indicated the contents. Karen opened the box and pulled out a small glass container oval in shape with a liquid inside.

"Read it." Logan turned the glass bottle around.

"Song of the Spring." A whiff of flowers reached her nose. "You bought me perfume."

"I didn't exactly buy this gift either. You remember me writing to you about an elderly woman named Mrs. Akerman?"

"I do."

"She gave me this bottle of perfume and told me to give it to my new wife. She's so happy for me to get married. Her husband fought in the Civil War and never came home. Watching me prepare for marriage brings back her old memories. She needs a reason to recall them. I'm happy to help her remember because it helps her heal. Do you remember reading the name of the Akerman orchard in one of my letters?"

"They were Dutch words that said something about orchards and love." Karen set the perfume on a nearby stand.

"You're right. Orchards of Love. Fruit trees bloom in the spring. Getting married is teaching my heart how to sing a whole new song. I love you, Karen, and I pray that what is blossoming now at the beginning of our life together will reap a rich harvest of love in the years to come."

Karen's eyes misted over, but she blinked the moisture away so it wouldn't prevent her from memorizing how Logan looked at this moment. Preacher and poet, he'd spoken a beautiful prophecy over their tomorrows. She picked up the bottle and spritzed a bit onto her wrist. The floral fragrance filled the room.

Logan reached for her scented wrist and kissed her hand. Memories from Christmas night a year ago flooded her mind. Seated before a cozy fire and talking about building a life together, this night had much in common with that one. Even the late hour noted on the grandfather clock was similar. For two years in a row, the best gift Christmas gave her arrived after every other celebration had ended.

17

Bundled in his coat and scarf, Logan stood on the platform of the Oswell City railroad station. The train from Chicago was due to arrive any minute. Mama, his sister Tillie and her husband Andrew had traveled from Silver Grove that morning. Logan's best friend, Pastor Peter Betten, and his wife, Anna, along with their baby, Charlotte, had come to town on the same train.

Pete had agreed to perform the wedding ceremony for his good friend. After years of failed attempts to match his shy friend up with the perfect woman, Logan's news of an engagement produced great celebration in the letters exchanged between the Betten household and the groom-to-be. Nothing less than officiating the service himself would satisfy Pete's desire for involvement on Logan's special day.

After a check-in at the hotel and a quick lunch at the Kramers' café, everyone except Anna and the baby waited with Logan for the rest of the wedding guests to arrive.

The De Witts weren't the only ones at the train station this afternoon. Most of the town crowded the platform, waiting and watching. Logan could guess why. Jake had managed to slip an announcement, no longer than two lines of print, into this week's newspaper informing Oswell City of the date and time of arrival for Pastor De Witt's bride.

The day of her arrival had never been a secret. Everyone knew the rehearsal was scheduled for tonight because the Ladies Mission Society planned to host the dinner. But how Jake discovered the time of arrival for Karen's train, Logan couldn't say. Jake must have made a lucky guess and happened to get it right. Or maybe the town's citizens were so determined to catch a glimpse of his bride, they would have stood in a chilly wind to welcome every train that pulled into the station until finally meeting the one Karen rode.

He shivered. Whatever level of excitement infused the town couldn't match the euphoria pumping inside him. His bride was coming to town to marry him and stay here to share a life with him. He couldn't imagine a larger, richer blessing God could possibly shower upon a person.

Billows of black smoke appeared in the gray sky above the roofs along the track. A shrill whistle blew. The smell of soot filled the air.

"She's coming." Logan turned to Mama and worked with all his might to keep his voice controlled. If he wasn't a grown man expected to fill the serious role of a clergyman, he'd jump up and down, clapping his hands and pointing while shouting at the top of his voice, 'The love of my life is almost here! Karen is coming!'

The engine ground to a stop. A hissing cloud of steam rolled from the giant iron wheels. Men in station uniforms scurried about. The door to the coach car opened. Karen's uncle Henry and her aunt Fran emerged first, followed by her mother, Margaret. They looked around for a moment. When Margaret spotted Logan, she smiled and led the others to his group.

Karen's sister Julia and her husband Arthur stepped off the train, each one carrying a small boy. Following her mother, Julia brought her family over to where Logan stood. Hugs were exchanged all around. Laughter and conversation rounded out the reunion as Logan kept his attention on the coach. Finally, he saw her. His fiancée appeared as gracious and lovely as ever.

"Logan!" She waved and rushed straight into his arms.

Overcome with the delight of holding her again, he planted a kiss square on her mouth. He could almost feel Jake lurking somewhere behind him, snapping the photos he'd coveted for so long.

Jake could snap all the pictures he wanted. This might be the first time Logan had been witnessed kissing in public, but it wouldn't be the last. The town would need to prepare for more displays of his affection for his new bride. No longer did he need to hold himself in restraint. His wedding was tomorrow, a day on which a new world of beauty and of love opened up to him.

"Welcome to Oswell City." Logan gestured to the brick station behind them, the first building in a row lining the main street. "Mama has been here before, but for everyone else, let me show you to the hotel. George has rooms ready for you."

Logan turned to the station and discovered that the townspeople still crowded around, blocking his path. For months, the citizens of Oswell City had waited and watched with him for this moment. They deserved to have a share in it. Logan reached for Karen's hand.

"Everyone, I'm happy to introduce my fiancée to you, Miss Karen Millerson." He gestured to the crowd. "Karen, meet Oswell City."

People reached to shake Karen's hand. Others congratulated her on her marriage to him. As they ventured onto the street, the group followed, chatting with Mama and learning the names of Karen's family. The trip to the hotel crawled along at such a slow pace, the men from the station in charge of delivering luggage waited for them at the front door. The crowd scattered, leaving only Paul Ellenbroek. He pulled Logan aside.

"What's wrong?" The look in Paul's eyes told Logan all was not well on this January afternoon in Oswell City.

"There's been an accident at the Haverkamps'. You

remember the farm they bought before Christmas north of town?"

Logan nodded.

"The two men were working together harvesting ice from the pond when one fell in. The other broke his arm trying to help him."

Logan rubbed his forehead. He knew the agony of a broken limb. "Does the man who fell in the water have a pulse?"

"I'm not sure. The doctor is probably trying to revive him since he is there now, but the family is asking for you to come too." A serious look claimed Paul's face.

Pete and Andrew gathered around.

"What's going on?" Pete asked.

Logan explained. "It might be a good idea for me to bring some people with me. Chores might need to be done."

"I'll go," Pete volunteered.

"So will I." Arthur joined the group in time to hear Logan's explanation. "You should come with us," he said to Henry, who leaned in to listen. Henry didn't argue but nodded his head.

"Find Karen. I'd like to take her along." Logan glanced at Pete.

He nodded and went over to the women who were busy sorting through satchels.

Karen returned with him and sent Logan a questioning glance.

He relayed Paul's information along with an invitation. "I'd like for the congregation to start getting to know you."

She nodded with understanding in her eyes.

The crowd at the station made a nice welcoming party, but Karen would never learn peoples' names if she was always surrounded by a mass. The best way for her to make connections was a little at a time. He hadn't expected to immerse her into his life quite so soon, but she'd do well, bringing peace to this crisis. Her place among them would solidify with ease as soon as people learned of her gentle nature.

He grasped her hand. "Paul, can we take your car?"

"You sure can." Paul nodded.

After a hasty conference with Mama and a promise to return in plenty of time for the rehearsal, Logan went with Karen and the men down the street to City Hall, where they crowded into Paul's car and drove out of town.

The two Haverkamp families shared the house on the land they'd bought together. One of the wives met Logan and his group at the door and ushered them to an upstairs bedroom.

Dr. Kaldenburg worked at making a cast on the arm of the man lying in bed.

He straightened when Logan entered. "This man only broke his arm. His brother didn't fare as well. Falling into the freezing water of the pond gave him a severe case of hypothermia. You may go in there if you wish, but he may not respond."

Logan nodded and took Karen with him to the room next door. Dr. Kaldenburg's prediction proved true. The man lay unresponsive, but he did appear to be breathing. Logan picked up the man's arm, and after discovering a pulse, he offered a prayer for a full recovery. Logan and Karen returned to the first room and joined the conversation the doctor held with the other men.

"The sled and tools are still out at the pond. Those items should be put away before dark. The Haverkamps also keep some livestock. Check with the women and see if you can give them a hand in the barn."

The group split up. Karen stayed in the house to help with washing dishes still left from the mid-day meal. Arthur and Pete went to the barn. Logan and Henry went to the pond. One horse foraged in the snow. The sled, partially stacked with blocks of ice, was parked near a slushy pool of water. Saws and picks lay scattered on the bank.

Logan turned to Henry. "Hitch the horse to the sled. Then come help me move these tools and the ice to the farm."

Henry ambled to the horse while Logan loaded up the tools.

He drove the horse to the farm and worked with Henry to stack the harvested ice in the ice house. The older man's face turned bright red, and he huffed in a great effort to catch his breath. But he didn't slow his pace, and he kept up with Logan until the job was completed.

They met Arthur, Pete, Karen, and the other two women in the kitchen. Logan prayed with them and then returned to town. He parked Paul's car at City Hall and walked his guests to the hotel. During the remaining hours of the afternoon, Logan and Pete, with the help of George Brinks and his sled, hauled the trunks full of Karen's belongings to the parsonage.

The spare bedroom at the end of the hall made the perfect place for storage until Karen had time to unpack. With the task completed and the men on their way to the hotel, Logan changed his clothes in preparation for the wedding rehearsal.

He went to the church early and spent time at his desk, making notes on the Haverkamps. Since the wedding and his honeymoon filled the next few days, Logan wanted to be sure and remember to call on them at his first opportunity.

The sound of heavy doors opening and closing carried down the hall. A mixture of voices followed. His family and his bride had arrived for the rehearsal and dinner.

Footsteps grew closer and stopped at his door. Logan glanced up and discovered Henry Millerson standing in his study.

"Good evening, Henry. What can I do for you?" Logan extended the same greeting he offered to all of his visitors.

A look of discomfort claimed Henry's features. He sat down and rubbed his hands together. "Pastor De Witt, I owe you an apology."

Logan couldn't recall anything offensive that had happened since Henry's arrival, so he stayed silent.

"I saw you today surrounded by loyal townsfolk when we arrived on the train. They welcomed us because they like you. I worked alongside you at that farm. Lifting ice is hard work, but you handled the strain better than I did. I'm sorry for the way I treated you when you were in Chicago last summer. Fran found our concert tickets the day after you left. I shouldn't have accused you of stealing."

"I appreciate that." Logan held Henry's gaze. "While I was in Chicago, I discovered that you are a devout man and have been hurt by the poor choices your brother-in-law made. I respect that. I can't promise that I won't make my own share of mistakes, but I can give you my word to take the best care of Karen I know how. I love her, and I would never intentionally disgrace her or any of you."

"I know." Henry's eyes turned watery. "I haven't wanted to see, but I do now that I'm here in your town. You have my blessing, Logan. Please marry Karen with the assurance that I approve."

The man had remembered to use Logan's first name. Miracles did still happen. He stood, accepted Henry's handshake, and went with his new friend to the sanctuary.

Pete collected everyone together and directed them where to stand. Arthur and Andrew, as Logan's groomsmen, joined him on Pete's left side. Julia and Tillie, as Karen's bridesmaids, stood with her at Pete's right side. Next, Pete guided Logan and Karen through their vows. Practice at slipping the ring on and off Karen's finger followed with an explanation of the words both of them were to say.

If Logan could have his way, the wedding band would already be melded to Karen's engagement ring and would stay in place on her hand, declaring them married tonight. No fuss. No large crowds, just him and his new wife, committing themselves to each other before the Lord.

The clink of pans and the scent of cooking food coming from the kitchen told Logan his hope was a figment of his imagination. The Ladies Mission Society had shown up in full force tonight to serve him and his wedding party a meal as soon as the plans for the wedding service were clear in everyone's minds.

He shook himself away from his thoughts and back into the rehearsal in time to follow Pete's instructions through the entire service from start to finish. Pete gave a practice benediction before Cornelia Goud entered the sanctuary with the announcement that the meal was ready.

Logan went with the group to the hall, where tables and chairs had been set up. White cloths and bouquets of evergreen boughs decorated the tables. Plates and glasses from the church's supply completed each place setting. Candles burned in the windows, casting a warm glow over the room. His chest expanded, and any tension left over from the day's events drained away. These women had invested much time and careful attention in their preparations.

"Pastor Logan, you and your bride should sit here." Grace Koelman pulled two chairs out from the nearest table.

He followed her directions.

"Your mothers may sit here." She indicated two more chairs at the same table. "Wedding attendants and their families may sit here." She pointed to another table nearby.

"Would you pray for us?" Cornelia glanced at him.

He nodded and offered a prayer thanking the Lord for his blessings.

The meal began with the entire group of women emerging from the kitchen, anticipating each need that arose. They heaped food onto the plates, filled water glasses, and ran for coffee. One of them even held the Bettens' baby daughter, so Pete and his wife Anna could enjoy the meal.

The women served the dessert, and while the group savored pastries handmade by the Zahn family, Clara Hesslinga and Lillian Ellenbroek approached the table where Logan sat with Karen. Between them, they carried a basket large enough to hold an entire day's work of clean laundry.

"Miss Millerson, we have a gift for you." Clara worked with Lillian to set the overflowing parcel on a chair. The movement claimed everyone's attention, and the room grew silent.

"The Ladies Mission Society wants to help you get off to a good start with your housekeeping. It can be a challenge to find decent canned goods in January, so we included those in this gift. Please accept it as our welcome to the town and to the church family." Lillian gestured to the basket. As the mayor's wife, she'd just proven that she did just as well as her husband in the delivery of meaningful speeches.

Karen removed the towel covering the contents and lifted items out of the basket. The table filled with quart jars of a wide variety of preserved vegetables. Jars of canned meat followed. She discovered smaller jars containing a variety of jams and jellies. Next, she pulled out an array of breads and rolls, even a pie. Bars of soap, a collection of candles, embroidered tea towels, and lace-trimmed pillowcases completed the gift.

Logan's heart swelled. Everything Karen had tried to get him to believe that night in Chicago last summer was true. His congregation viewed him as their friend. He might have begun as their only option of leadership, but somewhere along the way, he'd become a companion, another traveler at their side on the journey of faith.

Now Karen was accepted as a friend and companion. Henry's words came back to him. People welcomed Karen because they liked him. They respected him and cared about him. Tonight, the women demonstrated that they cared about his bride as well.

"Thank you. This is so kind and unexpected. I don't know what to say." Karen looked at the group of women who'd gathered around.

Cornelia's eyes crinkled at the corners when she smiled. "Just say you'll take good care of Pastor Logan. We call on him at all hours of the day and night, so we're happy to give back, even in small ways."

The party ended as the women cleared dishes from the tables. Logan slipped into the kitchen and maneuvered around cupboard drawers, a stack of pans, and animated conversations until reaching Lillian at the sink, her hands immersed in soapy water. Clara stood near whipping a towel across every surface with a swift and practiced hand.

Logan squeezed Lillian's shoulder. "Thank you for the dinner tonight and for the gift. Karen and I appreciate it very much."

Lillian smiled at him. "Our pleasure, Pastor Logan. See you at the wedding tomorrow."

That one word—*wedding*—nearly buckled his knees. Tingling broke out in his arms and legs. Dizziness assaulted his head, and his mouth went dry. He managed to produce a smile for all of the women who, by this time, were listening in on the conversation. Stutters would surely chop up his speech if he attempted a reply, so he only nodded and made an escape.

Karen waited for him in the hall. Family surrounded her, discussing final details for the big day.

His friend Pete slapped him on the back. "Ready to go through with it?"

"You know the answer to that." Logan recovered enough calm to return the teasing.

Pete laughed. "Be here by two o'clock."

"Count on it. Use my study if you like. Here's the key." Logan fished in his pocket and turned the key over to Pete.

"Thanks. See you for lunch?"

"Sure. Let's get everyone together in the hotel dining room." He'd welcome a meal with Mama and Tillie before the wedding. It might be his last chance to spend time with them since he and Karen would leave from the reception for their wedding trip.

"I'll spread the word." Pete left to find his wife.

Logan turned his attention on Karen. "You still want to do this?"

"Too late to back out now." Karen's eyes danced.

"I wouldn't want to back out anyway." He grew serious when his gaze landed on Henry, who visited with Arthur a short distance away. Logan lowered his voice. "Your uncle and I talked. He approves. Ask him about it when you return to the hotel."

"Really?" Karen's eyes widened, and she clasped her hands. "What did you say to convince him?"

Logan shrugged. "I didn't say anything much at all."

A knowing smile claimed her lips. She'd grown aware of those times when he hesitated to take credit for positive outcomes. Her smile told him she suspected he had more to do with it than he admitted. She didn't try to refute him. Instead, she stretched up on tiptoe and placed a kiss on his cheek.

"Until tomorrow." She walked away to find her coat so she could leave with her family.

Logan picked up the basket of goods and went across the snowy lawn to his house. Once inside, he lit a lamp and unpacked the basket. The jars he placed on the counter. The pie went in the pie safe. The towels he hung near the stove. He took the pillowcases to his room. He switched out the case on his pillow for the fancier one. Plumping it up a bit, he returned it to its place near the headboard.

The other pillowcase lay limp and empty on the quilt. A jolt of energy shot through him as if he'd been struck by lightning.

His queen-size bed had only ever known one pillow. Karen would share his bed with him starting next week. He needed to track down another pillow. Logan ran out of the room and down the hall. A fling of the blankets away from the spare room's bed revealed an unused pillow, the only one in the house. He snatched it up and took it to his room, where he worked with special care to prepare it for his new wife.

Shoving his hands in his pockets, Logan studied his work. Tomorrow, he was getting married. Bachelorhood had come to an end. Karen's trunks occupied space in his house. The canned goods and other household items waited in the kitchen. His bed had two pillows. The time had come to step into a new era, one of commitment, devotion, and blessings that stretched farther than the broadest horizon.

18

Logan stood at the front of the church dressed in his black suit and borrowed bow tie. The space he occupied to the left of the preacher was reserved exclusively for nervous grooms watching for their brides to emerge from the back of the sanctuary. He'd pitied the poor men in the past that stood at his side, awaiting the fateful moment of matrimony. Today, it was his turn.

Anywhere else in the world, this gray and clouded winter afternoon held no significance except for the hint of moisture in the air promising another snowfall. But for Logan, this was the day his heart had waited for. It was a moment in time, exquisitely orchestrated by the Lord, for him to enter into the sacred vows of marriage.

He worked as a minister in the church, the body that was declared in Revelation as Christ's bride. *The wedding of the Lamb has come*, the apostle John wrote about the end of time. *His bride has made herself ready. Fine linen, bright and clean, was given her to wear*. More of John's message. Logan had dedicated his life to proclaiming that message of redemption. Today, he would begin his own journey of faithful love that lasted until eternity.

The organ music paused. Pete glanced at him with an

expression of empathy mixed with joy. His friend felt happiness for him. He'd focus on the joy and forget about the nervous feelings churning his stomach. The music Karen and her mother had chosen for the entrance of the bridesmaids began. Arthur and Andrew appeared from his study and stood at his side. The presence of these brothers bolstered him, helping him breathe a little easier.

He looked out across a full sanctuary. Mrs. Akerman sat with Clara in their usual pew. Florence sat next to her aunt with Mick Farnsworth on her other side. She must have decided Logan meant what he said when he'd told her he was engaged to be married. She'd left him alone through the holidays. Maybe her withheld attentions meant she'd spent Christmas with Mick instead. Problem solved. He gulped in a deep breath.

Tillie walked the aisle wearing a dark red dress and carrying a cluster of white flowers. She looked lovely. Logan had the presence of mind to offer up a quick prayer of thanks for the growth in his sister's life over the past months. Julia came next. She wore the same style dress and carried the same flowers as Tillie. She flashed him a brilliant smile as she drew near.

If only he could return it and accompany it with a wink. But he dare not do anything ornery moments before the bride appeared. He chose to give her a slight nod instead as she took her place beside Tillie.

The music changed to a bright strain. Karen's mother stood. The congregation stood. The doors opened. Henry stepped forward with his arm linked in the arm of the most heavenly vision Logan had ever seen.

Her dress shone in pure white waves, flowing as she walked. A mass of white roses hid her waist from his view, but he caught a glimpse of the fair, unblemished skin above her lace neckline. Her eyes radiated love behind the misty veil. He couldn't stop looking at her. In spite of a trickle of moisture at the corner of one of his eyes, he did his best to radiate love back.

The organ music faded away. Henry brought Karen to a stop at the front of the church.

Pete cleared his throat. "Who gives this woman to be married to this man?"

"Her mother and I." Henry lifted Karen's veil and pecked a kiss to her cheek.

Logan stepped forward. Karen held onto his arm and went with him to stand before Pete. The service unfolded like a pleasant dream. He said what he'd rehearsed at the proper times and with no stutters. Someone must have prayed for his speech to flow so smoothly in this crucial moment. His heart did the talking, not his intellect.

Pete prayed, and then he preached a sermon. Karen handed her roses to Julia and turned to hold Logan's hands. Pete guided them through the vows and exchange of rings. The wedding band Mama had given him months ago had gone to the Gouds' jewelry store along with Karen's engagement ring earlier that morning to be melded together as one ring. Arthur had picked it up for him, and now it lay in Logan's hand.

At Pete's prompt, he repeated the words affirming this sign of covenant and slipped the ring onto Karen's finger. It sure looked good there, stating to the world that she was his. Karen did the same, repeating her vows and placing a wedding band on his finger.

Pete prayed once more. Everyone sang a hymn, and then Pete looked at Logan with twinkling eyes. "I now pronounce you man and wife. You may kiss your bride."

His heart pounded. He'd looked forward to this moment. Now that it had arrived, joy flooded over him, making him shake. Karen was his wife. He was her husband. The fact pressed him to reach for her, cup her chin, and savor this new reality.

For the first time he could recall in the history of Oswell City Community Church, the sanctuary erupted in applause.

Pete's voice boomed out, forcing Logan to break the kiss. "It is my pleasure to introduce to you for the first time, Pastor and Mrs. Logan De Witt."

Mrs. Logan De Witt. Boy, did he like the sound of that. If the organ hadn't started playing, he'd turn around and ask Pete to say it again. But Karen tugged on his arm as an indicator the time had come to stand in the back of the church and greet their guests. He walked the aisle with her wearing a smile that threatened to stretch beyond his ears.

The members of their families joined them and participated in the receiving line. Mrs. Akerman slapped his cheek with an affectionate pat to congratulate him. Florence reached to give him a hug. He returned it. The poor girl's only chance to receive a hug from him came on his wedding day. He could spare some sympathy and accept her well-wishes. Florence moved on to shake Karen's hand and offer her congratulations.

Paul and Lillian overflowed with happiness as did the other members of the consistory. Their wives hugged Karen and started in telling her all kinds of stories about Logan's years with them. Most of the tales were flattering, but a few of them he'd prefer Karen heard from him and not from someone else. Karen laughed and appeared to enjoy these new relationships, so Logan let the stories flow around him. Any correcting that might need doing, he'd take care of later.

Dr. Kaldenburg offered his congratulations in his typical serious yet light-hearted way. He talked with Karen's mother for a length of time and moved on. Pete and Anna were last.

He engulfed Logan in a sturdy hug. "I'm so happy for you, buddy. You deserve the best, and you got it. I'm proud of you."

Logan thumped his friend's back. "Thanks."

Anna and Pete both smothered Karen in hugs. Their display of care told Logan he really had made a good decision in taking that step into the unknown by proposing. The photographer prepared to take pictures of the bride and groom, so Logan grasped Karen's hand and led her to a corner of the sanctuary.

When the photo session was complete, Logan and his bride

joined the reception. The same women who served the previous evening's meal gathered around serving punch and coffee. Trays of sandwiches and bowls of salads lined a long table.

Tillie and Andrew and Julia and Arthur were already seated at a table designated for the wedding party. Grace Koelman beckoned for him to bring Karen over to the table with the wedding cake.

Alex baked the cake, and his wife had decorated it. Four tiers tall, the cake lavished with white icing and dark red rosebuds stood as a testament to one of the finest works of art the Zahns had ever created. Grace showed him how to hold the knife and where to cut. With Karen's help, he carved out the first slice of wedding cake.

After that, the women were content to let him and his bride sit down so they could take over. Logan ate the slice of cake one of the women served him, snacked on the sandwiches and salads, and then spent his time mingling with the other guests until the moment arrived to open the gifts.

Pete left the reception and was gone for quite a long time. Logan didn't give it a thought until his friend returned just as the wrapping paper fell from the last gift.

"Meet me in your study, please." Pete leaned in and murmured in Logan's ear.

Logan left his seat and followed Pete down the hall.

"What's going on?" Logan stood near his desk and faced his friend. Surely a problem hadn't arisen in town requiring his presence. Most of the town was in attendance at the reception. He couldn't think of anyone, other than the Haverkamps, who might have fallen into trouble.

"I've discovered some bad news." Pete's voice carried a tone of apology.

Something must have happened in town or on a farm in the community. Logan held his breath. Whatever circumstances called him away from his own wedding reception, he could handle.

"I thought it might be wise to get a weather report since predictions had been made for snow to fall in our area today," Pete said.

"It's not snowing here. Not a lot anyway." Logan glanced at the dark windows.

"Right. The light snow here isn't the problem. I went to the train depot to see if they had a report on the weather. It turns out a blizzard developed north of here. The tracks are drifted shut, canceling all train travel until further notice. I'm sorry, Logan."

His brow furrowed. He couldn't imagine why Pete felt the need to apologize to him. His limbs went numb as the answer sank in. He and Karen must ride the train in order to leave on their wedding trip. No train travel meant no honeymoon.

Nausea rolled in his stomach. He turned to the bookshelves, so his back met Pete's gaze in case he really did throw up.

"Maybe you and Karen can make other arrangements. I'm sure you can work this out." The apology in Pete's voice shifted into desperation.

Logan gazed at the dark town through the window behind his desk. This news couldn't be as bad as his mind was determined to make it. Surely he could find a way to still take his new wife on her wedding trip.

"Can I do anything? Call someone?" Pete asked. Logan's silence on the subject appeared to cause his friend a great deal of distress.

But he couldn't speak. All he could do was replay the devastating words. The tracks are drifted shut, canceling train travel.

"You all right?" Pete thumped his back.

"Get Karen, please," he croaked out. Even those few words taxed him. He dropped into his desk chair.

"Sure. Karen. I'll get her." Pete hastened from the room.

Moments later, Karen stood in the doorway. "Logan, what's wrong? I saw you and Pete leave the reception."

This moment was the first they'd been alone all day. He should use the time to tell her how beautiful she looked and how much she'd changed his life. He should let her know that ever since her arrival at his farm that summer day, he'd looked forward to tonight. The words lodged in his throat. He couldn't find the key to loosen them. Karen frowning at him didn't help.

He beckoned for her to come to him. One other time, he'd held her on his lap in a moment when he'd delivered bad news. He found himself in that place once again. Karen settled in, her skirts rustling with her movements. She arranged them to flow in the proper direction and looked at him.

"Pete checked with the train station about the snow." He swallowed. "Turns out there's a blizzard north of here shutting down train travel."

Karen stayed focused on him through the explanation.

Finding strength in her gaze, he mustered up the courage to deliver the blow. "We can't leave on our honeymoon tonight."

"Oh." The syllable came with a deep inhale of air. Instead of crumpling against him and weeping as he expected, she sat quietly as if lost in thought.

"What are you thinking about?" he asked in a soft voice.

"I'm trying to decide what our options are. Is there somewhere out in the country around here where we could go?" She studied him.

"If the snowfall gets heavier and the wind picks up, we'd be stranded."

"We probably shouldn't stay at the hotel." She bit her lip.

"With our families staying there, I'd prefer to go somewhere else."

She considered his words. A smile brightened her face. "What about your house—I mean, our house? What's wrong with just going home?"

His lungs forgot how to work. He stared at her for a long moment. The words pressing on his throat made him cough. "You want to spend our wedding night at the *parsonage*?"

"Why not?" She shrugged. "It's the place where we will begin our marriage and start our family."

He stared again. He couldn't think of a worse location for a couple in need of a little privacy. Why, his house didn't even have a back yard. The church bordered it on one side, the street on the front, and two neighbors on the other sides. No one had better get the terrible idea to head up a chivaree or pull some other ridiculous prank. Maybe he should pray right here and now for that blizzard to move in and blow enough snow around to make everyone stay home.

"Except for the clothes at the hotel, my belongings are already at the parsonage. Saves me the trouble of packing." Karen twisted her new wedding band around on her finger.

Logan caught a glimpse of the shiny band on his own hand. He'd never worn a ring before. He wore it now because of the vows he'd made to her. Karen's idea did have some merit. If they weathered out the snowstorm at his house, he could offer her a full and realistic beginning to their shared life.

"Maybe we can postpone the honeymoon and leave next week after the snow clears. We're only headed to the hotel in Des Moines. No reason why I can't adjust the dates of our stay."

"The theater tickets are for Friday's show."

"We should be able to make that." Logan smiled.

"Let's return to the reception before anyone misses us." Karen shifted her weight off of his lap and stood.

Pete met them in the hall. "What did you decide to do?"

"We're going home." Logan kept his voice low. Just the idea of the possible chivaree gave him a good reason for confidentiality.

"Good idea." Pete smiled wide.

"Go over there for me. Light the lamp. Start a fire. We'll wait." Logan could pass for the leader of a city gang the way he passed on these secretive instructions.

"Got it. Be back soon." Pete took the keys Logan handed him and left the church.

He and Karen joined the group in conversation with their mothers. Attention shifted to him, and the discussion died.

"Is something wrong? I saw you leave with Pete." Mama's brow furrowed.

Logan exhaled. "There's been a change of plans. Karen and I are staying in town tonight. A blizzard up north closed the train tracks."

"I'm sorry to hear that." Mama patted his arm.

"We'll meet you for breakfast at the hotel in the morning." No matter how hard he tried to stay serious, the thought of having Karen at home with him threatened to make him giddy and send him running around the room, shouting and laughing like a toddler. Karen's idea had grown on him until it became the best he'd ever heard.

Pete returned and came to find him. "Ready to go?"

"Yeah." He'd better leave before the giddiness set in and led him to do something foolish.

Pete smiled, went to the door, and announced in a loud voice. "Karen and Logan will be leaving shortly. If you would like to see them off, please follow me outside."

So much for the attempts at confidentiality. Now everyone would watch him take Karen home. Logan shrugged. Nothing he could do about it now. This situation was slipping further and further out of his control.

Karen and her mother exchanged hugs before she made the rounds hugging each family member and thanking them for their part in her special day. Logan followed behind, shaking hands. Guiding Karen out the church doors, he took her down the street, which was lined with people throwing rice and cheering.

He waved, opened the door of his house, and swept Karen into his arms. He carried her across the threshold and set her down in the entryway while shutting the door behind him. A lamp glowed on the table. He picked it up to light the way.

"Would you care to see your new home, Mrs. De Witt?"

"Please."

He led her through the house while he gave her a tour of the bedrooms, the water closet, the kitchen, the dining room with the piano, and the parlor. He set the lamp down on the table. A fire crackled in the fireplace sending warmth into the room.

"How do you like it?" Logan leaned on the mantle.

"I love it." Karen glanced at the window where snow tapped the glass. "So cozy on this winter night. I will be very happy here with you."

"We've shared a home before, but now we will share so much more." Logan tore his attention away from her long enough to poke at a log in the fireplace.

"What will you remember about today?" Karen's voice floated soft and reflective to his ears.

His attention returned to her. "How you look in your dress. The expression in your eyes as you walked the aisle. Placing my ring on your finger. The welcome the town has given you. Their wish to be involved in our wedding is their way of expressing friendship. I understand that now."

"So, you don't mind the fact that we didn't have a small ceremony with only family?" Karen asked.

"Not at all. Your way was the best way." He took her hand and kissed it. "What will you remember about today?"

"This. Standing here with you before our own fireplace after a lovely wedding service. That's what I'll remember." Karen's eyes softened.

In them, Logan read the depths of love she felt for him.

He cupped her chin as he cocked his head in the direction of the room, housing a bed that now had two pillows on it. "Go on in. I'll bank the fire and be there in a minute."

Karen nodded and turned from him, and he watched her walk away.

The word *holiness* thumped in his brain and in his heart. *Be holy as I am holy*, the Lord had instructed the Israelites. God is holy, and he is also love. Where the two meet is sacred space.

Holiness and the expression of love were the ways God wanted Logan to live in relationship with him.

It was also the way God wanted Logan to live in relationship with his wife. The covenant they had made to each other during their wedding service was designed by a holy God and intended to be lived out every day through expressions of love.

Logan stood on sacred ground. He finished his work with the fire, draped his suit coat over a chair, and went to Karen. Snow fell. The wind picked up. The lamp burned out.

Together they explored hidden places awaiting the proper time for revelation.

19

A white world swept and sculpted under a brisk wind met Karen's gaze as she looked out the kitchen window of her new home. Snow swirled around the house, dusting tree trunks and collecting in the corners of the windowpanes. No one would be leaving town for several hours. She must prepare for another day's delay in their honeymoon plans.

Karen sauntered around the kitchen in a study of the items she'd received as a gift at the rehearsal dinner. The towels hung near the stove. The jars lined the counter. She opened a cupboard and found the soap and candles. Logan had done a good job preparing the kitchen for her. His years as a bachelor had taught him well how to maintain order in this area of the house.

Her thoughts shifted to her new husband and ushered in recollections of the past days. So much had happened in a short span of time. She'd walked out the door of Uncle Henry's home for the last time, traveled to Oswell City, and joined her life to Logan's. As soon as she'd stepped off the train, ministry waited for her. She'd seen a large number of onlookers at the station, their response a mixture of curiosity about her and pride in Logan's decision to marry.

The opportunity to touch lives expanded once they arrived at the hotel. The situation at the Haverkamp farm immersed her in the unpredictability of Logan's existence. Adventure and challenge illumined the blessings and rewards of his calling.

Karen loved it. She'd been as homesick for the adventure that followed Logan around as she'd been for the man himself. Articulation of her longing hadn't come until this very moment as she watched the snow dance and swirl before the wind in its own unpredictable and adventurous manner.

The faint scent of *Song of the Spring* reached her nose. Too intense for a church service, the scent was just right for the hours she spent at home with Logan. She'd spritzed a little of the perfume on her neck only moments before Logan entered their room last night. The scent still clung to her skin this morning, adding its own touches to treasured memories.

Thoughts of Mrs. Zahn and the other women brought with them a swell of emotion as Karen turned from the window and uncovered a loaf of bread from the bakery. These women were so kind in offering Karen their gift. Each jar and baked item represented hours of work. She picked each jar up to study its contents. How thoughtful of them to share the bounty of their pantries with her. Karen wouldn't have thought to plan ahead with such insight.

The face of Clara Hesslinga's niece imposed on her thoughts as she found a knife and sliced the bread. The way she hugged Logan in the receiving line yesterday raised Karen's blood pressure. If Florence's actions were an accurate indicator of the level of affection people held for Logan, then he was more popular and better loved than he ever dreamed.

Karen's introduction into Oswell City society required a significant shift in how this community viewed their pastor. The older women doted on him like a favorite son. The younger women, if they were anything like Florence, probably held onto secret hopes of courtship.

He was a married man now, and married to her. She was off

to a good start with the Ladies Mission Society. If the rest of the town followed their lead in the acceptance of this new commitment in Logan's life, then these possible triggers for conflict may not flare as large or as heated as she suspected.

The bread sliced, Karen turned to the stove. A few embers still sparked in the fireplace, but the stove sat cold and black. She pulled her robe tighter around her middle. Her new home sure could drop in temperature overnight. At Uncle Henry's, household staff cared for the stove and overall warmth of the rooms, but here in her house, these responsibilities fell to her.

She might as well get busy and figure out how to operate this cast iron range. It was now her companion in caring for a family. Their relationship would go much smoother if Karen learned now how to make it cooperate. She gathered chunks of wood out of a bin near the wall, discovered the location of the matches, and worked to start a fire.

Logan's stove possessed different quirks from the stove in the Silver Grove School. Since this one was much larger and designed for cooking, Karen would have a bit of an education to acquire before attaining full competency. But she'd manage. Starting a marriage in the winter months would provide her with lots of opportunity for practice.

Oswell City might be small, but at least it had running water. She took a pan to the sink and filled it with water. She'd been delighted last night to discover this house had a water closet. Her adjustments to married life would go much easier with the aid of this comfort so closely resembling the luxuries she'd left behind in Chicago.

"Good morning, sweetheart." The words were whispered into her hair as two strong arms encircled her from behind.

Karen turned from the pan of water she heated on the stovetop and shifted her attention to her new husband. He wore no shirt. How he dared to venture out here into the cold, wearing only his trousers baffled her.

"Do you remember we're going to the hotel for breakfast?" he asked.

"Yes, but I thought you might like some coffee first."

"We've got time. Thank you." Logan moved to retrieve two cups from the cupboard.

They settled at the small table in the corner and drank until the clock told them they should leave.

Wind whipped snow into their faces on the walk to the hotel. No one stirred outdoors. Drifts piled in the yards and across the streets. Lamplight glowed in the hotel dining room. The scent of frying pancakes and cooked sausage hung in the air. Smiles and greetings from family members already seated at the tables added to the warm atmosphere.

"Looks like the weather is going to keep us in town another day," Pete said with a glance at the window.

THE WEATHER DETAINED their guests for two days. George Brinks gave everyone from Silver Grove and Chicago an extension on their room reservations. The group spent Saturday at Karen's new home. She found another reason to feel gratitude for the gift she'd received at the rehearsal dinner. Without it, she would've had no way to provide meals for such a large number.

Paul Ellenbroek came mid-afternoon with the news that the minister they'd arranged to preach in Logan's absence couldn't make the trip to Oswell City because of the drifted roads. After a brief conference, Paul and Logan decided to cancel the Sunday morning service so people could stay out of the blowing snow and cold temperatures.

The news of a canceled church service didn't slow down the Ladies Mission Society. Those who lived closest and could travel opened the church for the noon meal and fed the entire group of stranded guests the most succulent Sunday dinner Karen could remember.

Logan used George's telephone later that afternoon to call the hotel in Des Moines and rearrange their honeymoon plans. The hotel had accommodations available starting Tuesday night, so he changed their train tickets and made arrangements with Paul for Karen and him to be gone until the following Monday.

More snow fell Sunday evening, but the wind didn't blow, which gave the railroad crews a chance to clear the tracks. Finally, Monday afternoon, a train headed in the direction of Silver Grove arrived at the station. Karen stood with Logan on the snowy platform and exchanged hugs as he said goodbye to his family.

"Goodbye, Mama. I'm so glad you were here for the wedding." Logan released his mother from his embrace.

"I wouldn't have missed it for anything. I'm relieved the snow waited to fall until after we arrived in town." Logan's mother smiled up at him and then turned to Karen.

"Congratulations, dear. I'm so happy for both of you. That summer day, when we received the unexpected news that you were going to live with us during the school year, I never thought you'd remain permanently in our family. But I'm so glad you will." Karen's new mother-in-law gave her a hug.

"I'm glad too. I love you all so much. Thank you for making the trip." Karen's cheek brushed the fur collar of her mother-in-law's coat.

When the hug ended, Logan's sister Tillie took her turn, giving Karen a hug. Pete slapped Logan on the back.

"All the best, Karen." Anna gave her a hug, then backed away and smiled. "Pete and I are so happy for the two of you."

Karen nodded, and tears filled her eyes as Logan's family and friends boarded the train. A piece of her heart was headed back to Silver Grove. She didn't want to think about how much time might pass before she would see any of them again.

THE RELATIVES from Chicago waited longer for their train. Snow still fell at the eastern end of the route. The station master was confident clearing would get completed before the train reached that area, so Uncle Henry and Arthur bought tickets. Their trip would stretch far into the night before they arrived at their homes in the city.

"Goodbye, Mother." Karen gave her a hug.

"I love you, my dear. Life in Chicago will feel so different without you." Mother's breath teased Karen's hair and warmed her ear.

"I know."

Her mother would adjust. The moment had come to say goodbye. Karen loved her family, but they occupied a different place in her life now. She'd stay here with Logan as his wife and living a new life.

"I'm so happy for you, Karen." Julia flung her arms around Karen and smothered her with a hug. "What a lovely wedding! All of the townspeople chipped in to make it special. Everyone loves you. But I'll miss you so much."

Karen would miss her sister too. But the loneliness for Julia couldn't outweigh her love for Logan or her excitement to share a life with him.

"Congratulations, Karen. Beautiful wedding." Aunt Fran gave her a stiff hug. "I'm so glad we came."

Uncle Henry kissed her forehead. "We'll miss you."

Karen nodded as he shook Logan's hand.

"Take good care of her. She's pretty special." Uncle Henry gave a serious nod.

"You can count on it, sir. Thank you for coming to the wedding." Logan mirrored Uncle Henry's serious demeanor.

Karen and Logan walked with the family to the coach.

"Bye, bye, Auntie Karen," Ben yelled out and threw a little kiss her way.

Laughter bubbled in her throat while tears misted in her eyes once more. Ben and Sam would grow and change so much before she saw them again.

Grinding iron wheels on the metal tracks announced the train's departure. Karen waved at the window as her mother's seat inched past. This goodbye put closure on more than just the extended weekend they'd spent together. It closed the door on the past and asked her family to welcome a different future, one that Karen made for herself instead of the broken standards handed to her by her father.

He was gone. The past was over. Karen was married now and living in a new town where she might forge her own path of influence and security.

The train's whistle blew as it picked up speed. Mother, Aunt Fran, Uncle Henry, and Julia and her family were off to Chicago, going home. So was she. With Logan's arm around her, she turned away and completed the walk into a fresh and new beginning.

THE NEXT MORNING, Logan and Karen left on their trip. A clear and sparkling day, the sun glinted off the drifts covering the fields along the tracks.

In Des Moines, they arrived at the Rock Island Depot and traveled the few blocks to the Hotel Kirkwood, where Logan had their room reserved.

"Such an elegant place," Karen said as she walked with him through the lobby.

Their room on the third floor continued the theme of luxury. It could find a place among the fanciest accommodations in Chicago. She went to the window, drew back the lacy curtain, and watched the cars and buggies in the street below.

"I wanted nothing but the best for you, Karen." Logan came to her side. "I'm so glad we could still take this trip."

She smiled her pleasure at him and then went to change her

dress so that they would have plenty of time for their mid-day meal before attending a performance at the theater.

The week ended too soon. Karen could've gone on and on at this relaxed pace with Logan all to herself. The moment he arrived back in Oswell City, all sorts of demands would clamor for his attention. Karen soaked up the leisurely hours of quiet their wedding trip gave them.

JUST AS SHE'D EXPECTED, Logan's first day home from his honeymoon was scheduled full. He reported to her over their evening meal of the day's activities. He'd called on the Haverkamps and found them recovered. The man with hypothermia was sitting up in his bed and alert, and the other man still wore a cast. Everyone in the household held their breath to see if the arm might function again or go lame.

The pipes had frozen at Clara Hesslinga's home while Logan had been gone. The household of women had called on Paul Ellenbroek at the City Hall to help them make repairs. Neighbors brought them water. Alex Zahn and Artie Goud had kept an eye on them in Logan's absence.

He'd even managed to squeeze study time in between his visits. He planned to preach on Sunday, which meant he needed to stay on schedule in the development of his sermon.

After the meal, Karen sat on the sofa in the parlor, reading out loud to Logan from a book he'd brought home from his study. The theology of Jonathan Edwards leapt off the page as Karen progressed through the chapter. Logan lay with his head in her lap, relaxed yet attentive to her voice. In an instant, he shot to an upright position, his nose barely missing the spine of the book.

"I've got it!" His eyes lit up.

Karen frowned at him.

"The use of the house and land on the Akerman farm. I

know what the church should do with it." He stood, settled his hands on his waist, and looked at her.

Karen shook her head. Her mind remained buried in the sermons of Jonathan Edwards and had not yet entered into Logan's realm.

"Here's what we do." Logan paced before the crackling fire. "We open the house up as a place where relatives of Oswell City residents immigrating to this area can stay until they find a home of their own, just like we did with the Haverkamps and the Van Drunens. It worked so well when we used the house as a hotel this fall. I can't believe it's taken me so long to see."

He sat down next to her. "The best part is you can use your teaching skills. People need to learn English when they come here. So do their children."

"Transitional housing." Karen's mind finally caught up with him.

"Exactly. We offer a service for people who are moving here from another country."

"Sounds like outreach to me. If a little of the gospel message happens to get mixed in with the English education, people can find more here in Oswell City than just the chance to make a living." Karen closed the book. The look in Logan's eyes told her he'd lost all interest in reading.

"You read my mind." Logan tossed Jonathan Edwards onto the table and gathered her into his arms.

Karen's brain spun with the possibilities Logan's idea generated. She could teach again. God was so gracious in his mapping of her life. The adventure of this newlywed existence ignited a spark deep within her. She couldn't wait to see what she and Logan might create together.

20

Karen hung up the dish towel and finished tidying up the kitchen. Everything in order after the evening meal, she took the lamp with her to the dining room. Sheet music stretched across the music stand of the piano where she'd left it the evening before. Ever since her return from the wedding trip, Karen had fallen into the pattern of sitting at the piano and playing her favorites in the span of time following the evening meal.

Her husband remained a captive audience, declaring her music better enjoyment than the insights found in his books. But Karen had no one to entertain this evening. Logan was at the church meeting with the members of the consistory. He'd had to wait two weeks to share his idea with them.

Now that the date of the monthly meeting had arrived, she sat alone, watching the clock and waiting for his return home. Turning a page, Karen chose a section to review in a Bach prelude and began to play. She completed that song and moved to the next one before the clicks of a turned doorknob reached her ears.

Logan entered the house, came to her, and kissed her cheek.

"What did they say?" She turned away from the keyboard to face him.

"They approved." Logan removed his coat and scarf. "Everyone thought my idea for the use of the Akerman farm a sustainable solution. The only problem we had to work through was funding. Cooking and maintenance require employees who earn a salary. We don't have the funds in the church's budget for these sorts of expenses, so the consistory came up with an idea."

"What is it?" Karen went with him to the sofa.

"An auction. Planned for the first week in March. Paul will check with Martin over at Oswell City Auto and see if we can use his showroom. It's the only place in town we could think of that is large enough to house the equipment and household wares we hope to place in the sale. All proceeds will go to the church for use in establishing our transitional housing."

"That's genius." Karen's eyes widened.

"Sure is." Logan chuckled. "Leave it to Paul, James, and the rest of the businessmen in town to hatch such a creative plan." He took his shoes off and reclined. "The auction will need a large amount of organization to make it a success. Contacting potential sellers, communication, and publicity are a big part of it. I volunteered you to take charge of this organizational piece. You'll have the assistance of the Ladies Mission Society. They'll answer to you."

Logan kept talking, but Karen's brain got stuck on the words, 'I volunteered you.' Every muscle in her body went rigid.

She straightened away from the comfortable position she'd found at his side and looked at him. "You what?"

His monologue broke off, and he flinched when he met her gaze. "I volunteered you to head it up."

"Logan, how could you?" Karen squeezed her eyes shut. Tears threatened to fall, but she refused to give them release.

"What do you mean? You're good at those jobs. It's only natural that you'd take them on." Defensiveness edged his voice.

"But you didn't even ask." Karen's eyes flew open, and she glared at him.

So what if a tear or two glistened on her lashes. Logan must understand that just because he now had a wife, it didn't mean he could throw her name around in meetings as a person eager to take on tasks no one else wanted to do.

"Why would I need to?" He shrugged.

Karen frowned at him, stood, and stomped to the kitchen.

"This is really important." He followed her. "Karen, come on. That work needs to be done. The idea will fail without it."

"Then, get one of the people at that meeting to do it." Karen turned to him, her blood coursing through her veins and setting them on fire. "And leave me alone."

Moonlight reflected in Logan's eyes as they faced each other in the darkened room. Her words must have sliced him in a tender place because he blinked and stepped back.

She shoved past him, went to the bedroom, and shut the door. Changing into her nightgown, Karen still dealt with the heat of her racing pulse. She took her hair down, brushed it, and braided it. Her preparations for sleep were completed to the background sounds of Logan's footsteps from the kitchen to the dining room, the shuffling of papers on the table, and the running of water. She lay in the darkness on her side of the bed, stiff and tense.

Logan entered, changed out of his clothes, and claimed his side of the bed. He lay still for several moments until he reached for her and wrapped his arm around her.

"Karen, I'm sorry. I want you to share with me in ministry to this town, but I went about it all wrong. Please forgive me and tell me how I need to change."

Those tears threatened again. This was the Logan she loved, the man who saw her calling and was humble enough to give her a place. Her insides no longer flamed. Instead, they melted.

She turned to him. "Oh, Logan. I'm sorry too. I want to be involved and to help and to give support. But it scares me to think that you could come home any day at any time with projects for me to do that I didn't expect."

"If I hear you correctly, you need me to discuss with you ways for you to help and support instead of taking you by surprise with my own ideas of how that should be done." His breath fluttered her hair as he spoke.

"Yes, that's it." Not only was he apologetic, but a good listener too. She felt him nod.

"I can do that." He sat up and reached for the lamp that resided on his side of the bed. He lit it and turned to her. "Let's start over. Deal?"

"Deal."

A tiny smile tugged at the corner of his mouth, but his eyes remained serious as he cleared his throat. "Mrs. De Witt, it has come to my attention that the pastor and consistory of Oswell City Community Church are in need of a talented and capable young woman to assist them in the organization of their upcoming fundraiser.

"Pastor Logan can think of no better candidate than you. He would be honored to have your help and your support. But if you do not feel this role is a good fit for you, he will confess to getting ahead of himself and search for someone else."

Karen swallowed to repress the ache building in her throat. Logan had respected her feelings.

"I appreciate your offer, and I'm honored. Would you please pray with me first? I will give you my final answer in the morning."

Logan said nothing. He only winked at her and reached for the book they read from each night for their devotions.

The next morning, Karen dished scrambled eggs from the skillet on the stove into a bowl. Logan sat at the table dressed in a shirt and tie and sipping coffee from his cup. She set the bowl on the table and took her seat. He reached for her hand and prayed. With the growing suspicion of being watched, she spooned food onto her plate. She ventured a look at her husband.

"So?" He gazed at her.

Her brows lifted in a mimic of his question.

"What did you decide?" Logan reached for his cup.

"You may count me in."

Logan grinned.

"Please don't do that to me again." Karen infused as much school-teacherish authority as she possessed into the request.

"Lesson learned." Logan held his free hand up as though taking an oath.

"Good. When do I start?"

"Paul is coming to church for a meeting with me at ten o'clock. I'll know more when I come home for lunch." Logan picked up his knife to butter his toast.

Karen smiled. Now that she and Logan had arrived at an understanding, their marriage was surely off to a great start.

OVER THE NEXT WEEKS, Karen's days were filled with meetings and the resulting projects. The Ladies Mission Society took an active part in growing the list of contributors to the sale. Farm implements, quilts, furniture, and baked goods comprised the variety of items available for sale on the day of the auction.

Grace Koelman and her daughter planned to provide snacks and drinks during the auction. Other women in the group promised to assist in collecting money and keeping track of any paperwork. The tasks delegated out, Karen looked forward to an evening of light burdens that might allow her time to spend with Logan and chatting with neighbors instead of scurrying around worried about last-minute details.

The responsibility of accepting Jake Harmsen's request for an interview fell to her. With no avenue of escape from his camera or questions, Karen met with Jake and provided the information he wanted. The entire interview appeared on the front page and a majority of the second page, and a large photo accompanied the article. A thoroughness to rival the interest he'd stirred with his story and photo of Karen in Logan's arms at the train station the day she arrived in town infused the tone of Jake's writing.

She showed Logan the week's edition of the *Oswell City Journal* over the evening meal the day it came out.

He took his time looking at the photo of Karen in front of Oswell City Auto and reading through the lengthy article. "I'm proud of you, sweetheart. You've been working hard on this event." He glanced at the photo again and shook his head. "I guess Jake got what he wanted, pictures and news about you on the front page." Pride glowed in his eyes. "My wife is a sensation, but no one needed Jake's help to figure that out."

ON THE AFTERNOON of the auction, Martin Barnaveldt's showroom was packed full of potential buyers. The auctioneer stood on a platform in the corner, keeping up a stream of repeated syllables Karen had difficulty understanding. Other people must have caught the meaning, though, because Grace Koelman and Cornelia Goud stayed busy collecting money and making change.

At the end of the day, the women handed the cash box over to Karen. She took it home and stacked the contents on the dining room table. With Logan's help, she counted the bills and change.

When the last dollar amount had been recorded, she straightened and looked at Logan. "Four hundred and sixty-one dollars. Is that enough?"

He ran his hand through his hair. "For getting started, it is. But, we'll need more income to sustain the ministry long term."

Logan called a special meeting of the consistory to discuss this outcome. Karen came with him and stood before the group to give her report. She shared about the work that had been done in preparation for the event and then disclosed the total profit the fundraiser had generated. The group fell silent. She waited.

"Four hundred sixty-one dollars isn't enough." James Koelman broke the silence. "What do we do for the ongoing salary of a cook and a repairman?"

George picked up on James's train of thought. "He's right. A place like we're plannin' to run needs management. We might draw from this four hundred dollars for supplies, but what about salaries? Where will those come from?"

"George has a point," Alex said. "If you want to keep good help, you must pay them well."

Karen looked at Logan.

"My year of farming in Silver Grove taught me a farm must generate enough of its own funds to keep itself going." He licked his lips while his pencil scratched the paper before him. "If it doesn't, a man must sell out. That's what happened to me.

"This land was given to us. It doesn't cost us a thing. What would you think if we turned it into a working farm? We make the house available for people to stay in, but we use the barn and the orchards to turn a profit." Logan spoke while he wrote a list of numbers. Now he paused and looked up.

"The kitchen staff could make baked goods, cheese, or soaps," Alex suggested.

"The orchards always produce an abundant amount of apples. We could sell them. That money would go a long way," Paul said.

"What's our next step?" Logan asked.

"We ought to start takin' applications to staff the place," George said. "I can help ya out with that since I have a good idea of who has the kind of experience we're lookin' for."

"Sounds good. When we meet again, let's have a list of names to choose from. If we have people hired, we can move forward in opening the house up to new citizens." Logan glanced around the table.

The men nodded, so Logan ended the meeting with prayer.

Karen's heart felt ready to burst. She'd done a good job contributing to the auction's success. Important steps had been taken to build on that success and help Logan and the church execute their plans. She found his hand and held it as he prayed. Tonight was just the beginning of a long and important service to the citizens of Oswell City.

21

Logan really shouldn't allow Karen to attend any more meetings. The presence of his beautiful wife sent his mind to places it shouldn't go while trying to lead a group in making decisions. Amazing, he hadn't stuttered his way through the proposal of his ideas. He'd gotten lucky this once, shaving by with cohesive speech.

If Karen ever showed up at another meeting, his record was doomed to get broken, he was sure of it. Logan shook his head. Somehow he must get his brain off of Karen and onto his studies, but this task grew more difficult with each passing week.

"Good morning, Logan." Paul Ellenbroek entered the study right on time for their trip to the Akerman farm. After last night's meeting, they'd arranged to travel to the farm together. This morning's visit would allow them time to assess the buildings and decide how to best use the auction's funds. "Your wife did a nice job with the preparation for the auction. She's already an asset to the community." Paul smiled.

His approval made Logan feel like his buttons would burst. Karen was getting along famously with Oswell City, just like he knew she would.

"Before we leave, I want to ask what you think about an idea

I have for upcoming sermons." Logan came around his desk and put on his coat.

"What is it?"

"Well ... um ... I'd like to abandon the lectionary's suggested texts for the Lenten season and go off on my own preaching the delights of being married." Logan released the breath he'd held. He didn't necessarily need Paul's advice on what to preach, but the mayor was a good enough friend that Logan looked for chances to solicit his insights on important topics.

Paul stared at the floor for a moment as though deep in thought. "I don't see why you shouldn't. There are probably many people interested in the subject of learning and growing as a result of choosing commitment and faithfulness." His attention shifted to Logan. "Go ahead. I think you should."

"The summer Sundays of ordinary time will actually offer the perfect opportunity." Logan pulled his church calendar out of the desk drawer and studied it. "Better than Lent would. I'll wait, and then after Easter, I think I'll take the plunge. Maybe by the time summer rolls around, I will have been married long enough in the eyes of the congregation for them to take me seriously on the subject."

"Of course they will. Your messages are always good. People look forward to hearing what you have to say." Paul twisted his scarf around his neck. "Ready to go?"

Logan nodded and followed him out the door.

"I've contacted Mick Farnsworth," Paul said as they followed the road out of town. "He's watching for a report from today's assessment. He plans to travel here sometime and help us make the best possible investment in repairs."

"That's good news. We could use Mick's insights on where to start." Logan glanced around at the paint peeling away from the porch's pillars.

"More families are arriving in town with the warmer spring weather. Have you heard that Martin Barnaveldt's brother and his wife and children have come to Oswell City?"

"I haven't."

"They came in just yesterday on the same train with Conrad Van Drunen's two brothers and their families."

"Where is everyone staying?" Logan's brow furrowed.

"With George at the hotel. Conrad doesn't have room for them. He and Angelien have barely settled themselves."

"The sooner we get this place ready, the easier life will be for everyone." Logan pulled on a chip of white paint. A long strip left the pillar and fell to the porch floor.

"George will agree with that. His brother, Lester, is moving here from Meadow Creek."

"Oh, really? I know Lester from when I lived in Silver Grove."

"Lester is retiring from farming and wants to live near family. It wouldn't surprise me if George wrestles him into a job at the hotel." Paul smiled.

"There is certainly enough work at the hotel to go around." Logan laughed.

At that moment, Fred Akerman walked up the lane leading a dairy cow. He waved. "Don't mind me, Pastor Logan. I'll just put this cow in the barn."

Logan waved back and watched him disappear into the barn. After a few moments, Fred emerged and joined Logan and Paul on the porch.

"I'm donating a cow as my way of saying thanks for taking this place off my hands. I read the article in the paper about the auction and the outreach you hope to set up here. Use the milk for your guests or for any other endeavor that might help. I'll care for the cow until you've hired someone else to do it." Fred gestured toward the barn.

"Thanks, Fred. We appreciate it," Logan said.

Fred shook hands with him and with Paul.

Paul watched him walk the lane. "We must make sure our new kitchen staff knows how to make cheese."

Logan shared his smile and followed him inside to get started.

MICK CAME to town the following week and took a seat in Logan's study. "Here are my findings."

Logan studied the documents Mick spread out on the desk.

"If you spend one hundred and fifty dollars on the house and that same amount on the barn, you will have two hundred and fifty remaining. That can sustain you until fall when you harvest the apples. Over the winter and going into next year, have the employees work at the creation and sale of household items. By this time next year, your working farm should be well established." Mick gave his suggestions while Logan considered the numbers on the page.

"Thank you." He glanced at Mick. "I appreciate your guidance. The church board and I will talk this over."

Mick nodded.

"How's Florence?" Logan asked in a serious, pastorly voice. That's all she'd been to him since her arrival in Oswell City, a member of the congregation under his care.

"Fine." Mick's face turned red, but he managed a smile. "I'm following your advice, and I'm taking her to dinner while I'm in town."

"Don't forget to buy her a gift." Logan pointed in the direction of Main Street.

Mick patted his pocket as an indication he already had that important piece of business covered.

Logan gave him an approving smile.

Later that afternoon, Angelien led a shy-looking Conrad into Logan's study. "Good afternoon, Dominee. We're sorry to bother if this isn't a good time."

"Not at all. What can I do for you?" Logan asked.

"Conrad. He is *de timmerman*, I mean, he is carpenter. He

build furniture, lay flooring. He even paint and put shingle on roof. We read Mrs. De Witt's article in newspaper. Conrad ask if he can have job."

Her brogue-weighted English made Logan feel weightless. If he had wings, he just might lift off and start to fly.

"We could certainly use a skilled carpenter on the Akerman farm. Much work needs to be done there. I'd love to give you a job this minute. But the church board and I agreed to follow a process of gathering names first before deciding who to hire. May I put your name on the list?"

Angelien repeated everything Logan said to Conrad.

"Ya." Conrad's eyes shone.

"I'll make a note of it right now." Logan reached for his pen. "What about you, Angelien? Do you have any skills we might utilize?"

She blushed. "*Ik heb het kinderen*." She shook her head. "I mean, I have the children."

"You'd be welcome to bring them along. Karen will be teaching English as soon as the repairs are made. Your son could take the class if you want him to."

"I don't know. I never thought of this." Angelien appeared flustered at the possibility.

If Angelien and Conrad both drew a salary working at the Akerman farm, they'd receive many benefits, helping them get established in Oswell City even quicker. The opportunity was worthwhile to Logan.

"Do you know how to make cheese?" He ventured to question her even though he ran the risk of flustering her even more.

"Ya." Angelien nodded.

"What about soap?"

Another nod.

"Pastries and bread?"

"Since I was ten. *Mijn moeder* taught me. I mean, my mother. She taught me. I make brooms too."

Logan scratched notes onto the paper with no show of excitement, but on his insides, a party burst onto the scene. Angelien knew how to do every art necessary for the farm to turn a profit. He held his composure the best he could while shaking hands with her so he wouldn't gush all over and frighten her away.

LOGAN SHARED his information with Paul, and at the next meeting, the list of potential employees was narrowed. George made the contacts, and by the end of the following week, the staff was in place at the Akerman farm, including Conrad and Angelien Van Drunen.

Repairs were a work in progress, but enough were completed on the upstairs rooms to offer George relief at the hotel. The Van Drunen brothers and the Barnaveldt family moved into the Akerman home one mild afternoon in early April.

Accommodations were made in the parlor to transform the shabby, shadowy space into a sunny classroom. On a lovely spring day, Karen held her first English class for the Dutch-speaking children of these families. Showers of white apple blossoms in the orchard were visible through the windows. Their sweet scent carried on the wind as Logan spent an afternoon helping Conrad re-shingle the roof.

They paused in their work to allow Conrad some time to sit in on the English class. Logan took advantage of the break to drink coffee in the kitchen.

When the class dismissed, Logan sought out the pretty blonde teacher. "I have an idea for another way in which I need your help and support."

"What might that be?" Karen halted from stacking books.

"Do you remember Sunday afternoons in Silver Grove helping me lead the singing for the Meadow Creek services?"

"Yes." A look crossed Karen's face as though she could read his thoughts.

"How would you like to do that again—helping me with singing here on Sunday mornings?"

"You know I'd love it." Karen rewarded him with a smile.

"You're hired, Mrs. De Witt." He winked at her and met with success in his attempt to steal a kiss.

Karen turned back to gathering books, and Conrad needed his help with the roofing job, but Logan's inbred dairy farmer clock told him the time had come to go to the barn. Fred just might welcome a little help from a preacher who had a knack for coaxing milk from a cow.

"MY SOUL in silence waits for God, my savior he has proved; he only is my rock and tower; I never shall be moved." Prepared to preach his sermon, Logan sang along as Karen led the congregation in singing Psalm 62. This was the moment Jake should capture with his camera and notepad, Karen sharing ministry with him as his helper and his partner.

Today marked a moment of arrival. His bachelor days were ended, displaced by the beautiful and talented Karen taking up space in his heart. Her love for him struck him as the biggest surprise of his life. Her call to serve at his side filled him with joy beyond words. How close he'd come to missing out on so many rich blessings. Thank goodness he'd had the sense to catch on to God's leading in the direction of marriage, or Karen might have slipped away.

Sown like the seed of the farmer among all conditions of ground, Karen's willingness to share his life had at first encountered a rocky reception. Only because of the gradual change in his thinking did his heart become fertile soil. He'd taken the risk to allow love to sprout and grow there.

Now he had a flourishing crop, bountiful enough to sustain

him for the rest of his days. *Orchard of Love*. The words on the arch over the lane to the Akerman house entered his thoughts. Logan smothered a smile. He had an orchard of love blossoming inside him.

"My honor is secure with God, my savior he is known; my refuge and my rock of strength are found in God alone." Instead of joining Karen in the next verse of the psalm, Logan paused in his singing.

He'd been married for three months. Those months had been bliss. But that beginning was behind him. Karen was his for the rest of his life to love and to cherish. More than anything, he wanted to care for her well. Then she would know without a doubt she could count on him for unfailing stability and security.

"On him, ye people evermore rely with confidence. Before him pour ye out your heart, for God is our defense." Logan picked up the phrase and sang along.

He wanted to do everything for Karen that the psalm said God did for his people. Karen should have good reasons to place her confidence in him as her husband. He'd strive to provide refuge as a rock and solid defense all of their days together.

A glimpse of Karen brought the vows they'd spoken at their wedding ceremony rushing back into his memory. He promised to love her, comfort her, honor and protect her, to rejoice with her in times of gladness, to grieve with her in times of sorrow, and to be faithful to her for as long as they lived.

Karen glanced at him. The expression in her eyes promised him the same. He looked forward to a rich, full life in union with her, preserving a love strong enough to welcome whatever came.

"For God has spoken over and over and unto me has shown, that saving power and lasting strength belong to him alone. Yea, lovingkindness evermore belongs to Thee, O Lord; and thou according to his work dost every man reward." With the Lord's help, Logan could offer his wife everything he wanted her to receive from him.

The song ended, and he drew in a deep breath as he stepped

forward to offer a prayer. The words came easy. With so much love flooding his heart, a declaration of devotion found unhindered passage from his lips. He clasped Karen's hand for a moment before opening his Bible. The new era had arrived. Standing here before a group of people he cared about and talking of the Lord's grace was the perfect way to begin.

22

Summer came to Oswell City, immersing Karen into a new season of beauty, but also of challenge. This morning, breakfast dishes lay stacked on the table. Karen should wash them, but the week's supply of laundry demanded her attention. She must take care of it early, so the rest of the day would be available to prepare food for the group gathering at her house tomorrow.

For the first time in its history, the annual luncheon of the Ladies Mission Society would be held at the home of Pastor Logan De Witt. His new wife, who had recently joined the group, had made the gracious offer to host.

Karen had bought the eggs on Saturday for the angel food cake dessert. She retrieved them from the wire basket on the counter and broke them into her mixing bowl.

As she worked, the light in the kitchen dimmed. She glanced at the window. Not only had the clouds moved in, but raindrops, large fat ones, fell from the sky. Her focus shifted to the clothesline. She must rescue the laundry before any more rain fell on it, or she'd never get it dry and ironed by the time the women arrived tomorrow.

Karen flung her apron over a chair and raced outside with

the basket. The clothesline was situated near enough to the garden that Karen could assess the health of her mid-July vegetables whenever she tended to her laundry. Logan had worked the ground and helped her plant the seeds. Now the plot of green vines and shrubs thrived. Blooms covered the tomato plants. Pumpkin vines stretched beyond the boundaries of the garden and into the grass of the lawn.

A crawling sensation spread up Karen's leg. She glanced down to discover ugly brown bugs scurrying across her shoes. Somehow they found a passage under her skirts and were traveling her leg. She yelped and shook her skirts. Bugs fell onto the wide leaves of the pumpkin vine, where many more bugs of all sizes scurried for cover.

Karen stared in horror at the infestation invading her pumpkins. She didn't have time to deal with the pests right now, but Logan loved pumpkin pie. She'd learned from his mother how to make it, and she did so want to provide him with his favorite dessert this fall when the pumpkins turned a ripe orange. Those insects must get dealt with, but never would she touch a squash bug.

A trick Logan's mother had taught her for the control of pests in the garden came to mind. Karen picked up her basket of wet laundry and raced into the house. The laundry needed hung up to dry, and the cake needed baked, but the black-legged army invading her pumpkin patch demanded the highest priority. Karen filled a bucket with hot water, swished soap into it, and returned to the garden.

Long, healthy green beans dragged at Karen's skirts as she worked on the pumpkins. They should be canned tomorrow, but with the luncheon planned, the task must wait until the following day. Maybe she could at least pick the largest beans and store them in the icebox until she had time to work with the canner.

In her observations of the meals Logan's mother served, green beans were a staple vegetable through the winter months.

Karen would do well to gather every bit of harvest from the healthy plants.

The rain continued to fall. Moisture seeped through the layers of Karen's dress and petticoats. Water dripped from her hair. A large section of hair left the pins on the side of her head and flopped in her eyes.

Fewer bugs crawled on the pumpkin leaves, but she wanted to eliminate all of them. Karen worked until the mud caking her shoes interfered with her ability to keep her balance. Grasping the fence where snap peas climbed, Karen surrendered her battle for today and went to the house.

A glance at the clock told her Logan would soon arrive home for the noon meal. Karen slipped out of her muddy shoes and went to the counter. She must get that angel food cake in the oven so that it could bake, or she'd never stay on schedule getting food prepared. She poured the batter into the pan, shoved it into the oven along with some more kindling into the firebox, and went to change her clothes.

The cake baked while she and Logan ate their lunch. After he left, she pulled the pan from the oven. It should be done by now, but the batter hadn't risen anywhere near the top of the pan. Tears sprang to Karen's eyes. Her special dessert was ruined, not to mention a whole dozen eggs wasted. She had no time to go downtown and buy another supply. The laundry still needed hung up, and the other food on her list needed prepared.

Karen dumped the shrunken mass onto the table and reviewed the recipe. She must have forgotten to add more flour after the rain interrupted her work. Sighing, she went to the icebox to look around for ingredients to make a different dessert. There was still plenty of flour, and a large crock of butter took up space on the shelf. Karen reached for it and adjusted her plans to include shortbread on the menu instead.

The next morning, Karen awoke to a house strewn with the laundry she'd hung to dry the night before. A line of it ran across the spare room. Another ran above the stove. Two lines crisscrossed the parlor. She had some work to do to get it all ironed and put away before her guests arrived. At least the clothes were dry. That had been her biggest concern after the rain cleared and the afternoon had turned hot and humid.

Karen set up her ironing board and got busy in her warm kitchen. Already the day's temperatures were high. Good thing she planned to serve cold food. She believed the women would appreciate her choices.

By eleven o'clock, Karen had her laundry done, her table set, her hair done, and her Sunday dress properly in place. She might work harder as a new bride than she'd ever imagined keeping a home for her husband and finding her place in the community, but that didn't mean she must part with refined manners and current fashion. Karen smiled approval at her reflection in the mirror and went to the kitchen to boil water for tea.

Over the next half-hour, her guests arrived. They filled the parlor and dining room. What a relief Logan had brought extra chairs over from the church. This gathering would not have fit in her house without them. A large ring of chairs circled through the main part of the house. The women sipped tea and took in everything about Karen's home. Most of them had never been in Logan's house before today. Their curiosity probably ran as high as Karen's desire to host well.

"May I help you serve?" Angelien Van Drunen joined Karen at the table.

"Yes, please." Karen smiled at the woman near her age who had become a good friend.

Angelien poured the tea into the cups that she handed to the ladies as they passed through the line.

Along with the lace tablecloth and set of china dishes Mother had given her as a wedding gift, Karen had also received the most elegant tea set. A teapot, cups, and saucers sprinkled with delicate blue flowers and rimmed with silver completed the collection.

Karen had been thrilled at the gift when she discovered how

closely the tea set matched the décor in Logan's dining room. Visions of afternoon gatherings around her tea set in her pretty dining room filled her dreams. This luncheon was the perfect time to begin fulfilling those wishes.

Next on her menu came the chicken salad sandwiches. Ida had given Karen her own delicious recipe, last enjoyed with her family and Logan at the lakeshore. With rolls from the Zahn's bakery, Karen was eager to see if they tasted as good as they looked. The menu also included a fruit salad with a cream dressing and molded cheese with toasted crackers.

"Mrs. De Witt, tell us about your classroom," Ethel Brinks prompted around a bite of fruit.

"There are ten children. Four from the Barnaveldt family and six from the Van Drunen families. They are catching on quickly. The older ones should be ready to go to school in the fall." Karen settled into a chair and balanced her tray of food on her lap as she looked around at the other women.

They appeared relaxed and content with her party. So far, the training she'd received from Mother, Aunt Fran, and Ida secured her reputation as a gracious and capable hostess.

Karen had not gone out of her way to find a reason to host such a widely publicized event. But her turn in the rotation for hosting the monthly meeting fell on the very date of the special luncheon.

The previous year, Lillian Ellenbroek had hosted. Two years ago, Grace Koelman acted as the hostess. With the honor of opening her home to the group also came the self-imposed pressure to measure up. The Ellenbroeks and the Koelmans were the most affluent families in town, but Karen came from a household with more money and luxuries than both of these small-town families put together.

Logan didn't care about such matters. Some days, Karen believed he didn't even notice the nuanced distinctions in the social classes that made up the communal fiber of the town in which he ministered. But Karen noticed. The years she spent as a member of Uncle Henry's household had shaped her sensitivity.

Never would she use her affluent upbringing to her advantage or lord it over others, but neither was she ignorant of the credit she could be to the adored local minister if her efforts of hosting went well.

"Paul tells me Martin has invited his brother to go into partnership with him selling cars." Lillian scooped cheese onto a cracker.

"You will lose those students soon. The Barnaveldts have already found a place to live," Grace said between sips of tea.

"Logan and I knew to expect turnover when he invited me to teach. I'll try to do all I can to help the children learn in the time I have with them." Karen patted her mouth with her napkin.

"Did you hear that a seamstress is coming to town?" Cornelia Goud asked.

The others shook their heads, so she continued. "Her name is Eva Synderhof. She's a widow. Lost her husband and now is traveling here with her grown children. I found this out from my husband because she bought the store right next to our jewelry store." Cornelia sipped her tea.

"When is she arriving?" Lillian asked.

"As soon as she can. Artie expects her by the end of the month."

"It will be nice to have a seamstress in town. We need one," Grace said.

At that moment, the most horrific crash sounded from the kitchen. Conversation stopped as the sound of shattering glass filled the air. The blood drained from Karen's face. She raced for the kitchen.

Shards of broken glass covered the floor, the table, and her workspace at the counter. Warm afternoon wind took full advantage of the empty window frame and rushed into the house. Youthful voices and laughter carried on the wind. Karen picked her way across the kitchen and glanced in the direction of the sounds.

Three boys and two dogs scampered across the yard and through the garden uncaring of the heavy crop of beans hanging in the rows or the marigolds and petunias blooming at one end. One of the dogs even took a break to dig out a section of the strawberry plants.

Karen's veins heated. She should run out there and chase them away while yelling at them about how naughty they were. But she was the minister's wife hosting a respectable party. She couldn't just go chasing off after grade school boys in a demonstration of anger. This must get handled in a different way.

"What happened?" Angelien entered the kitchen.

Karen glanced around for answers. There, under the stove, a worn baseball rolled in a circle. She reached to pick it up. "This."

Angelien's eyes widened.

Grace and Lillian came to the kitchen. "Everything all right in here?" Grace asked.

"Some boys were playing outdoors and hit a ball through our window." Karen laid the offending piece of sports equipment on the counter while her bread supply caught her attention. The loaf lay under a towel and was surrounded by splinters of glass. A sigh escaped her lips. She and Logan had better not eat any more of that bread. The only option left to her was to make more.

But by the time she restored order to her kitchen, cleaned up from the luncheon, and canned her beans, Karen didn't know when she'd get more baking done. The canner would add enough of its own heat and steam to the air. She didn't want to even think about staying in a hot kitchen to bake bread too.

"I'm sorry, ladies." She led the women to the parlor. "I'd hoped you could enjoy this special occasion, but now it's been ruined."

"Nothing has been ruined," Lillian said. "You've done a marvelous job entertaining us, and the food was delicious."

The others agreed.

"Let's find a broom and help you clean up." Cornelia rose from her chair.

"Oh, no. Please. You don't need to do that. Logan and I can handle it later." Karen couldn't think of anything more horrifying than guests dressed in their Sunday best cleaning up a dangerous mess in her kitchen. "Allow me to serve you more tea so that we can enjoy dessert." Karen moved to the dining room table and picked up the teapot.

With reluctance, Cornelia sat down. Angelien moved through the group with the tray of shortbread and offered some to each guest. The group turned their conversation to happenings in town and in each other's families until the broken window was forgotten. The women stayed for another hour, chatting and snacking on the shortbread.

After everyone left, Karen used the broom to sweep up the glass and went outside to assess the damage to the garden. Beans had been knocked off the plants, so Karen went ahead and picked all of them. She'd have an early morning getting a start on this much work. The strawberry plants lay in the grass, so she replanted them and gave them some water. Maybe they would recover from the assault that ripped them from the ground.

When Logan came home later in the day, she showed him the window and explained what happened.

"The worst part is, I don't know when I'll get a new loaf of bread baked. We don't even have any eggs." She leaned against the wall and talked while Logan fit a board over the window.

"After supper, I'll go over to Harley's and ask him to order some glass for us through the lumberyard." Logan retrieved his hammer from the toolbox and pounded.

Karen turned her attention to setting the table with food from the luncheon. After the meal, Logan went downtown while Karen washed the dishes. He returned with a basket of eggs, set them on the table, rolled up his sleeves, and set to work measuring flour into a bowl.

"What are you doing?" Karen turned away from stacking china dishes on a shelf.

"Only two people in this world know that I can bake bread." Logan reached for a wooden spoon and stirred. "My mother, because she taught me, and now you. Don't tell on me." He gave her a teasing grin and continued with his work.

"Thank you." Karen placed a kiss on his cheek. She might stand a chance now at managing the amount of work facing her if she didn't need to worry about the bread too.

Logan's loaves baked up with perfection. Karen pulled them from the oven before heading for bed. She turned down the lamp and went to the bedroom while the comforting scent of fresh bread filled the house.

"We have the kitchen cleaned up, the window repaired, and a new supply of bread baked. I think I'll call it a day. Tomorrow I'll track those boys down and return their baseball. Maybe they'd be willing to work with me in coming up with a plan to pay for the new glass." Logan joined her in the bedroom and bent to remove his shoes.

THE NEXT DAY, Karen tackled the tasks that waited. Logan came home for the noon meal to a kitchen overflowing with jars, bowls of green beans, and much steam in the air. Karen sat with him at the dining room table for their meal to escape the heat and disorder of the kitchen.

"I have good news." He poured water into his glass. "I caught up with the owners of the baseball. They live in our neighborhood and understand they should find a different location for their games."

Karen drew in a deep breath. Surely her garden was also safe.

"The glass for the window arrives tomorrow. Conrad is going to install it for us."

"That is good news." Karen buttered her slice of bread.

"Here's the best news." Logan looked at her and smiled. "I found out this morning I can take a week of vacation this summer like I did last year. How would you like to stay at that cottage on the lake we'd talked of?"

"I'd love it, Logan." Cool lake breezes and days with Logan all to herself were much more appealing than the monotonous task of canning garden produce in an overheated kitchen. "Even though this trip will occur several months after our wedding, we can still consider it as our honeymoon."

"Our official honeymoon." Mischief glittered in Logan's eyes. "I almost forgot. A few of the women who were at our house yesterday were at the church this morning. They raved over your party. Sounds to me like it was a success."

"Even with a broken window?" And with a flopped cake, squash bugs on the pumpkins, laundry that wouldn't dry, and the fear she might not measure up as Logan's wife.

"Even with the broken window." Logan laid his fork down and reached for her hand. "I'm proud of you, Karen. Thank you for sharing my life. I know it isn't easy at times, especially considering what you left behind. Not a day goes by that I don't marvel over the fact you really are here with me. I don't know what I ever did to deserve you, but whatever it was, I'm grateful."

Karen's vision blurred. Logan saw the toil of her life. He understood it, and he appreciated the efforts she made. She wanted to reply, but all she could do was nod and savor the taste of the bread cut from the loaf Logan had baked just for her.

23

Logan sat at the dining room table with the account book. The numbers on the page confirmed the churning in his stomach. Funds from the auction were low. Really low. Mick had been right. Their working farm needed the harvest of apples from the orchard to sustain it. Those apples couldn't ripen soon enough.

Another week's worth of pay to Conrad as the handyman and to Angelien as the cook and housekeeper, and the account would be drained. Logan rubbed his hand over his eyes. Surely the time to sell apples was quickly approaching. If the apples were harvested and shipped within the next two weeks, money would be available to keep everything at the farm running smoothly. He didn't want to think about what might happen if the harvest were delayed.

A knock came at the door.

"I'll answer it." Karen left the dishes she stacked and opened the door.

Conrad stood outside. "Good evening, Karen. Is Logan at home?"

"He is." Karen gestured to the table.

Conrad nodded and entered the house. The solemn

expression on his face told Logan something had happened. Angelien was expecting another baby. Maybe his visit related to the pregnancy in some way. Or maybe an emergency had arisen requiring the pastor's attention.

"How can I help you?" Logan stiffened in anticipation of Conrad's news.

"The apples in the orchard are ripe." He claimed the chair across from Logan. "But there is no fruit on the ground or in two of the trees near the road."

Logan shrugged. Conrad's English had improved under Karen's instruction, but the speech failed to alert him to any crisis.

"Pastor Logan." Conrad leaned forward. "I believe someone is stealing our apples."

"Stealing?" This might turn into an emergency if Conrad's words were true.

"Yes."

"But who?" Logan shook his head.

"Not sure. The orchard has not had upkeep for many years. People in the area might be helping themselves to the fruit. The apples are good. Angelien baked a pie with them yesterday. No one would let them go to waste."

Logan shrugged. Neighbors coming over and picking up dropped apples wasn't anything to get worked up about.

"We should let the sheriff know and have him come out to ... what do you say ... investigate." Conrad snapped his fingers as he recalled the English word.

"No. That isn't necessary. We don't have enough evidence other than a few apples missing. And if the neighbors are the ones picking the apples, then I don't see that they are committing a crime. Let them have a few to use. It won't cut into our profit."

"Sure." Conrad nodded. "But, I will keep watch."

Logan offered him a smile. They talked for a while about the farm and Conrad's work. Then Conrad left to go home.

THE NEXT MORNING, Logan sat at his desk in his study, looking over Psalm 103. He'd completed the series of sermons on the subject of marriage. Now that he'd gotten that out of his system, he should probably preach a few sermons that reminded his flock of God's true nature.

Footsteps sounded in the hall and stopped at the door. Logan looked up.

Conrad stood before him.

"What can I do for you?" Logan asked.

"Three more trees have lost their fruit." Conrad approached the desk. "That makes five trees we can't harvest."

Logan frowned. "When did this happen?"

"Not sure." Conrad shrugged. "Must have been during the night. I will stay there tonight instead of going home. Maybe I will catch the thief."

If the apples really were taken under cover of darkness, the stealthy work probably couldn't be blamed on the neighbors. "Would you like me to contact the sheriff?"

"Please."

"I'll come out tomorrow to check on you, and I'll bring him with me."

A smile crossed Conrad's face.

THE NEXT DAY, Conrad met Logan and his passenger in the yard before they climbed out of the buggy.

"More apples are gone."

"Did you see anyone?" The sheriff asked.

Conrad shook his head. "I don't know how they stay so quiet."

"Let's take a look." The sheriff followed Conrad into the orchard.

Leafy boughs heavy with red-skinned fruit brushed Logan's shoulders as he walked with the other two men along the rows of trees. Bees flew from the grass and settled on the ripening apples in search of sweet scents carried on the autumn air.

"This entire row has been picked." Conrad came to a stop near the wooden fence separating the orchard from the road and pointed. "More trees along that far border are also empty."

Logan looked around. If Conrad's words were true, then over half of the orchard had already been harvested.

"Come on." He beckoned the others to follow. Surely the outcome wouldn't be as grim as he feared.

But Conrad was right. Desolate trees stretched along the property lines. Only the trees nearest the house remained untouched. No one could guess how long the robbers might wait before taking those apples too.

"We need to pick all the apples still on the trees. This must be done today. Conrad, go to the house. Get Aneglien and anyone else who is willing to help." Logan pointed at the house.

Conrad took off on a run and soon returned with his wife, his brother, who still lived on the Akerman farm, and the newest resident, Eva Synderhof.

The bushel baskets Logan and the sheriff found in the barn began to fill. Conrad brought the wagon to the orchard and loaded the baskets onto it. The sheriff returned to town, taking with him the message for Karen to expect Logan home late.

He helped Conrad get the apples to the barn where they could find storage and protection until morning. As he traveled the darkened road back to town, a sinking sensation filled his stomach. The church needed every last apple from the orchard in order to make enough money to sustain the farm. Now their profit was cut by over half.

Karen met him at the door. "Did you find the thieves?"

"No. But that doesn't matter right now. The damage has been done. Without the sale of the apples, we have no way to pay the

Van Drunens or to cover our other expenses." He dragged in a deep breath.

"Oh, Logan." Karen clutched his shirt sleeve. "Does this mean Conrad will lose his job?"

"I hope not." Logan crossed the room and sat at the table. "They already have two children and another due this winter. Conrad can't afford to go without a job. But we may not be able to provide him with one any longer."

Logan dropped his head into his hands. A chair nearby slid over the rug. Karen's skirt brushed his knee. Her hand rested on his back.

"I don't want to have to be the one to tell him, but I don't see any way around it." He ventured a gazed at her. "Please pray."

"I will." Karen nodded.

"Tomorrow morning, I'll go back out there and have a meeting with everyone." Logan swallowed against the harsh reality of the task before him.

He took Karen with him to the farm. Angelien opened the door and admitted him into the parlor. Paul came too. After Logan had shared with him the turn of events, Paul offered to spread the word to the other members of the consistory and to give Logan his support.

"Could you please call Conrad in as well as the residents?" Logan met Angelien's questioning gaze. "I have news I need to share with everyone."

Angelien nodded and left the room. Over the span of several minutes, a group gathered.

Logan cleared his throat. "As you know, much of our apple crop has been stolen, which means we have fewer apples to sell. The consistory, at the advice of Mick Farnsworth, was counting on the profit from the harvest to pay Conrad and Angelien their salaries and sustain this ministry. Without the full profit, we no longer have the funds to cover expenses. I hope we don't have to close this operation down, but that looks like what will happen. I'm sorry."

Eva's mouth fell open. She exchanged glances with the other women in the room. "Are you saying we must move out?"

"I'm afraid so." Logan nodded.

"But we don't have anywhere else to go. Not yet, anyway. I'm looking for my own home, but haven't found it yet." Eva's eyes grew wide.

"We still look for land. Our family need place to live too." Conrad's brother spoke up. His English was less fluent than Conrad's, but his concern still came through loud and clear.

"I know. I wish there were something I could do." Logan puffed out his cheeks and ran a hand through his hair.

"Wait. I have an idea." Angelien looked at him. She captured the attention of the entire room. "I make brooms in my spare time. I've also made extra batches of soap. You told me when I started my job that you wanted me to have those items ready for sale during the winter. If we had a place in town to sell them, we could sell them now."

"What about my dress shop?" Eva suggested. "I'm just getting started building up my business, but my shop is downtown, right on Main Street. I could put Angelien's items in the window. That would surely draw attention."

"It's worth a try." Logan's gaze traveled between the women. Good thing he'd asked Karen to pray last night. Answers were coming. Who would've thought Angelien had planned ahead and already had a stash of merchandise ready to go?

"I'll take Angelien's brooms and soap with me today." Eva beamed.

"Does this mean we are staying?" Conrad asked.

"Carry on as usual. Let's see how well the products sell. Then we will make a decision." Logan watched for Conrad's response.

He smiled.

Logan could believe the man was quite relieved to hear he could keep his job.

"Let's sell what apples we do have. Every little bit of profit helps," Paul suggested.

The group agreed and assisted Paul and Logan with the work.

LOGAN RETURNED to his schedule of sermon preparation and keeping up with the daily visits and correspondence. The following week, he stopped in at Eva's store to check on sales. He held his breath as he examined the products in her window. An unpleasant conversation with the Van Drunens may still await him.

"Good afternoon, Pastor De Witt. I'll be with you in a moment." Eva greeted him and then returned her attention to the woman standing near the cash register.

Logan nodded and sauntered over to the stacks of soap on a shelf in the display window. He picked up a bar of soap and studied it. The price was visible in the corner, but that wasn't what caught his attention. The label, in the shape of a circle with the silhouette of an apple tree, marked the packaging of the bar of soap. Around the tree, the words, *Orchard of Love* filled the space. Below, in smaller print, was the phrase, *handmade by Angelien Van Drunen.*

She'd designed a label for their working farm and given it the perfect name. No longer was the land given to the church known to him in a distant, generic manner as someone else's property. It was an orchard of love, a place where new citizens heard the gospel, made friends, and had space to call their own until settling into a more permanent home. It was also a place of beginnings, scented with the fruits of harvest.

If only Nellie had known what a gold mine she'd possessed. Thoughts of the little lady brought to his mind the gift she'd insisted on her young pastor giving his new bride for Christmas.

Song of the Spring. The perfume lingered in various corners of the home he shared with Karen—on her pillow, in the parlor, in the kitchen—whenever the stronger smells of cooking food didn't overpower it. His home had become its own orchard of love, a place of beginnings, of living daily in holiness and faithfulness.

"Angelien has been making cheese." Eva's voice reached him before she did. "Look. Here is a round of it." She picked up a circular package with a label similar to the bar of soap in his hand.

"Isn't that label charming?" She pointed at it. "Angelien and I noticed the arch over the lane one evening as we were out walking. She decided it would make a good name for our orchard."

Logan accepted the cheese when she handed it to him.

"I've sold out of brooms twice. The soap is in demand. Sales are good. I'll bring the money to you as soon as I get a break." Eva hastened to the counter where she cut fabric when another customer entered the store.

Logan paid her for the soap and the cheese and took it home for Karen. She'd love that label, he was sure of it.

24

"Hey, Karen, listen to this." A smile bloomed on Logan's face as he sat at the kitchen table.

She paused from pushing around the food on her plate. It failed to tempt her appetite.

Logan waved the letter he'd discovered in the mail. "Pete says he and Anna would like to stay with us when they come to Oswell City so Pete can attend the denominational meetings our church is hosting. They plan to bring Charlotte with them."

"It will be nice to see them again. When do they arrive?" Karen sipped from her glass of water.

"They plan to come on Sunday night, just in time for the start of the conference on Monday morning." Logan folded the letter and returned his attention to his plate of food.

"Pete and Anna may use the spare bedroom. That will work well, but we will need a crib for Charlotte. Maybe I can ask the Ladies Mission Society. One of them might know of a crib we could use." Karen took a bite of bread with no butter. Nothing seemed to agree with her stomach lately.

Logan chuckled. "Let's wait on that. If word gets out that you and I are looking for a crib, it will create a stir. I'll go rummage around in the house at the orchard. Surely there's one in the attic or in one of the bedrooms I can sneak home without drawing too much attention."

"Good idea. I didn't think about how that would look." Karen's face heated. She hadn't thought of Logan's point, but it became obvious to her. If she made arrangements to move a crib into the parsonage, people would certainly draw an incorrect conclusion and maybe even spread rumors. Just when she'd begun to gain confidence in her ability to measure up to her own standards as the minister's wife, another lesson to learn confronted her.

"When the day comes that we are in need of our own crib, I won't be borrowing it from anyone. It will be a permanent fixture in the parsonage and will likely draw more attention than either one of us will know what to do with." Logan winked at her and then fell silent while he ate.

Karen watched him eat. If only her appetite stayed as interested in food as his did. The ham loaf and potatoes she'd cooked for their lunch were two of her favorites. She couldn't imagine why the food didn't taste good to her. In fact, it even smelled unappealing.

She'd opened a window while it cooked. The brisk autumn wind had swirled into the kitchen but had done little to revive her appetite. Karen had fled to her room until Logan came home in order to escape the smell. She must be coming down with a sickness of some sort for as tired and uninterested in eating as she felt these days.

Logan pushed back from the table, kissed her temple, and left the house. Karen looked around at all the dirty dishes. So many dirty dishes. She didn't know how she'd ever get them clean. Most of her afternoon would pass before she completed the task. And when it was finished, she'd go to her room and lie down for a lovely nap until Logan arrived home at the end of the day.

The rest of the week, Karen dragged herself through the task of cooking. Not only did she have a husband to care for, but now she had guests arriving. Groceries must get purchased. She needed to wash and dry linens for the spare bedroom. Jobs she usually took pleasure in loomed large and impossible in her weary mind. She must do them, though. For the sake of the respect Logan enjoyed, she must maintain a clean and orderly home. But oh, how difficult her goal had become.

At noon on Sunday, Logan came home from church to find her lying face-down on the sofa. The pillows buried her nose, preventing odors from reaching her nostrils and offered a steady surface on which to rest her throbbing head. She'd managed to go to church and lead the singing, but she'd skipped out on the greetings and shaking hands after the service.

Instead, she'd come home to prepare their dinner. The smell of the succulent roast beef cooking in the oven had become too much. Karen didn't know how she'd ever stand in the kitchen surrounded by those smells to make the gravy.

"Karen, aren't you feeling well?" Logan grasped her shoulder.

How she wished she didn't have to admit to him that the dinner he deserved and looked forward to made her nauseous. She must indeed be coming down with something, a disease that stole her energy and was growing worse with no improvement. If she didn't have guests staying with her this week, she'd make an appointment to see Dr. Kaldenburg. She made the great effort to lift her head and look at Logan.

"Your face is so pale, sweetheart." Concern furrowed his brow as he gazed into her eyes.

Karen achieved a seated position. "I still need to make the gravy."

"Stay here and rest. I'll finish preparing lunch." Logan smoothed her hair.

"No, I'll do it." Karen shook her head. She stood and welcomed Logan's arm around her waist as a steady support.

"Are you sure you feel well enough for the Bettens to stay here?

Maybe I should tell Pete to reserve a room at the hotel instead." Logan found the pan and a whisk and set them on the stove.

"I want them to stay here." Karen opened the oven door and held her breath while odors wafted from the roasting meat. If her memory served her correctly, these were delicious smells, but today the savory aroma assaulted her and left her stomach rolling once more.

"Karen?" Logan knelt beside her.

"I'm fine." She swallowed and willed herself to believe it.

"Let me help you. That roasting pan is hot." He took the hot pads from her hands and lifted the pan onto the stove's surface.

Karen shut the oven door and took her time rising to her feet. She picked up the whisk and gritted her teeth. Her husband deserved a good meal. She'd do everything in her power to provide it for him.

After the meal, Logan washed the dishes, and Karen dried them, an arrangement that made her stomach quite happy. Logan got the job of looking at the mess and tolerating the smells while she only had to manage the clean and sparkly items he handed to her. This kind of assistant in her kitchen made the work much more tolerable. Maybe with Anna in her home over the next few days, Karen could count on having an assistant until she had the chance to visit the doctor.

"Ready to go?" Logan asked after throwing out the dishwater.

Karen nodded. He helped her with her coat and walked with her to the train station. Their wait was brief since the train from Silver Grove ran on time. The Bettens emerged from a coach and joined Logan and Karen.

"It's so good to see you. "Anna hugged Karen the best she could with Charlotte on her hip.

"I've missed you." Ten months was way too long of a span of time between visits with Anna Betten.

"And I've missed you. So much." Anna pulled away and smiled.

"How is this little dear?" Logan stroked the chin of sixteen-month-old Charlotte. The baby responded with a giggle.

"She has her daddy wrapped around her little finger." Anna laughed.

"Just wait until your turn comes, my friend." Pete slapped Logan on the back. "Nothing compares to being a father."

Karen blinked against the mist clouding her vision. She'd always known Logan would make an excellent father. In that moment, she wanted to give him a reason to become one. As soon as she felt better, she'd share with him how this moment stirred the longing of her heart.

Logan led the way inside to find the luggage and then down the street to their house. How nice that Logan had helped her clean up the kitchen before meeting the train. Now her guests could enter an orderly and peaceful home where they could find comfort.

"Your family may use our spare room." Logan carried the bags down the hall with the Bettens following him.

Thank goodness Logan took charge of the situation. Karen's stomach rolled again. She swallowed and went to the kitchen for a glass of water. Maybe sipping a little at a time would help calm her stomach. She went to the parlor and settled in with the group laughing and chatting as they caught up on the happenings of each other's lives.

THE NEXT MORNING after sharing breakfast and sending the men off to their meetings, Karen brewed tea and brought it to the dining room table. Anna sat in one of the chairs. Charlotte played with a stack of blocks on a quilt nearby.

"How are Logan's mother and sister doing in Silver Grove?" Karen asked as she poured tea into a cup for Anna.

"Very well. Sandy is enjoying life as a grandmother."

"Good. From what both Sandy and Tillie write, everyone is in good health."

Tillie's baby had been born that summer. Letters from her were filled with news of her son.

"They are. Will you and Logan make the trip to see them over Christmas?" Anna stirred sugar into her tea.

"We hope to. Logan will preach on Sunday and again Christmas Eve. We may try to see his family and mine in the week following." Those plans would work out if Karen started feeling better. She didn't want to think about the rock and sway of a train with the kind of treatment her stomach gave her recently. "What are your plans for Christmas?"

"We will visit my mother. Pete's parents are gone, so we only spend time with my family over the holidays." Anna took a cookie from the plate holding a variety of treats from the bakery.

Karen poured tea into her cup and sipped it. She didn't dare try to force anything into her inconsolable stomach, not even a small sugar cookie.

"What do you think of Oswell City by now?" Anna asked.

"I like it here. You've probably heard about the outreach we've started to help people moving here from the Netherlands."

"I have. Logan told Pete about it in his letters."

"I've met many new people. Angelien Van Drunen has become a good friend. So has Eva Synderhof. She recently opened a dress shop on Main Street. Her work is excellent. If Mother saw it, she would give her business to Eva." Mother's expectations were high, but Eva could meet them just as well as the seamstress in Chicago.

"Sometimes I wish Silver Grove had a dress shop, but our town is too small. Nora Carter might give a few suggestions when she measures out fabric I buy at the mercantile, but anything more complicated, I take to Logan's mother. She has helped me on several projects."

"I also teach English to the children of families who are new to town."

Anna smiled. "How nice for you, Karen, that you have a way to keep teaching. You are one of the best."

"Thanks. I missed a day last week because I didn't feel well. The week before, I missed two days for the same reason." Karen sipped from her cup. The hot tea had a settling effect on her stomach.

"Oh, really? Are sore throats or the flu going around in Oswell City? There were two cases of the flu in Silver Grove before we left."

"What I have feels like the flu, but I don't have a fever. No one else I've heard of has been sick. Just me." Karen scratched the back of her neck. She couldn't think why Logan hadn't caught the sickness from her or where she might have contracted it.

Anna's motions of breaking off a bite of her cookie stilled as she stared at Karen for a long moment. "You say your symptoms are like the ones that come with the flu?"

"Yes."

"Upset stomach."

"Terrible. I'm so nauseous. Especially in the mornings. Everything I cook smells awful. I don't even want to eat, but I know I should." Karen rubbed her forehead.

Anna bit her lip while a smile stretched across her face. "Karen, I don't think you have the flu."

"You don't?" Karen tried to come up with other ideas of what might be upsetting her stomach so much. Maybe she'd developed an intolerance for certain kinds of foods. The way she'd felt lately told her if this was her problem, she'd become intolerant to just about everything.

"No. It sounds to me like whatever you have won't be going away for several months. Nine to be exact." Anna grew serious and refilled her cup.

Karen's mind ran through a list of ailments. Only one made

any sense. It wasn't a disease really, more of a, well, a condition. It was a condition that would change her life.

"You mean ... you don't suppose Logan and I—"

"You've been married long enough. I don't see why not." Anna shrugged.

Karen's mind worked to absorb this new possibility. She thought over the state of her health during the last couple of months. The signs were all there.

Anna gave her a conspiratorial gaze. "As soon as you are able, talk to the doctor. After you've told Logan, write to me. Pete and I would love to be the first to know." A gentle smile replaced her earlier secrecy.

Karen's eyes grew round, and her breathing slowed. A baby. She and Logan might actually be expecting a baby. Her stomach churned. The one symptom she'd feared most overpowered her. Karen clamped a hand over her mouth and dashed for the water closet. So much for the tea's settling effects on her digestive system.

25

Friday evening, Logan walked with his friend to the train station. Anna carried Charlotte and walked with Karen. Thoughts of his wife shot little pains through his chest. Karen's color had not returned. She looked so pale, and she'd grown thinner. He hadn't seen her eat a full meal the entire time Pete and Anna had stayed with them. She must be terribly sick. If he hadn't been so busy leading meetings this week, he would have insisted that she visit the doctor.

He'd hinted at the idea one evening as they prepared for bed, but Karen refused to make an appointment before their guests returned home. She'd said she hoped any day to feel better and talked no further on the subject. He'd dropped the matter in trust that Karen knew how to take care of herself and would seek medical help before her condition grew too threatening.

But looking at her today, Logan believed, contrary to her hopes, she wouldn't improve from one day to the next. He must spend the entire day Saturday working on his message for Sunday. If his schedule were more flexible, he'd pick her up and physically carry her to Dr. Kaldenburg's office so Karen could receive the proper attention. For now, he had no choice but to stay aware and offer his help whenever she'd accept it.

Their group arrived at the station and waited near the tracks for the train. Logan wrapped an arm around Karen to shield her from the chilly air and to impart to her a bit of his strength. She leaned on him, frail and weary.

"Good to have you here this week." His heart thumped as he shook hands with Pete. "We will try to drop in on you some evening after Christmas when we come to Silver Grove."

Pete nodded. "Come by toward the end of the week. We'll be home from visiting Anna's mother by then. Anna and I will look forward to seeing you."

The train chugged to a stop as Anna gave Karen a hug. "Remember to write me as soon as you find out."

Her whispered words floated to Logan's ears. He frowned at the hidden meaning.

"I will." A smile broke out on Karen's face.

Pete and Anna boarded the train. After one more wave, Logan led Karen home. She acted normal, putting away dishes and working around the kitchen, but she went to bed quite early. Logan took advantage of the quiet evening hours and went to his study to prepare his sermon.

Saturday morning, he left the house before Karen awoke. When he came home at noon, he found the table set and Karen seated in a chair near the stove, stirring soup in a pot. Holding her head in her other hand, she looked ill.

"Karen, I'm worried about you." Logan fell to his knees before her and framed her face with his hands. "Maybe you should take time today to visit with the doctor. He might be able to help you."

"I just want to rest." Karen shook her head. "I'll go on Monday. I've already made up my mind to see him on Monday morning."

"Then maybe you should stay home tomorrow instead of leading the singing."

"That isn't necessary. If I rest this afternoon, I'll feel well enough to be at church tomorrow." Karen glanced at the pot of soup and gave it a stir.

"You're sure?" His forehead creased.

"I am. By tomorrow morning, I'll be fine." Karen looked at him with an edge of determination lighting her eyes.

In reluctance, Logan stood and released his hold on her. He forced a smile and went to the table to eat his lunch. The remainder of the afternoon he spent in study.

Sunday morning, he rose early, got dressed, and went to the church. Karen still slept. If she felt well enough to awaken on time and help him with the services, he'd welcome her assistance. If not, he'd stand in as song leader. The music wouldn't sound as nice, but it was the best he could do if Karen chose to listen to his suggestion and stay home.

But she came. She sat on the front row dressed in her stylish Sunday dress and looking quite proper. No one would know she'd struggled with sickness this week. When he finished the opening prayer, he beckoned for her to come to the pulpit.

Karen followed the order of worship through the first hymn and the prayer. He took a seat as she started the next song. A favorite of his, Logan gave his full concentration to the beautiful words of verse three.

"Here's my heart, Lord, take and seal it. Seal it for thy—"

A thump sounded from the pulpit. Karen's hymnbook fell to the floor. She went limp and followed the book's path. Logan jumped out of his seat to catch her, but he moved too late. Karen landed on the floor and sprawled over the stone tiles.

Logan turned her over so he could see her face. Her eyes were closed. He spoke her name, but she didn't respond. His stomach turned to rock. Whatever disease ravaged her insides had stolen her away from him. If she never awakened, his devastation would kill him.

"Karen? Karen, please. Wake up." Desperation trembled in his voice.

The organ had stopped. The congregation no longer sang,

and one person at a time sat down in the pews. The church hushed as everyone watched and listened.

Logan rubbed his eyes against the film of moisture threatening to fill them. He should have carried her off to the doctor yesterday and left his sermon incomplete. He could always preach another one, but Karen may not get another chance.

He should check for a pulse. That's the first thing anyone looked for in an unresponsive person. He lifted her wrist.

Dr. Kaldenburg left his place in the third pew and knelt at Karen's side to hold two fingers to her neck. "She has a pulse. That's good. Has she fainted before?"

"No." Not that he had witnessed anyway.

"Any changes in her behavior?" Dr. Kaldenburg lifted each of Karen's eyelids.

"Her eating. Karen hasn't had a full meal in at least a week." His hands trembled.

"Ah. Does she complain of dizziness or pain?" The doctor felt around the back of Karen's head.

"Only an upset stomach and nausea." Logan blinked as memories of Karen's struggles with cooking came to mind.

"Has she ever vomited?" The doctor glanced at Logan.

"Yes. Twice, I believe. Two mornings in a row." Logan stroked his chin and his brow furrowed.

A hint of a smile pulled at the doctor's mouth as he stood. "I'd like to examine your wife further. Could you please bring her to your study?"

Logan scooped Karen into his arms as gently as he possibly could and followed Dr. Kaldenburg down the center aisle. The congregation stared. Some of the women whispered. Logan sensed their concern and struggled with his desire to stop and thank them. But now wasn't the time. For all he knew, his precious Karen lingered between life and death. She needed him to stay on track following the doctor's orders. He rounded the corner and strode down the hall.

Karen's lashes fluttered. She stirred in his arms. "Logan? What's going on?"

"Shh. You fainted a few minutes ago. Dr. Kaldenburg wants to examine you." He picked up his speed.

Karen pushed at his chest. "What, now?"

"Yes. Now." Logan hadn't been more serious in his life. Fear of losing her and worry over her sickness put an edge in his voice that allowed for no negotiation.

"This should wait until tomorrow when I have an appointment." A moan accompanied her words.

"You shouldn't have waited so long. If I'd paid more attention, I would have made you go to the doctor even with guests in the house." His voice sounded tight. Fear still ruled.

Karen sagged into his arms as he took the last steps to his study. The doctor waited beside the open door. Logan settled Karen into a chair near the bookcase.

He kissed her forehead. "I'll be back to check on you as soon as I can."

Pain shadowed Karen's eyes as she looked at him. If the pain was from her fall on the floor or from something he'd said, he didn't know. They'd work it out later. Right now, Karen needed the doctor's attention.

Drawing a deep breath, Logan returned to the sanctuary. Standing behind the pulpit, he looked out at an assembly with a mixture of bewilderment and worry on their faces.

"Mrs. De Witt is with the doctor." He held up his hand. "I trust he will provide us with answers very soon."

His mind stayed behind with Karen, but he needed to focus if he stood a chance at preaching a sermon that made any sense. Logan cleared his throat and read the passage of Scripture, then continued straight from his notes. His thoughts were too distracted for any sort of improvisation. He might even cut the message a little short this once. If the others in the sanctuary were as curious as he was about Karen's condition, they'd appreciate a shorter sermon.

As he wrapped up his last point, Paul came to stand with him.

"Please join me in offering prayer for Mrs. De Witt." Paul bowed his head and petitioned the Lord for Karen's restored health.

Logan offered the benediction, but instead of hanging around in the back to shake hands, he made a beeline for his study. Surely the congregation would understand his wish to skip out this time. He burst into the room and looked from the doctor to Karen.

She sat in the chair where Logan had left her with her feet resting on the seat of the other chair.

Dr. Kaldenburg leaned against the desk and addressed her. "Keep your appointment tomorrow. I want to confirm my findings from this examination. I will leave now so you and Pastor Logan can talk."

Logan made eye contact with the doctor in hopes of gathering a clue to Karen's troubles. The doctor gave nothing away. He slipped out of the room and shut the door behind him.

Logan knelt at Karen's side and took her hand in his. "What did the doctor say?"

"Pretty much what I thought he'd say." Karen rubbed her eyes.

More questions lodged in his throat where he couldn't get them past the tightness that felt ready to strangle him.

Karen looked at him. "The doctor thinks we might be expecting a baby."

If a man could split in two from the inability to contain overflowing joy, he'd fall in halves to the floor. Fear drained out of him, and giddiness took its place. Karen wasn't going to die. She didn't even have a chronic disease. She would be a mother, which made him a father.

He must try to put this into words. "This is why you've been so sick."

"Anna shared her suspicions with me." Karen nodded. "But I

didn't dare to believe them. I want nothing more than for you to be a father, but I'm still trying to figure out what it means to be your wife. I could barely keep up with all of my work when I felt well. What are we going to do through this pregnancy and the days following the baby's arrival? I'm not sure when I'll start feeling better. Maybe the doctor can tell me tomorrow. I want to keep teaching, but a baby will change everything."

"We'll work it out one step at a time." Logan reached for her other hand and held both of them in his. "If your sickness lingers, maybe we can find someone to help you with housework. Not every day, but often enough to help you stay caught up."

"I would appreciate that. I can look forward to the baby's arrival more if I know I'll have help. Thank you." She smiled at him.

"Everyone is worried about you." Logan stood. "What would you like for me to tell them?"

"Let them know I have an appointment with the doctor tomorrow. If the results of his examination confirm our conversation from today, then we can share with the town our happy news." Karen shifted her feet from the chair to the floor.

Logan nodded. "Stay here to wait for me, and I'll take you home." He left the study and went into the hall. People clustered around him, asking about Karen. He repeated her words and assured them he'd have more news later in the week.

When the building emptied, he locked the doors, returned his notes and Bible to his study, and took Karen home.

MONDAY MORNING, Logan sat at his desk reading. Another Advent season was only three weeks away. He wanted to gather information and outline his messages. A quiet morning while he waited on Karen to finish at the doctor's office gave him the perfect opportunity to get this work done.

Footsteps sounded in the hall. He glanced up to find Karen

standing in the doorway.

"Good morning, Mrs. De Witt. What can I do for you?" He offered a teasing grin.

A smile tugged at her lips. "Pastor Logan, I'm in need of some advice."

"What kind of advice is that?" He couldn't recall Karen ever using his formal title before. Her attempt to create ceremony around this meeting humored him and caused a little burst of pleasure to erupt somewhere deep in his heart.

She approached his desk and sat on it in the same flirtatious way Florence did last summer. "I need you to tell me the best way to break important news to my husband."

"Will he think it is good news or bad news?" Logan raised his brows.

Karen bit her lip as though she gave the question much thought. "He'll probably think it is good news."

"You may start by closing my door." Logan leaned back in his chair.

She followed his direction.

"Come here." He pointed to his empty lap.

"Do you help all of your parishioners in this way?" Karen raised her brows in a mild school-teacherish rebuke.

"Only the beautiful ones." He grinned like a boy who'd gotten away with pulling a prank in school.

Karen laughed as she settled on his lap.

"What do you have to tell me, Karen?" He asked, enjoying the blue depths of her eyes.

"You are going to be a father, Logan." She framed his face with her hands. "The doctor confirmed it. Our baby will be born next year in May."

Each muscle trembled. He drew in a deep breath. His beautiful Karen carried his child. Together they would grow a family while gaining practice at loving, serving, and trusting. He crushed her to his chest. Every last one of his dreams was coming true.

26

Logan stood before a full sanctuary ready to begin the morning's service. Joyful thoughts of Karen's pregnancy thumped through his mind as they had all week. He'd contemplated the best way to let everyone know. Maybe he should have spilled the news to one person at a time as he'd met them downtown over the course of the past few days.

He'd received many inquiries about Karen's health, but answering individual questions wasn't the most efficient way to lay everyone's concerns to rest. Jake would have been more than happy to put an article in the paper, but Logan wanted the congregation to hear the news from him. A Sunday morning with everyone present was the easiest form of communication.

"Good morning." He cleared his throat. "Before we get started, I would like to share some news with you."

The complete attention of everyone in the room centered on him. People leaned forward. Others shifted in their seats to see around the person seated in the pew in front of them.

"Last week, my wife fainted while leading the singing. Dr. Kaldenburg examined her on Monday. I'm happy to tell you that the doctor confirmed Karen and I are expecting a baby, due in

May." Logan looked out over the assembly as a grin threatened to stretch off of his face.

For the second time he could remember in the history of Oswell City Community Church, the sanctuary erupted in applause. Logan gave the call to worship and led the singing of the hymns since Karen had stayed at home, too ill to leave her bed.

His preaching went better than he expected. Distraction was still his middle name these days. Between the euphoria of becoming a husband and the anticipation of becoming a father, Logan's brain had forgotten the meaning of the word focus. He did his best. Surely the day would come when he'd grow accustomed to standing under downpours of blessings.

The greeting time after the service was filled with hugs, well wishes, and celebration. He went home eager to share the happy response with Karen. Still in her nightgown, she crept around the kitchen. A pan sat on the stove. The last of the loaf of bread lay in slices on the table.

"Oh, Logan." Karen held her head. "More bread should be baked tomorrow, but I can't stand the smell of it in the oven."

"I'll take care of the bread." He removed his suit coat and draped it over a chair.

"You shouldn't have to do the baking. You are already so busy." Karen leaned on the table as if to keep her balance.

"I don't mind. I want to." He settled his hand on one of her shoulders. "How far are you on dinner preparations?"

"I haven't started." Karen frowned.

Logan raised his brows. "You've been sick this morning."

"Three times." Karen closed her eyes as if a fourth dash to the water closet loomed in her immediate future.

"Go lay down." Logan steered her to the bedroom. "I'll fix our meal. It won't be anything fancy, but it will at least save you from standing in the kitchen and looking at food."

Karen nodded and allowed him to help her into bed.

A knock came at the door. Logan dropped a kiss on Karen's forehead, then hastened into the hall and opened the door

"This is for you." Mrs. Brinks held out a steaming pan wrapped in a towel and entered with one of her daughters.

Logan took it from her and set it on the dining room table.

"We are so happy for you. Congratulations again on the news of Karen's pregnancy."

He smiled. "Thank you."

"Since your wife wasn't in church with you this morning, I assumed she probably is still not feeling well. We brought food from the hotel kitchen." She pointed to the pan on the table.

"Very thoughtful. Thank you, Mrs. Brinks." Logan smiled at her and her daughter.

"Come along, Katie. Let's not keep the pastor from his dinner." With a wave, Mrs. Brinks led the way to the street.

Logan had just removed the foil from the fragrant contents of the pan when a knock came on the door once again. This caller was Mrs. Goud with a cake, delivered for the same reasons as Mrs. Brinks' food.

The following week continued on in the same manner. Logan hadn't needed to bake any bread. The Zahns dropped by with a special delivery. Angelien brought cheese and jams from the farm. Eva brought over a baby blanket she'd sewn. The Ladies Mission Society made plans to host a shower. Jake ended up putting a notice in the newspaper, complete with a summary of Karen's fainting episode.

In the evenings, with Karen tucked in next to him on the sofa sipping ginger tea, Logan wrote letters to Mama and Tillie, to Pete, and to Karen's mother. Each one of them would be thrilled. He watched the mail for letters containing their responses.

The excitement in Logan's house suffered competition for his attention. The orchard was barely turning a profit. The money from the auction long gone, Angelien's contributions brought in only a slim income. Angelien and Conrad must get compensated for their work at the orchard, but the account had funds for one more paycheck. After James Koelman signed it, the consistory would be left with the tough decision to shut the farm and the orchard down.

Logan hated to do it. The rooms had stayed full ever since the beginning. He didn't know where the Van Drunen brothers or Eva's family would go. Turning them out seemed so unfair, like he'd somehow gone back on his word. But expecting Conrad and Angelien to work for free was a worse scheme.

Logan prayed. If the work at the orchard was meant to continue, God would give them the funds they needed.

One morning, immersed in thought and surrounded by stacks of books, Logan glanced up to find the sheriff standing in the doorway of the study.

"Found your apple thieves." The sheriff crossed his arms over his uniform.

Logan's brow furrowed. In his concern for Karen, he'd forgotten about the investigation the sheriff had conducted over the last month.

"Turns out you were right." The sheriff took a seat. Neighbors have been helping themselves to the apples. But these aren't just any of your typical Oswell City neighbors. These boys are dangerous. I've got them locked up at the jail now."

"What made them so dangerous?" Logan shuffled his notes.

"Guns. They've been stealing guns from area farmers. I've had reports come in over the past weeks of missing guns. Taken right out of houses and barns. Never thought the crooks were the same ones who stole your apples."

The information sounded unusual to Logan too. He couldn't think what gun thieves would want with apples.

"Turns out the crooks have connections with gangs back in

the city. They ship their stolen guns in barrels and then make a nice profit. Those apples were the perfect camouflage. The crooks filled their barrels full of apples. No one would ever know about the guns buried inside." The sheriff leaned back as though quite pleased with himself for foiling the gangsters' plans.

"How did you find all this out?" Logan tapped his chin.

"The beauty of their scheme is in their location." The sheriff chuckled. "These boys have been right under your nose, Pastor Logan."

"What do you mean?" His temperature rose.

"You know that old silo and rundown shed at the back of the Akerman property near the ravine?"

"Yeah." Logan's tentative answer betrayed his dread of whatever the sheriff might say next.

"Headquarters. They must have taken it over sometime this fall while they worked on accumulating their gun supply."

Logan ground his teeth. Outright robbery was happening on church property! And those vile crooks didn't even have the decency to use the apples as food. The crop would probably get dumped out and go to waste once the guns arrived at their destination.

"I must talk to Paul and James about this." Logan exhaled. Just when the church made an honest effort to help people, a crime operation is discovered on the land. It had better not undermine the reputation of the consistory or of the objectives the orchard was attempting to achieve. Those foxes. How insidious.

The sheriff stood. "I've recovered some of the apples. They are in a wagon in the barn. If I were you, I'd tear down those old buildings as soon as possible." He turned and left the room.

Questions about the background of these men swirled through Logan's mind. The thieves must have found accommodations in a neighboring town. Conrad had not mentioned suspicious tracks or evidence of trespassers. George would have mentioned mysterious strangers at the hotel. Maybe they were rovers, working their way across a region and staying on the move to avoid getting caught.

Whatever their story, Logan had no interest or reasons to learn more. He closed his books and walked to City Hall to seek out Paul's perspective on the matter. He strode into Paul's office and spilled the entire story.

"Wow." Paul smoothed his mustache. "The sheriff made quite an important discovery. Glad he has those men behind bars. He must have brought them in just this morning while I was in meetings."

"I fear this development reflects badly on the church and appears like we allowed crime on our property. I feel responsible." Logan ran his hand through his hair.

"I can see why you would. But don't worry about it. Once the story comes out in the paper, and everyone can read the facts for themselves, no one should suffer any loss of respect." Paul came around the corner of his desk.

"Would you have time to come to the farm with me this evening? I'd like to check how many apples came back to us."

"Good idea. I'll plan on it." Paul nodded.

"I'd like for James to come too. I'll pick him up and then drop past your house." Logan waved and went home to share his plan with Karen.

The three men arrived at the orchard after dark. Logan went to the house for a lantern and took it to the barn. The glow of the flames reflected off the painted side of a farm wagon. Logan climbed the ladder at the back and looked in.

A laugh rumbled from his lips. "This wagon is over half full."

"What? You don't mean it." Disbelief crossed James's face.

"I certainly do." Logan jumped off the ladder.

"This means we have apples to sell." Paul's face lit up.

Logan shook his head. "These apples aren't fresh. I'm not sure how high of a price they would bring."

"True. They will have a lower quality." Paul stroked his chin.

James moved to the corner and pointed at the apparatus in

the shadows. "This farm has a cider press. Maybe we could sell cider instead."

"That might be worth a try. I'll bring it up to Angelien and ask if she knows how to make cider." Logan led the way out of the barn.

Angelien didn't know how to make cider, but Conrad did. With Logan's assistance, they searched the barn for jugs. If the barn had a press, jugs were probably stored somewhere nearby.

Their search soon turned up crates full of jugs.

ONE SUNNY AFTERNOON, Logan and Conrad, along with Conrad's brothers and three men from the church, set to work making cider. The consensus was to make one batch and see how well it sold. If no one was interested in buying, then Logan would take his chances of attempting to sell the aged crop of apples.

Over the next two weeks, Logan kept an eye on the success of the sales. Conrad and Angelien must get paid by the end of the month. If the cider didn't sell, the farm and the orchard would have to close.

Late Saturday afternoon, as Karen lay on the sofa listening to Logan rehearse his sermon, a knock came on the door. Logan went to answer it. Eva Synderhof rushed in out of the cold.

"Pastor Logan, I've brought the money over from the sale of products from the farm. I've sold out of the cider. Bring me another supply, would you? With the holidays coming soon, it's a popular drink. Well, I must get back before dark. Good night." Eva swept out of the house.

He and the men would have to get busy churning out another batch of cider. Maybe they should take the risk and make two batches, or even three.

"Shall we take a look?" Logan exchanged glances with Karen.

Karen left her place on the sofa and came to the table to help him count the money in Eva's pile of bills and change.

A smile crossed Logan's face as the last coins were added to the pile. "There's enough here to pay the Van Drunens. Thank goodness."

Logan released the breath he'd been holding. Money for one more month had been provided. The intruders who stole the apples hadn't ruined the orchard and its purpose after all. He put the money in a drawer of his desk. Monday, he'd make the trip to the orchard and share with everyone the good news.

27

"The women of the church have been so kind." Karen stood near the dress form in Eva's shop.

"You received some lovely items at the shower. You and your husband should be well prepared for a little one to join your family." Eva settled her tape measure around Karen.

Already, her dresses had grown tight. She'd barely gotten the one she wore buttoned when she put it on this morning. She'd anticipated the eventual arrival of the day when she'd have to alter her dresses, but it had arrived sooner than she expected. These altered dresses would fit for the next month, but Eva would have to sew a few new dresses for her very soon.

Eva moved to the counter to write a measurement down. "I hear you have household help now."

"Yes, I do. Logan talked to Paul and Lillian. They made arrangements for one of their staff to come to our house two days each week. Her name is Joyce. On one of the days, she'll help me with the laundry and the other with the baking."

"Oh, that is a nice arrangement." Eva laid one of Karen's dresses on the counter. "What about teaching at the orchard? Are you still able to do that?"

Karen sat on a plush stool. "I am. I go out there two days a week on the days when Joyce doesn't work. We start later in the morning than we did in the past, but we're still able to get a full day fit in."

"Good for you. It sounds like you will have new students in the spring. A nephew of the Gouds is moving to Oswell City as soon as the snow melts. They have five children." Eva picked up her scissors.

"What are your holiday plans?" Karen asked as she watched Eva work with as much skill as Miss Rose in Chicago.

"My sons and I will have a quiet day resting and exchanging gifts. How about you?" Eva placed the head of a pin in her mouth.

"Logan and I decided to stay in Oswell City over Christmas." Karen pressed her lips together as if working extra hard to keep her mouth closed would prevent Eva from swallowing a pin. How seamstresses dared to hold pins between their teeth, Karen would never know. "I'm concerned the train would make me motion sick. I have to be so careful not to get sick, even when I'm perfectly still. I don't want to take any chances on a swaying train."

"That's wise." Eva thrust a pin into the fabric of the skirt.

"I'm hoping Joyce can help me prepare the extra food for our Christmas dinner."

"Your families are probably disappointed you won't be paying them visits over Christmas." Eva took out the tape to measure again.

"They are. Everyone is so excited about the baby. We'd have such fun talking it over in person, but letters will have to suffice until I feel better." Karen watched shoppers enter Eva's store and browse through the rack of dresses she sewed in her spare time.

"How does this look?" Eva held up the dress for Karen to view.

Eva had expanded the waistline with tasteful tucks of fabric in a complementary shade of the same dark blue as the skirt and bodice. The result looked stylish and modest.

"I like it." Karen nodded.

"All right, then." Eva laid the dress on the counter. "I'll start on it today. It should be ready by tomorrow afternoon."

Karen smiled and left the shop as Eva assisted her shoppers. Nausea, her constant companion, Karen skipped her planned visit to the grocers and went home. Logan would soon arrive for their noon meal anyway. As slow as she moved these days, Karen could use the extra time to prepare the food. As she worked, an idea percolated in her mind. Logan arrived just as she set the table, and she brought it up as they ate.

"I visited with Eva this morning while I was at the dress shop." Karen touched her napkin to her lips.

Logan raised a brow.

"She said her family is staying home by themselves over Christmas. The Van Drunen brothers and their families will likely have similar plans. We are staying in town over the holidays. What would you think of hosting a Christmas dinner at the orchard?"

Logan remained silent for a moment. "I fear it would make too much work for you."

"I could ask Angelien to help me."

"She's expecting a baby, too, and farther into her pregnancy than you are." Logan buttered his bread.

"Maybe both of her sisters-in-law can help, or Eva." Karen leaned over her plate.

"This means a lot to you." Logan glanced at her before taking a bite of bread.

"I guess it does. I hadn't thought about it at all until right before you came home, but I'd like to give it a try." Karen spooned applesauce into her mouth. The one food she could count on keeping down was the sauce she'd made with apples from Lillian Ellenbroek's tree.

"I'll talk with Conrad the first chance I get." Logan smiled at her.

KAREN ATTENDED the Christmas Eve service and managed to lead the singing of the carols. She'd perked up a tiny bit now that she had Joyce's assistance with her work. The improvement in her well-being wasn't substantial, but it provided her with enough energy to resume song leading. For this small change in her health, Karen was grateful. Singing the hymns on Sundays and the carols during the Christmas season increased her patience with her present condition.

The next morning, Logan spent the early hours of Christmas Day lighting a fire in the parlor of the old Akerman home and helping the Van Drunen children string popcorn on the Christmas tree. Karen worked with Angelien and the other women preparing food. Only once did she run outside to get away from the smells. She even managed to keep her breakfast in her stomach, where it belonged.

At noon, the party sat down to a table with enough plates, glasses, and silverware for eighteen people. The meal was delicious, and the company enjoyable. The afternoon was spent before the fire, exchanging simple gifts the women had bought in town the week before.

Mid-afternoon, as Eva's sons had the younger children engaged in a board game, Angelien left the parlor and went to the kitchen to make coffee. Karen followed to offer her help. Instead of reaching for a pan and the coffee grounds, Angelien leaned on the sink for support. A groan left her mouth as she gripped the underside of her belly.

"Angelien?" Karen rushed to her.

She shook her head. "These pains have come off and on all day, but this one is the worst."

"Sit down." Karen pulled a chair out for her from the small table in the corner.

"I didn't want to ruin our fun day together by mentioning my pain, but oh ..." Both of her hands gripped her abdomen as Angelien rocked back and forth in the chair. Beads of sweat broke out on her forehead.

"We need the doctor. Let me get Logan." Karen rushed to the parlor and summoned her husband away from the leisurely conversation the men carried near the fireplace.

Conrad came along.

"Angelien, are you in pain right now?" Logan bent over her.

She scrunched up her face and nodded.

"The baby?" Conrad rested his hand on her shoulder with concern in his eyes.

"It's too early." Angelien doubled over as much as her pregnant form would allow and began to cry.

Karen's heart raced, and her insides tensed. What if Angelien was in labor, and what if the baby came early? A memory from her childhood she'd thought gone from her mind surfaced. A woman in Father's congregation had gone into premature labor. Neither the mother nor the baby survived. The tragedy left a husband and younger children grieving and alone. The same couldn't happen to Angelien and Conrad.

Mother had stayed at the house of the family through the labor.

Karen would do the same. She swallowed back her tears. "Let's get you upstairs, Angelien."

"I'll go for the doctor." Logan hastened into his coat.

Conrad assisted Angelien to a standing position and guided her up the stairs.

Karen went to the parlor to inform everyone of the situation.

"The poor dear," Eva murmured.

Karen gathered Markus and Betje in her lap and offered them reassurance that their mother would be fine. She read them stories to get their minds off of the doctor rushing into the house in a blast of winter air and the screams of pain echoing from a room upstairs.

The little girl turned her face into Karen's blouse and whimpered. The little boy held tight to Karen's arm.

At Eva's prompting, her children joined the men in taking the cousins to the barn. Chores needed to be done, and if Conrad's brothers were astute, they would use up ample time feeding the horses and the dairy cow. Their wives assembled a simple evening meal. Everyone made their best attempt to eat, but no one's thoughts were on the food.

Logan remained upstairs with the doctor and Conrad. Karen should probably be there too, but Angelien's children needed her, so she stayed downstairs and endured the screams with the others.

The night wore on. The dishes were done, the children bedded down in the parlor, and the fires banked. All fell very silent, and then a man's cries, full of agony, tortured the group below.

Karen's eyes filled with tears. Those cries belonged to Conrad. Her pulse thumped in her ears. She could only imagine what those wails might mean.

"Mama! I want to see Mama." Markus stirred from his bed on the floor and began to cry.

"Not now, dear." Karen reached for him. "We must wait for the doctor."

If Karen's worst fears came true, this little boy would never see his mother again. She dragged in a deep breath and tried her best to comfort him.

Footsteps clumped down the stairs bringing Logan into the parlor. His face was void of color. His hair was frayed all over his forehead, and his eyes were haunted.

Karen's stomach lurched at the sight of him. Something terrible must truly have happened.

"Angelien is gone. She died giving birth to Conrad's daughter. The baby died too." Logan's voice turned deep and scratchy as if he wanted to cry and wail right along with Conrad.

The announcement pierced Karen's chest with a sharp pain. The news couldn't be true. Her friend, vibrant and smiling at the Christmas dinner, couldn't be dead. Taken from them on a day of celebration at a moment when she should be welcoming a new life into her family.

Karen covered her eyes. She wanted nothing more than to fling herself onto her bed and weep. Logan gave Karen a quick glance that shattered her heart with the sorrow reflected in it. He left the house. Moments later, she heard the sleigh runners on the snow. As the pastor, Logan had likely been assigned the grievous task of fetching the undertaker.

"The doctor might need help cleaning up." One of Conrad's sisters-in-law left her place on the sofa. With a sob, she hurried upstairs.

Karen gathered Angelien's surviving children into her arms. Someone must help them understand how Logan's announcement affected them. She fought the news with everything in her, but the sooner they absorbed the truth, the better they could adjust to life with only their father.

"Markus, Betje. Listen very carefully because I must tell you something." Karen gulped in air.

"Is it about Mama?" Four-year-old Markus watched Karen.

"It is, dear." She stroked his brown hair.

"Mama." Two-year-old Betje echoed her brother and pointed at the ceiling.

Tears blurred Karen's vision. This task of explaining cold facts to little hearts was proving to be harder than she expected. Maybe she wouldn't accomplish it.

"Your mother isn't upstairs any longer."

"She isn't?" Markus asked with wide eyes.

Karen shook her head.

"Jesus came to get her and take her to heaven." Karen wiped one of her eyes.

Confusion settled onto Markus's features.

Karen swallowed. "You remember hearing Pastor De Witt talking at church about the special homes God has prepared for his children in heaven?"

Markus nodded.

"That is where your mother is now. With Jesus in her special home." Karen couldn't bring herself to tell the children about the baby sister who they'd never meet. Maybe someday Conrad would choose to tell them this part of the story. If Karen attempted it now, she'd cry so hard, no one would understand her words.

"Jesus. Home." Betje echoed Karen as if she understood.

"Where's Papa?" Markus looked around. "Did he go to heaven too?"

A smile tugged at Karen's mouth. "No, dear. You'll see him again soon."

Logan returned. A man in dark clothing brushed with snow followed him upstairs. The other sister-in-law wept. Eva sniffled and wiped her eyes with her handkerchief.

After a short while, Logan came to the parlor and sought out Karen. His eyes were watery and rimmed in red.

She gazed at him through her own tears.

"Karen," he said in a low voice. "I've talked with Conrad. You and I are taking the children home with us until further notice. He's still upstairs with the doctor. The two of them are in for a long night."

Karen nodded and turned to the children. "Come. You are both going home with me tonight. We'll have cookies and milk. You can sleep in our nice, cozy spare room. How does that sound?"

Markus reached to hold her hand, and Betje buried her face in Karen's shoulder.

She went in search of the children's coats, pulled together enough frame of mind to pack a bag with their clothing, and led them out of the house behind Logan.

TWO DAYS LATER, Karen watched as he conducted the funeral. A somber congregation gathered to pay respects to the stricken husband. Logan preached a meaningful sermon and said all the right words at the gravesite, but Karen could see he was barely holding himself together. She wanted nothing more than to take him home with her, where they might be alone so she could comfort him.

But a luncheon must get eaten at the church first. After that, dozens of people would require his attention, seeking from him their own solace and comfort.

Karen took Markus and Betje home with her. The little girl fell asleep, so Karen laid her on the spare room bed. Markus agreed to sit in a chair at the dining room table and drink a cup of milk Karen warmed on the stove for him.

Near the supper hour, Logan came home. He laid his leather-covered Bible on the desk and took off his black coat. Underneath, he wore his crisp white shirt and tie with his well-tailored black suit. His blond hair had managed to stay perfectly in place in spite of the wind blowing at the cemetery. His spectacles rested on the bridge of his nose, reinforcing his studious and wise demeanor.

Karen's heart swelled. Heroes, according to the world, were soldiers in the army, cowboys who wrangled rugged beasts, or men of valor and undaunted courage. But Oswell City's true hero stood right here in her dining room. Logan De Witt was truly a man of valor and courage. He'd stood by a town full of grieving people while feeling deep pain himself.

In the hour when he'd needed his greatest amount of solace, he'd freely offered it to others. He'd never believe her if she were to share with him these thoughts in her heart, so instead of relying on inadequate words to express her love for him, she wrapped her arms around his neck.

He gathered her close and held her in silence for a long

while. When the meal was ready, Logan took his seat at the table and ate enough food to lead Karen to believe he found comfort just in being home and sharing this meal with her. She did her best to eat in spite of her finicky appetite as a way to show him support.

Not until Betje and Markus were asleep for the night did Karen have the chance to talk the day over with him.

"That funeral was the hardest thing I've ever done." Logan's jaw worked as though tears were ready to fall. "The coffin lowered into the ground containing his wife and child. I don't know how Conrad is going to stand it. I don't know how he's ever going to stand it!"

Karen could do nothing except listen. His strong emotion paralyzed her.

"Oh, Karen." Her name came out on a moan as Logan leaned over. With his elbows on his knees, he held his head in his hands. "The night Angelien died, there was so much blood. So very much blood. I've never seen anything so terrible."

Karen swallowed against her own tears.

"I don't know what I'd do if that had been you and our baby." Logan turned to her and placed both of his hands on her expanding abdomen. "It would kill me. It would just kill me. I wish someone could make a promise to me that I won't lose you like Conrad lost Angelien." Tears dampened his cheeks, and his voice trembled.

Karen could think of nothing to say. The events of the past days had frightened her as much as they had her husband.

"I'll always love you, Logan, even if death should part us. It won't stop me from loving you." Her words sounded thin and insufficient, but they were the best she could do. Each day of their marriage had become a new revelation of the depths of Logan's love for her. She strived daily to demonstrate her love for him and wanted more than anything at this moment to offer the right word or the best display of affection to ease his anguish. But she had nothing.

All she could manage was silence. Her heart was too busy marveling over the crevice his worry opened before her. The revelation allowed her a glimpse deep, deep down into the heart of her husband. His tears, his wish for a promise, confirmed that yes, she definitely was married to a man with a heart that rivaled the size of the vast Grand Canyon.

Every new day that dawned provided her with yet another opportunity to hold that spacious heart in her hands and care for it with delicate and tender strokes. She'd do all she could to ease his fears and help him find peace on this bitter winter night as well as in the weeks to come.

Their own baby would arrive in the world safe and healthy. She would survive the birth and live to share many happy years with Logan. She had to believe that, and so must her husband. There was no space in this difficult pregnancy for doubt and fear.

"Pray with me."

Karen reached for his hand. Together they went to the One who held their lives and their future.

Logan settled his head on her shoulder and let her do the talking as she poured out their concern before the Lord. He echoed her "amen" when she finished, but Karen saw the worry still present in his eyes. It told her that the prayer would swirl in his heart until the day came when he held both his wife and a new baby safely in his arms.

28

"Pastor Logan?"

Logan looked up from the notes spread across his desk to find Clara Hesslinga standing in his doorway and wrapped in a woolen shawl.

"Nellie is sick. Dr. Kaldenburg is at my house already. We'd like for you to come too." She wiped one of her eyes. The moisture may have come from the stinging cold morning, but was more likely from whatever situation had developed at her home.

Logan left his studies, threw on his coat, and followed her from the church.

Florence opened the door for them and led Logan down the hall while her aunt removed her winter wraps.

Nellie lay in her bed and gave faint responses to the doctor's questions. He bent over her as he moved his stethoscope over her chest.

When he noticed Logan, he straightened and announced, "She's suffered a heart attack. Her pulse is still regular, but weak."

Logan swallowed the lump in his throat. He'd grown attached

to the crotchety little woman over the past months. This news made his throat ache.

He stepped into the room and laid a comforting hand on her forehead. "Nellie?"

She glanced up at him. "Oh, Pastor. I'm so glad you came."

Logan managed to smile.

Dr. Kaldenburg turned to Clara, who by this time had joined the others at Nellie's bedside. "I've given her medicine for the pain. Keep her as comfortable as you can. I'll come back later this afternoon and check on her."

"Yes, Doctor." Clara nodded.

With a brief smile at Logan, Dr. Kaldenburg left.

"Sorry you're so ill, Nellie." Logan settled into a chair near the bed. "Can you tell me what happened?"

Several moments of silence passed. "I woke up around six with a terrible pain in my chest that made me break out in a sweat. That's really all it was, but the pain didn't go away. I had trouble breathing, so Clara called the doctor."

"You had quite a scare. Do you have pain now?" Logan held her hand.

She sighed. "I would if the doctor hadn't given me that medicine."

"Try and get some rest. You're a tough little lady. I'm sure you will feel better soon. You've had difficult things happen to you before, but you've pulled through." Logan gave her a smile.

Nellie patted his hand as if he was the one in need of comfort. "You better know it."

Logan chuckled. "May I pray with you?"

"If you want to." The same words Nellie always used to answer that question came with more interest than they had in the past.

He offered a prayer for strength and freedom from pain.

"Could you please tell her family? They need to know what happened." Clara's eyes pleaded with him.

"I'd be happy to." Logan left the house, went home to inform

Karen, and then saddled his horse for the chilly ride to Fred's farm.

LATER THAT AFTERNOON, Logan took a break from his study to turn his attention to the vacancy Angelien's death had left at the orchard. Her absence from this world, from her family, and from her job still stunned him. Their Christmas Day celebrations had begun with such joy, such anticipation of the meaning of the day and time spent together, but had ended in tragedy.

The reality of Angelien's death took his breath away. Her children had lost their mother and baby sister. Conrad had lost his wife and child. Logan's heart clenched every time he thought of Conrad.

With his sorrow came fear. Deep, terrifying fear. What had happened to Conrad could happen to him. Karen could die in childbirth. Nothing guaranteed a happy ending. Some women survived, and some didn't. These were the cold facts, and Logan must prepare for any outcome. And yet, he couldn't pretend.

If he were to lose Karen, part of him would die too. And if, like Conrad, he lost his wife and his child, his heart would get crushed beyond his ability to focus on preaching sermons. A loss of Karen and their baby would mean the destruction of his entire life. Like the thieves that stole a harvest from the orchard right under his nose, the foxes of death and tragedy could invade his orchard of love and steal his wife and child away from him, leaving him powerless to prevent the destruction.

Logan shook his head. He must pull himself out of these melancholy thoughts. Nothing had happened to him. Karen was alive and perking up, thanks to Joyce's consistent presence in the kitchen. Her pregnancy seemed normal, according to Dr. Kaldenburg's assessments. Logan was blessed, and he must remember that truth instead of dwelling on his worry.

Four more months and this would all be behind him. Karen's

health would be restored, and she'd have delivered a healthy son or daughter. He must believe that. He must, or another kind of fox, the one of fear, would invade every area of his life and interfere with even his most basic ability to function.

To clear his mind, Logan stood and walked a few laps around the sanctuary. He returned to his desk and pulled out the list of names the consistory had compiled at their last meeting. Several of the potential candidates for the position as Angelien's replacement looked promising. A couple of the women were younger, with small children at home. Others were older, who might welcome a job to fill their days.

Logan bundled into his coat once more and took the list with him to make calls on the ladies named there. But first, he must stop in on Conrad. The man and his two children had returned to their own home. One of Conrad's brothers, along with his family, had moved in with Conrad after the holidays so the grieving father wouldn't be alone, and so a sister-in-law could do the household tasks Angelien had performed.

If Conrad felt anything like Logan did about the loss of Angelien, he'd welcome a visit.

LOGAN BREATHED a sigh of relief when Lester Brinks' wife took the position as housekeeper and cook at the orchard. A capable, efficient woman, she had much experience with all the tasks required to keep the house and orchard functioning smoothly. She did not possess the knowledge of broom making, but the production of apple cider came naturally. The steady gain in profit the farm had just begun to enjoy was sure to continue under Mrs. Brinks' management.

Nellie Akerman managed to linger for a week in her feeble condition. At two-thirty in the morning, a firm knock awakened Logan from his sleep. Clara had once again come looking for him. He dressed and walked the snowy distance to her house, where he found Nellie pale and motionless in her bed. Perhaps she was already gone, and he'd missed his chance to offer her one more consolation.

She opened an eye and peeked at him. With tired movements, she beckoned him to her bedside. Clara rushed past him while a sob escaped from her lips, even though she tried to hold it back with her handkerchief. The door creaked in her wake until a small gap remained, offering him a glimpse of the hall.

They were alone in the lamp-illumined sick room.

Nellie's veined hand covered with paper-thin skin rose from the quilt that covered her and fell onto his arm. "I'll miss you, Pastor Logan. Even the lights and glory of heaven won't outshine what you've given me."

Logan swallowed the lump in his throat. She'd given him quite a bit too. From a slap on the cheek during their first meeting to the perfect Christmas gift for his new bride, his relationship with Nellie Akreman had been filled with unexpected displays of her persevering character.

She'd shaped him by helping him grow a little more rugged in those places on his insides where he'd find it easier some days to give up than to continue his frail attempts to fight the good fight.

"But, the time has come for me to surrender. I'm still going to come out the winner, you know." A bit of the old steel edged her voice.

"You've never lost at anything, Nellie Akerman." His voice went low to match his contemplative mood. He didn't want to lose at anything, either. Ever. If he possessed even half the courage of this dying woman, he could change the world.

A self-satisfied smile crossed her lips, and they sat in silence for a while.

"Fred will hang the sword in the house at the orchard. He'll be talking to you about it. I hope you don't mind." Nellie's feeble voice carried through the quiet room.

"No. Your house on the farm is the perfect place for it." Like Nellie, many of the guests staying in her donated house had fought and overcome their own battles. Surviving the trip to a new country and starting a new life required as much courage as signing up to fight in a war. The sword would serve as a fitting reminder that victory was never very far away.

Nellie looked at him. "I've seen you with your new wife. She's expecting your baby, isn't she?"

Logan nodded. Nellie must have missed the service on the Sunday he'd made the announcement, or maybe her other ailments stole a bit of her memory. The town had grown just as excited about the coming baby as they had about his wedding. How the sensation had failed to reach into Nellie's living quarters, he couldn't imagine.

"Hang onto love, Pastor Logan. Don't let anything steal it away from you." Spoken like a true warrior, Nellie had learned what was most worth fighting for.

It was the one battle she still waged, but only for a little while longer. Her arrival in heaven would secure all victories.

"Well spoken, Nellie." He patted her hand. "Thank you." If he could just figure out how to guarantee a safe delivery for Karen, he could assure Nellie he'd take her words seriously.

"Nothing can separate me from God's love." She turned away from him and stared at the shadowed ceiling. "Not trouble or hardship. Not danger or the sword."

The room quieted. Logan glanced over at Nellie. She no longer breathed. Her eyes were wide open.

She smiled.

Joy. Victory. Logan's heart exploded. The results of it trickled down his cheeks in streams flowing from his eyes. Another person he cared about had left this world. Sorrow and celebration danced together. He pulled the quilt over her face and left the room to find the appropriate people with whom to share the news.

SUNDAY MORNING, Logan sat in his chair to the side of the pulpit as Karen led the singing. He tried to sing along, but grew distracted, as usual, by the vision of his wife in her Sunday dress. No longer could it conceal her expanding waistline. The image really shouldn't delight him as much as it did. The congregation would declare him a fool, smiling as he was, while the rest of them sang about the more sober subject of confession and petitioning the Lord for his mercy.

Logan cleared his throat and attempted to sing his own request for mercy. If Karen's delivery didn't go as he hoped, he'd need all the mercy the Lord was willing to give him just to survive from one day to the next.

Karen ended the song. He prayed and offered the benediction. She went with him to greet people on their way out of the sanctuary but returned home to finish preparations on their noon meal while Logan spent time in his study, putting books away and hanging up his robe.

"Logan." The soft voice filtered through the room and teased his ears.

He turned to find Florence standing in his doorway. A weight settled on his chest. Surely the scene from the summer one-and-a-half years ago wasn't about to be repeated. Not here in an empty church building with his wife at home waiting for him.

She sashayed to his desk and sat on the corner of it.

If he dared to hold his head in his hands at this moment and groan, he would take full advantage of the opportunity. Instead, he asked the question he asked everyone who visited.

"What can I do for you?" He nearly choked.

Florence gave him a demure smile. "A girl could make good use of those words. You always knew just what to say to turn me into a pushover."

Logan's face heated. He'd never said anything to her other than what was required, according to the apostle Paul, for building one another up. Any flame of interest he might have felt for her had been extinguished long ago.

"But you and I are over, Logan." She stood.

Air rushed out of his lungs. Florence had finally caught on to what he'd been trying to tell her since her arrival in town.

"I came to ask ... well, to ask ..." She rubbed her hands together.

Logan waited.

"You're still my pastor, and I ... well. I need you to tell me if I'm saved." She ventured a glance at him.

His eyes were bugging out. He just knew it. But what else could a fellow do when the one person in town he tried his best to avoid came in seeking his advice on the weighty subject?

"Sit down." He dragged in a deep breath and gestured to one of the chairs, not the corner of his desk.

Florence behaved herself and claimed a chair.

"What has caused you to question your eternal state?" Logan settled into his chair. With the desk between them, he should be able to keep Florence at a safe enough distance to carry on a reasonable conversation.

"Mick has proposed. He wants to marry me." A smile tugged on her mouth.

"What do you want to do?" The inexperienced Mick sure had come a long way, and he'd taken a decent amount of time learning how to secure the affections of a woman like Florence. Logan hid his own smile.

"A fresh start would be nice. Reuben, he ... um ...he caused me much pain, and I ..." Her voice trailed off, and her eyes filled with tears.

Logan fished in his pocket for his handkerchief and gave it to her. "Do you think you could stay faithful to Mick?"

"Of course, I could." Florence's attention rushed back to Logan. "He's a lot like you, Logan. Steady. Caring. He has boatloads of friends. I know I'll be very happy with him."

If a contest happened to be running at the moment, then

Florence would win the prize for knowing what to say to turn him into a pushover. To think all these years, she'd held him up as her standard for how a man should act. He'd do whatever it took to restore her faith in herself and in the Lord. Logan flipped through the gospels to find passages that would refresh her on the message of salvation.

With tears in her eyes, Florence apologized for her unfair expectations of him since her arrival in town. Holding her hands in his, Logan led her through the prayer of rededication until Florence's heart belonged solely to her Lord and not to her unfulfilled wishes.

She hugged him and went home. Logan locked the church and made his way across the lawn to the parsonage. He walked a little taller and stood a little straighter. Freedom snipped the last thin strand that held Florence to him. Nellie would be proud. He'd fought the battle and won. Not only should a fellow hang onto love, but sometimes he needed to discover the best kind of love to hang on to.

29

"You want me to do what?" Karen failed to prevent horror from raising her voice. It probably screamed from the expression that crinkled her face as she stared at her husband. Logan, for sure, had gone crazy.

He reached across the lace tablecloth and grasped her hand. The gentle circular motion of his thumb on the back of her hand was probably intended to soothe her, but her heart raced too fast for the simple caress to do any good.

"Karen, this isn't as bad as you think." A bit of humor twinkled in his eyes. "All I'm in need of is one bridesmaid. Florence doesn't have any friends from her single days living in Oswell City. They are all married with families of their own and settled in other parts of the country.

"She and Mick want a small gathering for their wedding service. Mick's brother is standing up with him, and, well, given my longtime friendship with the bride as well as the fact that I'm conducting the service, it makes sense that you would participate too."

Karen would do about anything to ensure that Florence Hesslinga was good and married to anyone, giving the girl a reason to put an end to her relationship with Logan.

"I've observed over the winter months that Florence's attentions had gradually shifted onto Mick, but that didn't stop her from throwing an occasional longing glance your direction. I'm glad you never returned it. Did you even notice?"

Her presence in town had taught the younger women Logan was no longer an eligible bachelor. She'd even made friends with many of them. But Florence remained attached to him somehow. If standing up at the wedding was what it took to break that bond, she'd agree to Logan's request.

A smile, full of understanding, crossed his face. "Karen, sweetheart. Florence means nothing to me. She was Pete's idea from the beginning. I bored her and didn't buy gifts that were expensive enough to please her."

Logan sounded sincere. She could accept what he was saying as the full and precise truth.

"Something you have to remember is how much you've changed my life. I didn't expect to marry, but God had other plans. Those plans included you, and they were better plans than Pete or Florence or anyone else could have designed for me."

Karen bit her lip as she listened. When he finished speaking, she nodded in understanding and agreement.

"Stand up in this wedding with me. Let's show Florence that you and I will always belong together." Logan caressed the back of her hand again.

His proposal sounded reasonable, but a clear obstacle hindered her comfort level with these plans.

"You know I can't do that." She rose from her chair and gestured at her figure. "Just look at me."

Logan's gaze left her face and moved over her profile, taking in her bodice stretched to its limits over her changing shape and the skirt flowing in ripples around the baby growing within her. The term *waistline* belonged to another life. If Karen ever saw it again, she'd never waver in her belief of miracles. But her shape these days contradicted any hint of the stylish form that normally defined her figure.

The humor in her husband's eyes spread to his mouth. A smile stretched his lips while he studied her.

Karen flushed and scrambled back into her seat as much as her swelled middle would allow. She should have learned by now that Logan's response to her pregnant form had yet to match her own.

"I believe Florence is using dark colors in her wedding." He cleared his throat. "You could probably get by with wearing your navy blue dress. And besides, you'll be with me."

The light in his eyes told her he felt quite proud of the fact. Her cheeks heated even more. He went to the kitchen for a refill of his coffee cup and returned with the stack of mail from the desk. He slit envelopes and read the contents while Karen cleared the table.

"Oh, my goodness."

Logan's whispered words reached Karen's ears as she pulled a dishtowel from the drawer.

"What is it?" She returned to the table.

Logan read the letter in his hand with awe present on his face. "At those meetings Pete and I attended last fall, I mentioned our ministry in the orchard to the others. One of those men is a professor at a nearby college. He has asked me to come speak about it to the students in chapel."

"Will you do it?" Warmth spread through Karen's chest.

He glanced up from the letter. His attention settled on the widest part of Karen's body. "Not sure I should travel right now. It's not a good idea to leave you home alone."

Karen settled into a chair. "I think you should go."

His eyes held a question.

"The experience you've gained would help others." She clasped his hand.

Logan's mouth scrunched to one side of his face as he considered her words. "I could travel there and back in two days, which means I'd only be gone one night." His face lightened with a sudden idea. "Maybe you'd like to come with me."

She wrinkled her nose at Logan as if he was still crazy. Standing up in front of her own Oswell City congregation eight months pregnant was something she could get used to, but venturing out among strangers and so obviously with child would make her uncomfortable.

Not to mention her stomach's unpredictable response to the strain of travel. Her nausea had improved a little, but not enough to guarantee she'd last through a long buggy ride and important meetings. No, she'd better stay home. She pushed away from the table with a vigorous shake of her head.

"Just thought I'd check. It would be fun to have you along. You'd have the chance to talk about your classroom at the orchard."

"Maybe another time. If you're offered more invitations after the baby comes, then I'll join you."

Logan nodded with a smile and a wink. He stood, placed a kiss on her temple, and returned to his study at the church for the remainder of the afternoon.

He made plans to travel to the nearby academy, and was quite solicitous in the provisions he made for her in his absence. The first day would be spent with Joyce completing the baking. Paul was put on alert to tend to anything Karen needed. She read the concern in Logan's eyes as he rushed about between church and home, gathering notes and making arrangements for her. Nothing could possibly go wrong while Logan was away. He'd looked after everything so well.

LOGAN RESISTED one last glance over his shoulder of the home he shared with Karen. She'd gone inside by now anyway. He turned his attention to the street and waved at Joyce as she followed the sidewalk to the parsonage to assist Karen with her baking. He sucked in a deep breath. Karen should get along just fine until tomorrow when he returned to town.

He directed the horse to the west and attempted to shift his attention to the speech he would give that afternoon. His mind stubbornly stayed focused on his wife. Never had he dreamed marriage would be so enjoyable, so perfect for him. Maybe the pleasure came as a result of having Karen as the woman who was his wife.

Some truth might exist in that thought. Marriage to her was better than marriage to anyone else. Karen had become the center of his whole world. Every decision he made, every action lived out was done with her mind. Karen had become a part of him in ways he'd never even known were possible.

And now they were having a child together. Even without the help of his spectacles, Logan could see what lay ahead of him. Not just on the road he traveled this morning, but on the journey he and Karen shared. Their future held promise. The dreams God had spoken into Logan's heart long ago were taking shape. A wife, family, and fruitful ministry in a town full of people who loved him were his gifts to Logan.

After hoping and waiting through seasons of grief and impossibilities, Logan had now arrived in a place of revelation. The view that broke forth before him brought deep satisfaction and gratitude. He recalled the Psalms sung in last week's church service and hummed the melodies all the way to his destination.

"Greetings, Pastor De Witt. Thank you for making the trip to join us today." Dr. Blake, the college president, met him at the grand, two-story brick building housing the college.

"My pleasure. I'm honored that you invited me." Logan followed Dr. Blake across the street to a stone church building where the student body gathered for chapel services every afternoon.

"Good afternoon." Logan addressed the student body and then shared his message at the proper place in the service. "I've been invited here today to share with you about the unexpected ministry God has given us. We help new residents in our town who have immigrated to Iowa from Europe."

The students listened with full attention. Many of them asked thoughtful questions afterward. Logan did his best to answer them, and then he met with a group, including the president, other professors, and the colleague who had invited him for dinner at the local restaurant.

Low clouds, heavy with rain, gathered and sent out bolts of lightning during the meal. Logan entered the hotel just as great booms of thunder rattled doors and picture frames. He removed his suit coat and tie and then settled in to read a book he'd brought along as rain poured from the sky. The storm continued through the night. He made his best effort to sleep in spite of the lightning flashes and thunder rumbles, but his thoughts stayed fixed on Karen.

Tonight was the first they had been apart since the day he married her, and Logan chafed at the separation. If only he could be at home tonight, shielding her from the noise and danger of a storm.

The rain continued through the next morning. Puddles in the road and muddy tracks slowed Logan's return trip by a considerable rate. He stopped for a brief lunch at a café in a town hardly half-way on the route. A long and slow afternoon of travel lay ahead.

By four o'clock, storm clouds redeveloped and hung low over the buggy's roof. The wind rose, so Logan guided the horse and buggy into a field along the road and waited out the gusts in an abandoned shed. Hail joined the pounding rain and piled in the doorway. Logan pulled his coat tighter about him and soothed his horse with an apple from the feed supply under the buggy's seat.

Thank goodness he'd sought shelter from the wind when he did, or the feed would have become soaked and ruined. For the next hour, thunder boomed, and rain poured. The afternoon light, already dimmed by the clouds, faded to evening. He must get home as soon as possible. Karen was probably worried about him. Under dry weather conditions, he would have arrived in Oswell City by now.

Logan poked his head outside. The wind had calmed, but rain still fell. If he didn't want to spend the night in this shed, he must return to the road. Any effort he made brought him closer to Karen, and that was what mattered.

He backed the horse and buggy into the field and walked them along the fence to the road. His shoes soaked and caked with mud, Logan slipped on the narrow step as he climbed into the buggy. He rubbed his shin a brief moment where his leg scraped the step and tried again. This time he succeeded. The rain streamed from the buggy roof and into rivers at the side of the road while Logan guided the horse toward his home.

Waves of water rushed downhill, flattening the grass in the ditches. Puddles filled patches of the road. Creeks swelled and overflowed their banks. Still, Logan traveled on. Darkness overcame the last bit of light in the sky as he reached the edge of town.

Water flooded Main Street and blocked passage. He turned down an alternate street and approached the parsonage from a different direction. Lamplight glowed in the windows, inviting him into the warmth. He'd been wet for hours. His feet and nose were cold. His fingers were numb in their grip of the reins.

He rounded the corner and drove the horse into the small barn behind the church. After unhitching the buggy and forking hay into the manger, Logan closed the door and sprinted to the house. Since his shoes carried so much mud, he avoided the front door. Karen would probably appreciate his effort to protect the clean front hall from mud. He turned the knob of the back door and burst into the kitchen.

Karen stood at the sink. She whirled around and caught sight of him. "Logan!" Her eyes went wide, and her hands flew to her cheeks. "You're drenched."

He looked down at his sodden clothing. Water dripped to the floor.

"We have to get you dry." She hastened from the room and soon returned with a stack of towels. Her hand rested on his neck, his forehead, and then one of his own hands. "You're freezing. Oh, dear. I hope you don't get sick. Go undress by the stove."

He shivered and slipped out of his shoes while Karen took his hat and peeled off his coat. She tugged him over to the rug before the stove and helped him unbutton his shirt.

He sneezed.

Karen gave him an anxious gaze and moved even faster to help him get out of his wet clothes. "Go to bed, Logan. Get warm. I'll bring you the supper I kept for you and a cup of coffee."

He turned away and inhaled the scents and comforts of home. What a perfect welcome, to have Karen fussing over him. How she must have worried as the day turned to evening with no sign of his arrival. He reached their bedroom and lost no time in following his wife's directions.

In that moment, his wife did a much better job taking care of him than he'd done taking care of her. After some rest, he'd resume his efforts to protect and shield Karen, giving her the best support he had to offer.

30

Karen stood at the back of the sanctuary and listened to the organ music's soft strains. Clara fluttered around Florence, adjusting her veil and smoothing the train of her dress. A man, Florence's father, perhaps, stepped closer and offered the bride his arm.

Clara glanced at Karen. "It's your turn now, Mrs. De Witt. We're ready."

Karen nodded and walked down the aisle to where Logan stood arrayed in his black robe, holding his Bible and wearing a smile meant just for her. He held his hand to his mouth and coughed.

True to her worst fears, Logan had developed a severe cold that settled in his chest. The cough still persisted. So did the damp weather. Rain fell again today, adding more water to the flooded rivers and streams in the area. Karen wanted to prepare the soil in her garden for another planting of vegetables, but the ground was too saturated.

She shifted her thoughts back to the wedding and concentrated on completing her journey to the front. Her legs ached. Her waistline stretched so far in front of her that she'd probably fill an entire doorway if she'd been required to pass through one. At least her dress covered all of her frame. She couldn't imagine how many yards of material Eva must have used in this gown's recent alteration.

Karen held her bouquet of white flowers a little higher. They may not help much in covering her swelled front, but they might offer an onlooker a bit of distraction from her pregnant form. Only for Logan would she agree to stand up in a wedding less than four weeks away from her due date.

He winked at her as she passed by him to her assigned place. A smile tugged at her lips, but a sharp pain around her middle forced it into retreat. Karen gritted her teeth and willed her attention onto the bride, who stood at the back of the church waiting to make her entrance.

Logan raised his hands, prompting the guests to stand. Another pain attacked Karen's middle. It lasted through Florence's walk down the aisle and didn't subside until Mick led Florence to stand before Logan.

A few brief minutes passed before another pain wrapped around her. She clenched her teeth to refrain from clutching her abdomen. Surely the pain would go away soon. If only she could sit down and ease her achy legs. But an entire wedding service stretched before her, and she must continue standing. She mustn't draw attention away from the bride and groom. Karen bit her lip and held her breath through each episode of pain.

Finally, Logan told Mick to kiss his bride. Karen could hang on a few more minutes. She had to. The bride and groom left the platform, and then the best man escorted Karen. She'd survived. In as much haste as her achy legs allowed, Karen went to Logan's study and collapsed into a chair.

He arrived moments later and knelt beside her. "Karen?"

"I need to go home." She rubbed her forehead. "No one will miss me at the reception, will they?"

"No, of course not." Logan's anxious gaze moved over her. "What's wrong? Do you have a headache? Are you feeling sick again?" He stood up and continued to study her.

"No. My abdomen, it just—" Karen grasped her sides as a sharp pain once again took hold of her.

"I wish we could call Dr. Kaldenburg, but I found out this afternoon that he's stranded on a farm south of town." Logan ran his hand through his hair.

Karen's eyes widened. "What?"

"Yeah. He left yesterday afternoon to make a house call, but the bridge got washed out overnight. Now he can't get back to town."

"I shouldn't need him, anyway." Karen attempted to straighten. "I just had an appointment with him a few days ago. If I go home and lie down for a while, I should feel fine."

Logan eyed her with concern. "Are you sure?"

She nodded.

"Do you need any help getting to the house?"

"No." Karen shook her head. "I'll take my time. It's not that far. You have to be at the reception anyway."

Logan's mouth flattened into a line that betrayed his doubt. "Let me at least help you stand. I'll cut my time at the reception a little short and come home soon."

She nodded and accepted his offered hand. Once she got to her feet, Logan wrapped an arm around her and assisted her out the door.

"I'm fine." She looked at him and gave him a faint smile.

"See you later." The concern left his eyes, and his features softened as he watched her leave.

Karen picked her way across the soggy lawn. Rain streamed from the gray clouds overhead. Droplets dampened her hair and trickled down her back, but she crept with caution. One slip on a muddy patch, and she would never be able to get back on her feet again.

She reached the house and went inside. Another pain came so quickly and lasted so long she doubled over and sank onto the sofa. Drawing in deep breaths, Karen calculated the distance to the bedroom. She must lie down. But first, she must get out of this dress and into her nightgown. Karen pushed off the sofa and steadied herself. She crossed the parlor and reached the bedroom doorway as another pain, stronger than the others, gripped her body.

LOGAN WATCHED Karen journey across the lawn. How he'd love to break out of the church and stay at home with her, but he had to attend the reception. Mick and Florence had requested that he meet their parents. That shouldn't take too long. He'd mingle long enough to eat a piece of cake. As soon as he finished it, he'd slip out and go home.

When he saw Karen disappear into the house, Logan hung up his robe and joined the party.

Florence saw him first and gave him a hug. "Thank you for the service. It was lovely."

Mick shook Logan's hand when Florence finished with her hugging. The couple led him to the cluster of folks gathered around Florence's mother and father. Someone handed him a plate with a slice of cake on it. He took it with him when Mick led him to meet his parents. Logan shook hands, smiled, and offered the best responses to the conversation he could think of, but his mind stayed stuck on Karen.

She could be in real trouble. The look on her face resembled too much the expression Angelien wore the night she died. Logan's pulse raced. He faded out of the conversation swirling around him, downed the last bites of cake, and left the gathering. As soon as he arrived in the wide outdoors, he sprinted to the house.

He found Karen seated on the floor and slumped against the parlor wall. Pain strained her voice.

"Karen?" He asked as tremors shook his whole body. "What happened? What's wrong?" He knelt beside her and clasped her shoulder.

"I—I'm in labor, Logan. Help me to bed." She gritted her teeth and squeezed her eyes shut.

"Karen, sweetheart." Logan's mouth went dry. "You can't be in labor. It's too early."

"Tell that to the baby." Karen clutched her sides and groaned.

He must do something. No way would he lose Karen and their child to the disaster of an early birth. If only he knew how to prevent a child's entrance into the world. Their son or daughter must stay put a few weeks longer. Babies should understand that an early appearance meant the death of their mother.

Logan brushed strands of hair away from Karen's face. "You need to get comfortable. Let's get you out of this dress."

He scooped her up with great care and set her on the side of the bed. Logan unbuttoned the row of buttons down her back and eased her dress off her shoulders.

Karen took care of the remaining layers of undergarments while Logan retrieved her nightgown from the closet. She slipped it over her head as another pain stiffened her.

"What can I do?" He held his breath as she doubled over.

Karen wagged her finger at her pillow.

He pulled the covers back and propped her up on her pillow as well as another one borrowed from his side of the bed. A deep breath of air left her lungs as if her new location brought a great sense of relief.

"Please check the baby. I'll tell you how to do it." Karen instructed him through the steps Dr. Kaldenburg had followed in her last appointment.

He reported his findings, which brought a bright smile to Karen's lips.

"The baby is definitely on its way. With no doctor in town tonight, you will have to deliver it, Logan."

Her announcement stole his breath, and dizziness assaulted him. Deliver a baby! He'd delivered plenty of sermons in his life, and he'd even delivered a bouquet of flowers to the banker's wife on behalf of her sister when she'd been in the hospital, but never had he delivered a baby.

This was their baby Karen talked about. He or she deserved a proper welcome into the world. Logan didn't know the first thing about medical procedures, especially delivering a baby. Logan shook his head to clear it. Karen was speaking. He must tune in and try to catch as many of her words as possible.

"... the towels from the water closet. I washed them yesterday. Bring those here." She scrunched her eyes shut while another pain stiffened her body. After the pain passed, she inhaled. "Build a fire in the stove and start boiling water. You will need it for sterilization and cleansing."

Logan took off on a run, shedding his suit coat and tie as he went. The white shirt for sure had to go. He'd learned of the amount of blood that accompanied a birth from Angelien's experience. A white shirt was of no help in the delivery room.

He stripped it off, leaving only his lighter-weight undershirt to catch the stains. How the doctor managed to stay clean during an emergency, Logan couldn't fathom. But he wasn't the doctor with a professional medical reputation to maintain, and this situation could get messy.

In the kitchen, he set to work at the stove, heating water and rounding up towels. He returned to the bedroom right as a scream ripped from Karen's mouth. In a rush, he moved to her side.

"That was so bad," she panted several moments later.

For the next several hours, Karen endured increasing levels of pain. Logan gravitated from her side to the window where lightning flashed, wind blew, and rain poured. The occasional rumble of thunder echoed across the sky. The doctor would not be returning to town anytime soon. Logan drew in a deep breath. This job of bringing his child into the world belonged to him, whether he'd asked for it or not.

Another scream from Karen brought him away from the window. He held her around her shoulders as he had through the previous pain, but this time it didn't go away. Karen writhed in pain and screamed by turn. He left her side to check on her progress. The very top of a tiny, dark-haired head met his gaze. His heart leaped into his throat.

"Keep going, Karen!" He held out his hands, ready to catch the newborn that would slide into the world at any minute.

Karen screamed, and her whole body tensed. A little face, red and wrinkled, appeared.

"One more time! Do that one more time." Logan yelled out over her screams.

She followed his direction. A baby boy slipped into Logan's hands.

"It's a boy, Karen. We have a boy!" Giddiness shook his voice. He was a father. He had a son. A surge of love flooded his heart as he looked at the infant in his hands.

"Get the scissors. Cut the cord." Karen's voice sounded like she'd run all the way to Chicago and back.

Logan did as she instructed, reaching for the scissors he'd placed on the dresser earlier that evening.

"Dry him off and help him breathe," Karen instructed him again.

The slimy little body threatened to fall from his grasp more than once. Logan reached for a towel from the stack and rubbed it over the back and legs of his infant son. The baby whimpered at first, but the sound grew stronger as it turned into a healthy cry.

Laughter came from the direction of the bed. Logan looked at Karen, and they exchanged a long, joyful gaze with each other. Logan turned away to work at wrapping the baby in a blanket to keep him warm.

Of perfect form and health, the baby filled his new father with an awe bordering on reverence. A miracle is what Logan held in his hands. A complete miracle. The baby was his to guide and teach, to love and—

Another scream from Karen jolted Logan out of his thoughts.

He turned to look at her. "What's wrong? What can I do to help?"

She tensed with pain as if the baby must still be born. But the baby had come. His precious Karen should not have any more pain. He might lose her yet. Just because she'd delivered a healthy baby didn't mean a complication hadn't arisen to threaten her own well-being.

If only the doctor were available. Logan knew nothing of how to ease Karen's distress if something went wrong.

"What's the matter?" He shifted the baby into the crook of his arm and hastened across the room.

Karen shook her head, and her eyes scrunched tight. She waved her hand toward the foot of the bed.

Logan's brow furrowed. He rushed to the place she indicated and bent down. Another head, covered with the same dark hair was visible. He sucked in air as dizziness once again swirled his world off balance. It couldn't be!

"Karen." His voice wobbled, and he couldn't decide if he should laugh or cry. He just might do both.

She opened her eyes and focused on him.

"It's another baby. Twins."

A look of amazement mixed with a bit of panic crossed her face.

"Come on, sweetheart. You can do it. Two more pushes and this baby will be born." Logan ran his hand through his hair. Two babies. He and Karen were father and mother to twins.

Karen's body tensed. She went through the sequence of screaming and stiffening while Logan rested the first baby in the crib he'd built and positioned his hands to catch another slimy infant.

"Another boy! Twin sons."

Karen began to cry. The firstborn baby wailed. Logan reached for another towel, turned the newest baby over, and rubbed his back. The baby cried. Tears streamed down Logan's cheeks as he wrapped it in a blanket. He handed him to Karen and then picked up the other crying baby.

He sat with her on the bed, their cheeks touching and tears mingling. Karen had lived. She'd survived through that long, sick pregnancy, delivered not just one, but two healthy sons, and sat here sharing his joy.

"I love you." He turned his head and planted a kiss on her temple.

He could have gone on kissing her until dawn broke on the horizon, but one tiny baby grew tired of his tightly wrapped blanket, or maybe he wanted to try out his eating skills. Cries erupted from him and soon alerted his brother that the state of things needed improvement. They both chorused in wailing together.

So, this is how life would be now—two little men in his house, competing with him for Karen's attention. Logan chuckled and took a baby with him to the parlor while Karen helped the other learn to eat.

They traded off this way through the early morning hours. Around ten o'clock, the babies slept. Logan brought Karen a tray filled with a simple breakfast.

Her exhausted eyes filled with love for him. "Do you know," her soft voice held wonder and a bit of humor, "I fell in love with you during a windstorm, married you on the night of a blizzard, and give birth to your children in a season of flooding?"

He hadn't recalled so many natural disasters associated with their relationship. Maybe Karen would have been better off pursuing her own teaching career and living independently instead of sticking with him through engagement, marriage, and starting a family.

"But I wouldn't trade those experiences for anything." She gazed into his eyes. "You're my whole world, Logan De Witt. The struggles and the tough times have only made my love for you stronger. Without all those storms, I wouldn't have the depth of trust in you or the unending love for you that has grown in my heart."

Such a tender declaration. He must hold it and honor it with the utmost care. He grasped her hand and swallowed while he measured every word. Only the truest ones deserved to be spoken at this moment.

"Karen, you are my wife, a holy gift from God sent to shape me and form me closer to his likeness. I'm a better man because of you." He tilted Karen's chin and placed a tender kiss on her lips. His love for her would only continue to grow in the months and years to come.

When they finished eating, Karen settled in for some rest. Logan washed the dishes and put his shirt back on along with a jacket. He ventured downtown to see if he could learn anything more on the doctor's whereabouts, grinning a foolish grin as he walked.

No one in town suspected Karen had given birth in the night, and even if they did, never would anyone guess she'd birthed twins. The surprise of his life!

He knocked on the door of the doctor's house. The housekeeper answered. Millie was an older woman and had kept house for the doctor many years. When Logan asked about the doctor, Millie informed him she was unsure when he'd return. Logan went home again with nothing he could do but to wait until the doctor found safe passage into town.

LATE THE FOLLOWING AFTERNOON, the sun shone through a break in the rain clouds. Logan puttered in the kitchen, baking another batch of bread. Karen sat propped in bed with one of their sons. Both babies had caught on well to the mechanics of nursing, and Karen rotated them at regular intervals. The schedule took time. Good thing Joyce was already in place as a helper. Karen would need her more than ever with newborn twins in the house.

A knock came at the door. Logan left the kitchen and went to answer it. "Dr. Kaldenburg! Come in."

"Millie said you stopped by yesterday." The doctor entered the house and looked around. "Everything all right?"

"Fine. Just fine." That foolish grin stretched Logan's face again. He led the doctor to the bedroom where one baby lay in the crib, and the other snuggled close to his mother.

The solemn and steady doctor lost all composure. His eyes bugged out, and his jaw dropped.

"Logan delivered them Thursday night." Karen smiled at the doctor.

Dr. Kaldenburg's astonished eyes fixed on him.

Logan's face heated. In the crisis of the moment, all he'd thought about was the health of Karen and the baby, well, babies, as it turned out. He hadn't given one ounce of care to how this all might look to the doctor. He attempted to explain now.

"Look, Dr. Kaldenburg. There was nothing else I could do. Those babies were on their way, and they needed delivered. We had no way of reaching you to let you know."

"Incredible," the dazed doctor muttered as he ventured into the bedroom. His gaze passed between the crib and the bed and back again. He bent to look at the baby in the crib and then studied the baby in Karen's arms. "You did a wonderful job."

Logan's flush deepened.

"If you ever get tired of preaching and decide to go into medicine, let me know," the doctor said with a chuckle and shook hands with Logan.

"Do they have names? What are they?" The doctor asked Karen.

"Simon and John. Simon after my father, and John after his." Karen tilted her head in Logan's direction.

"That's nice." A smile broke out on the doctor's face. "Good, strong, family names. Your mothers will be proud."

Logan smiled this time. "Yes, they will. I'm looking forward to telling them."

"After supper, I'll return for a more thorough examination." Dr. Kaldenburg made his way to the door. "I just arrived in town, you see, after a rather harrowing ride in Fred Akerman's boat across the river, and would really love to sit down to one of Millie's meals before resuming my work."

"Understood. There's no rush. Karen is getting along fine." He followed the doctor to the door and closed it behind him. Logan turned back to his household. His family. He was in for many restless nights and care-filled days. But the surprise and the pleasure of these two new gifts to his home outweighed the fatigue the work would bring. A grin on his face, he went to the bedroom to ask Karen what time she would like to eat her evening meal.

31

Karen leaned against the rough bark of the apple tree trunk. Overhead, a spray of white blooms wafted sweet scents into the fresh spring air. Similar in fragrance to her antique bottle of perfume, the blossoms reminded her of the frail old lady who had owned this orchard and given the bottle of *Song of the Spring* to Logan as Karen's Christmas present. She treasured the memory of his surprise arrival in Chicago with the gift only days before their wedding.

Nellie was gone now. So was Angelien. The winter had been merciless in its claim on cherished lives in their community. Logan had served at each and every funeral, bearing the losses and feeling the sorrows right along with his flock.

She watched him now, mingling among the various clusters of folks gathered on the lawn and waiting for the call to enjoy the noon meal. How nice that the Sunday School Superintendent had asked to use the orchard as the location for this year's picnic. Everyone needed this day in the sun to count their blessings. The fresh outdoors offered strength and vigor that the griefs of the winter months had stolen.

A laugh rang out as Logan tossed his head back in response to a story Martin Barnaveldt and his brother shared. Lester and

George Brinks joined the group and chimed in with conversation that required many animated hand motions. Their faint voices floated to Karen's ears. Logan laughed again. His utter joy in the moment brought a smile to Karen's lips.

She shifted her attention away from the entertaining group and located her mother seated in a wicker chair, holding Simon, and surrounded by adoring ladies. Mother had arrived in town as soon as possible after receiving Logan's call. She had traveled by train to Oswell City from her comfortable home in Chicago, armed with two adorable white gowns. Miss Rose must have made them and had probably put in at least one sleepless night to complete them in time for Mother to bring.

Karen shook her head. The fuss that has been made over the babies outdid her wildest imaginations. Flowers, cards, meals, and tiny articles of clothing had arrived at her door from every corner of their small town. Girls offered to babysit. Mothers stopped her on the street with advice.

Clara Hesslinga and Cornelia Goud had claimed the babies as their own. These older ladies sought Karen out in social settings and insisted on holding a baby. It gave her a break and a chance to mingle, they said, which was true. But Karen never expected to have so much voluntary attention heaped on her.

Clara stood behind Mother now, with John in her arms as she listened to the conversation. Cornelia hovered nearby as if putting herself on call to take over the care of a twin should Clara or Grandmother grow tired.

Karen's eyes grew misty as she heeded Mildred Zahn's call for the group to gather around the tables lining the lawn and heaped with food. Logan stood in the middle of the assembly. He bowed his head to pray. Karen reached his side and slipped her hand into his as he spoke the first words. Firm pressure on her hand accompanied the brief glance he gave her. He smiled and closed his eyes once more.

As soon as he uttered the "Amen," herds of children of all ages raced past in their competition to seek out the front of the line. Older people left their chairs and sauntered across the lawn. Women worked at uncovering dishes and preparing the table.

Logan whispered in her ear. "Take a walk with me."

The babies were in good hands for the moment, so Karen nodded. In the flurry of the potluck picnic, no one would miss the minister and his wife as they slipped out of sight and walked the lane. Logan had done well during the weeks following the birth of their children in making the most of these opportunities for them to catch a few minutes alone together.

They reached the end of the lane and turned around. Karen's gaze took in the well-tended orchard, repaired fences, the re-shingled barn with its new coat of bright red paint, and the roofline of the restored old home, grand in its situation among the flowering trees, reposing and gracious as royalty seated on a throne. Money was no longer an issue, thanks to the steady demand for cider.

Her husband was a genius in his stewardship and was now becoming famous in their area from his successes. More speaking engagements came his way. Karen would accompany him when she finished making arrangements for the care of the babies during these trips.

"There was a time when I'd considered tearing this arch down." Logan came to a stop, his voice floated calm and reflective to her ears.

Karen gazed up at the Dutch words that reminded guests this was an orchard of love.

"But it fits us pretty well, don't you think?" Logan asked in more of a statement than as a question demanding an answer.

"I'm glad you left it in place. Even though you didn't know at first how to use the orchard or if the ministry would last, God did. He's been showing you his plan a little at a time."

Logan chuckled. "I would have never guessed that this old rundown house and these overgrown trees would amount to so much."

"Faith, Logan." Karen laid her hand on his arm. "That's all it takes to see the good."

He turned to her and took her hands in his. "I think you're the one with the vision. Not me."

"But you are the one who wears the glasses," she said with a teasing tone in her voice.

A smile crossed Logan's face. "Remember that evening in Chicago when you alerted me to my opportunities for influence?"

Karen nodded. "I do."

Logan scanned the tree branches above them. "The Lord saw further than I could. He knew what we could become as a couple, as a congregation, and as a town."

"Do you believe me now when I say you are popular, respected, and loved?" She tilted her head to give him a teasing smile.

"Of course I do." A thoughtful expression claimed Logan's face. "I started believing it when those women presented us with that lavish gift on the evening of our wedding rehearsal."

Karen turned serious as she looked into his eyes. That same expansive heart of depth and sensitivity gazed back at her. This time, the love was not shadowed by fear or worry. Happiness swelled there instead.

"Ever since, I've been watching my dreams come true." He raised one of her hands and kissed the back of it.

"There you two are."

Mother's voice cut through the air, jolting Karen out of their sacred moment.

"Simon is fussing. I've tried everything to calm him, but he wants his mother." Mother handed the baby over to Karen.

"Thank you for looking after him for so long. I'll take care of him. Why don't you go and get some food?" Karen patted Simon's back to help him settle.

Mother smiled and hurried away.

"And you, little man." Logan bent over Karen and brushed the baby's cheek. "I didn't envision two of you arriving together."

The baby calmed at the sound of his father's voice. Logan always did have a way with infants. Karen should recruit him more often to settle the babies for their naps like Arthur did with his and Julia's children.

Logan took Simon into his arms and held the baby against his shoulder. The motion of the walk down the lane must have offered the baby enough of a distraction to help him forget his hungry tummy, because he traveled against Logan's chest in silence.

Karen inhaled a large satisfied breath as she strolled at Logan's side. She enjoyed her own degree of influence among the citizens of Oswell City as she carved out her place as Logan's wife. Much work and patience went into the endeavor, but she'd reached the goal of learning how to maintain an orderly home as well as earning the trust and respect of the other women in town.

The babies had arrived healthy and strong. Friendships abounded. Strands of relationships stretched across her life in all directions weaving her into the close-knit fabric of the daily life that comprised her and Logan's existence. Life looked beautiful. With Logan, she could say that every last one of her dreams had come true.

LIST OF CHARACTERS

The Millerson Family from Chicago

- Karen—Karen Millerson
- Mother—Margaret Millerson
- Uncle Henry—Henry Millerson
- Aunt Fran—Fran Millerson
- Julia—Julia Bauman, Karen's sister
- Arthur—Arthur Bauman, Julia's husband
- Ben and Sam—Julia's two sons, Karen's nephews

The De Witt Family and Friends from Silver Grove

- Mama—Sandy De Witt, Logan's mother
- Tillie—Tillie Carter, Logan's sister
- Andrew—Andrew Carter, Tillie's husband
- Pete—Pastor Peter Betten, Logan's best friend
- Anna—Anna Betten, Pete's wife
- Charlotte—Pete and Anna's baby daughter

The Citizens of Oswell City

- Logan De Witt—Pastor of Oswell City Community Church
- Matthew Kaldenberg—the town's doctor
- Paul and Lillian Ellenbroek—the town's mayor and his wife
- Artie and Cornelia Goud—the owners of the jewelry store
- Alex and Mildred Zahn—the owners of the bakery
- George and Ethel Brinks—the owners of the hotel
- James and Grace Koelman—the town's lawyer and his wife
- Jake Harmsen—the editor of the town's newspaper
- Florence Hesslinga—a girl from Logan's past
- Clara Hesslinga—Florence's aunt
- Fred Akerman—a local farmer
- Nellie Akerman—Fred's widowed mother

Immigrants to Oswell City

- Eva Synderhof—a seamstress
- Conrad and Angelien Van Drunen—a carpenter and his wife

ABOUT THE AUTHOR

Michelle lives in Iowa with her husband and two teenage sons. She is a graduate of Northwestern College in Orange City, Iowa, with an associate's degree in office management. She is also a graduate of Central College in Pella, Iowa, with a Bachelor's degree in Religion with a Christian Ministry emphasis and Music. Michelle is the spiritual services provider for an organization that offers services for people with physical and mental disabilities. In this role, she offers grief care, teaches Bible studies, leads retreats, and writes devotionals. Michelle is also a worship leader on Sunday mornings directing the choir, playing piano, or singing.

You can learn more about Michelle by visiting her website: MichelleDeBruin.com.

ALSO BY MICHELLE DE BRUIN

Hope for Tomorrow

When Logan De Witt learns of his father's sudden death, he returns home to the family's dairy farm. During his stay, he discovers his mother's struggle with finances and his younger sister's struggle with grief. Concern for his family presses Logan to make the difficult decision to leave his career as a pastor and stay on the farm. As a way to make some extra money, he agrees to board the teacher for their local school.

Karen Millerson arrives from Chicago ready to teach high school but her position is eliminated so she accepts the role of country school teacher. Eager to put her family's ugly past behind her, Karen begins a new career to replace the trust she lost in her own father who had been in ministry when she was a child.

Logan and Karen both sense a call from the Lord to serve him, but neither of them expected that one day they would do it together.

Can Karen learn to trust again? Will Logan lay aside his grief in exchange for God's purpose for his life?

Promise for Tomorrow

Living a life of faith isn't going the way Logan and Karen hoped until some special visitors arrive and offer them their future back.

Karen Millerson dreamed of teaching high school but now finds herself boarding with a farm family and teaching country school. She is engaged to marry Logan De Witt and is getting prepared to share in ministry with him. But when she gets blamed for the tragic fire at the school, Karen's future grows uncertain.

Logan De Witt is working to clear his family's name with the bank. But when he breaks his leg, hindering his ability to work the farm, Logan is faced with life-changing decisions. When his best friend can't offer the help he requested, can Logan find a way to care for his family and court Karen at the same time before his love for her destroys all of them?

NEW HISTORICAL ROMANCE FROM SCRIVENINGS PRESS

Scarred Vessels

by Elaine Marie Cooper

In a time when America battles for freedom, a man and woman seek to fight the injustice of slavery while discovering love in the midst of tragedy.

In 1778 Rhode Island, the American Revolution rallies the Patriots to fight for freedom. But the slavery of black men and women from Africa, bartered for rum, is a travesty that many in America cannot ignore. The seeds of abolition are planted even as the laws allowing slavery in the north still exist.

Lydia Saunders, the daughter of a slave ship owner, grew up with the horror of slavery. It became more of a nightmare when, at a young age, she is confronted with the truth about her father's occupation.

Burdened with the guilt of her family's sin, she struggles to make a difference in whatever way she can. When she loses her husband in the battle for freedom from England, she makes a difficult decision that will change her life forever.

Sergeant Micah Hughes is too dedicated to serving the fledgling country of America to consider falling in love. When he carries the tragic news to Lydia Saunders about her husband's death, he is appalled by his attraction to the young widow. Micah wrestles with his feelings for Lydia while he tries to focus on helping the cause of freedom. He trains a group of former slaves to become capable soldiers on the battlefield.

Tensions both on the battlefield and on the home front bring hardship and turmoil that threaten to endanger them all. When Lydia and Micah are faced with saving the life of a black infant in danger, can they survive this turning point in their lives?

A groundbreaking book, honest and inspiring, showcasing black soldiers in the American Revolution. *Scarred Vessels* is peopled with flesh and blood characters and true events that not only inspire and entertain but educate. Well done!

- Laura Frantz, Christy Award-winning author of *An Uncommon Woman*

MORE HISTORICAL ROMANCE FROM SCRIVENINGS PRESS

Under This Same Sky

She thought she'd lost everything -

Instead she found what she needed most.

Illinois prairie - 1854

When a deadly tornado destroys Becky Hollister's farm, she must leave the only home she's ever known, and the man she's begun to love to accompany her injured father to St. Louis. Catapulted into a world of unknowns, Becky finds solace in corresponding with the handsome pastor back home. But when word comes that he is all but engaged to someone else, she must call upon her faith to decipher her future.

Matthew Brody didn't intend on falling for Becky, but the unexpected relationship, along with the Lord's gentle nudging, incite him to give up his circuit riding and seek full-time ministry in the town of Miller Creek, with the hope of one day making Becky his bride. But when his old sweetheart comes to town, intent on winning him back—with the entire town pulling for her—Matthew must choose between doing what's expected and what his heart tells him is right.

Valley of Shadows by Candace West

Valley Creek Redemption Book Two

A shattered heart.

A wounded spirit.

A community in crisis.

Lorena Steen gave up on love years ago. She forgave her long-time estranged husband, but when circumstances bring her to the Ozark town of Valley Creek, she discovers forgiving is far from forgetting.

Haunted by his past acts of betrayal, Earl Steen struggles to grow his reclaimed faith and reinstate himself as an upstanding member of Valley Creek. He soon learns that while God's grace is amazing, that of the small-town gossips is not.

When disaster strikes, the only logical solution is for Earl and Lorena to combine their musical talents in an effort to save the community. But even if they're willing to work together, are they able to? Or will the shadows that descend upon Valley Creek reduce it to a ghost town?

Safe Refuge

Newport of the West—Book One

In two days, wealthy Chicagoan, Anna Hartwell, will wed a man she loathes. She would refuse this arranged marriage to Lyman Millard, but the Bible clearly says she is to honor her parents, and Anna would do most anything to please her father–even leaving her teaching job at a mission school and marrying a man she doesn't love.

The Great Chicago Fire erupts, and Anna and her family escape with only the clothes on their backs and the wedding postponed. Father moves the family to Lake Geneva, Wisconsin, where Anna reconnects with Rory Quinn, a handsome immigrant who worked at the mission school. Realizing she is in love with Rory, Anna prepares to break the marriage arrangement with Lyman until she learns a dark family secret that changes her life forever.

Made in USA - Kendallville, IN
1183121_9781649170828
10.20.2020 1001